THE ELITE

DJ WILSON

WrittenWord Press   Indianapolis, IN

I 'intend' to dedicate this book to my wife Robynn - Always & Forever.

Please forgive the insider reference, but I do want to thank Robynn as well as my daughters Tammy and Stacy. They shared editorial duties and seemed to enjoy the first draft. I imagine it became a laborious task by the third or fourth reading. Without them, I am sure I would have never caught on to the 'i before e' thing and the other intricacies of spelling, let alone grammar. It's convenient to have kids who are smarter than you.

I would also like to thank my sister-in-law, Sheryl Eccles. She offered to read the first chapter one morning over coffee. One chapter led to another and by lunch, she had read the entire manuscript. I will never know if she genuinely found it to be a literal page-turner, or she was just flattering me. Either way, it was kind of her.

Finally, I want to thank my mother who read the first half of the manuscript before her long and happy life ended. I hope there was no connection. Love you Mom!

CONTENTS

◆PROLOGUE◆◆◆◆◆ 7

◆CHAPTER 1◆◆◆◆◆15

◆CHAPTER 2◆◆◆◆◆31

◆CHAPTER 3◆◆◆◆◆55

◆CHAPTER 4◆◆◆◆◆79

◆CHAPTER 5◆◆◆◆◆95

◆CHAPTER 6◆◆◆◆117

◆CHAPTER 7◆◆◆◆139

◆CHAPTER 8◆◆◆◆157

◆CHAPTER 9◆◆◆◆169

◆CHAPTER 10◆◆◆185

◆CHAPTER 11◆◆◆199

◆CHAPTER 12◆◆◆213

◆CHAPTER 13◆◆◆229

◆CHAPTER 14◆◆◆249

◆CHAPTER 15◆◆◆273

◆CHAPTER 16◆◆◆293

◆EPILOGUE◆◆◆◆307

◆PROLOGUE◆

Adon Remington had thought it impossible for life to get any worse, but yesterday's meeting had proven him wrong. He had been offered a position that should have been flattering. He wanted to take it. His wife, Joyce, wanted him to take it. The cost of accepting, though, was enormous; almost unimaginable. He and Joyce had sat up all night agonizing over the decision, but in the end, they had agreed. He would accept – and pay the awful price.

It seemed so recent that he and Joyce and their twin sons had been a happy family without a care in the world. In fact, Adon remembered the day it all ended as one of their happiest. Adon was a young, but accomplished engineer. He worked on several of the moon landings and advanced quickly at the space administration. They had a beautiful oceanfront home just forty miles south of Mission Control Center. The boys had both come home from school for the weekend. Colin was about to begin an apprenticeship, following in his dad's footsteps as an aeronautical engineer specializing in rocketry. Adon remembered how much he had looked forward to having Colin at work with him. Mandatory service required a certain degree of separation from family, but Adon had been able to pull a few strings and, at least, get Colin assigned to the specialty.

Alek came home to shill for more money. His doctoral thesis in marine biology was costing far more than they had ever guessed, and he was running low. Adon had made no secret of the fact that he was anxious to help any time he could and Alek had long since overcome his timidity in asking for help. Joyce rarely approved of the ongoing support they gave Alek. She felt he had become a professional student, dragging his studies on and on to put off mandatory service. It may have been out of some blind loyalty to his famous mentor, a founder of the modern environmentalist movement, who Alek idolized for years. Either way, she felt his father was doing him no favors by continually giving him money that they really couldn't afford.

Nevertheless, Adon just could not cut Alek off. The thought of it was like eating Brussels sprouts: you knew they were good for you; you wanted to do as your mother told you; you tried. But once in your mouth, you simply could not swallow. The reflex just wouldn't come. Instead, you gagged. Then you sat at the table all evening because your mother would not let you get up until those cold, nasty-looking Brussels sprouts were gone. That's how it was with helping Alek. Adon just could not cut him off. He knew Joyce was right, and now he was going to have to say no in a far more painful way.

But back then, on the day it had all ended, everything had been perfect. The weather could not have been better. It was a very comfortable sixty-three degrees. There wasn't a cloud in the bright blue sky and the water was that deep pink which even a picture of could make a person relax. Adon splurged on some thick steaks to grill while they all played at the beach. Both boys had always loved the ocean, and they had spent the day competing on surf boards. They thought to build a fire and hang out on the beach through the evening, but the call from Mission Control put the kibosh on those plans. Adon had less than an hour to report for a meeting. It was an extremely unusual demand, especially when there were no missions in progress. In fact, it had never happened before. He thought for a second that he might be getting fired but dismissed the idea as crazy. He could not imagine what was up. All his boss had said was that it was of the highest possible importance. As it turned out, that was an understatement.

***

That first meeting had been a shocker, and it had been contentious. The news was big, no doubt, apocalyptic in Adon's view. Their neighboring planet, just thirty-five million miles away, had suddenly exploded. Scientists at the Space Administration knew exactly what had happened – a meteor had hit the planet head-on, right at its largest fissure and penetrated to the planet's core. What the scientists did not know was the effect it would have on them.

Some felt it was little more than a curious event without any direct effect on them. They argued that most of the planet's pieces would stay in their present orbit. There was, after all, a gravitational balance that would act to contain the planet's remnants. It would even pull all the pieces back together over the next millions of years and reassemble the celestial body. Others mostly agreed, but felt that the few pieces that had escaped the planet's orbit would alter the entire solar system's gravitational balance, including their own. They believed their planet might be pulled into a slightly more distant orbit from the sun, cooling the planet and creating something of a nuclear winter.

There were a few that predicted the absolute worst. They felt it was inevitable that they would be struck by one of the exploded pieces. If that happened, even a small piece could devastate them. They went into painful detail.

Such an impact would throw huge amounts of matter into the atmosphere. It would cause two-thousand-foot waves that might completely empty an ocean. Such an event would create years of darkness, interfere with photosynthesis, and cause much cooler temperatures globally. Much of the atmosphere would escape through the hole in the protective belt created by the entering piece. The resulting harsh conditions would, in turn, lead to the extinction of many species, including humans.

In any case, whatever was going to happen would happen within a week. After a lot of shouting, they agreed to keep things quiet for twenty-four hours while the government made plans to move as much of the population as possible to safe ground. The entire globe was dotted with underground shelters from back in the early days of nuclear research. Those old shelters were still supplied and available to accommodate more than half of the world's population.

When the announcement was finally made, most people agreed with the scientists who saw the explosion as merely a curious event. About two-thirds of the population refused to go to the shelters. Joyce wanted to be one of them. She argued that even if the worst happened, she would rather be dead instantly than suffer a slow and miserable death sheltered underground on a dying planet.

Adon tended to agree with Joyce's logic,

but he just could not bring himself to submit to a near certain death and stay aboveground. He had insisted and had almost been vindicated in his decision when the worst happened. It was not a large piece of the exploded planet that struck them – it was an enormous piece. All life on the surface came to a nearly instant end. The atmosphere was almost completely lost. The planet's orbit was changed. Even worse, Joyce had been proven correct – life in the shelters was hell.

***

Nearly all the scientists came to the same conclusion – that the shelters would not be able to sustain life for more than a couple hundred years or so. The survivors would need a longer-term solution. Two plans quickly emerged. The idea of building an artificial environment that could be sustained almost indefinitely was the most popular. The environment could drift through space, maybe for tens of thousands of years, until it came upon a suitable habitat. After all, scientists were almost unanimous in their speculations that there were actually thousands of life-sustaining planets throughout the universe. As a famous environmentalist, Alek's mentor would have been a natural choice to lead the artificial environment expedition into deep space, but he had stayed aboveground and had perished immediately. In his place, they would choose his protégé Alek.

The other plan was less radical. Many liked the idea of fleeing, like refugees, to their neighboring planet one orbit closer to the sun. The space agency was well into its research and had sent several missions there already. There was a breathable atmosphere; there was an abundance of water; they had not only confirmed the presence of life, but had evidence that it was highly evolved; and they knew they had the technology to move a large number of people to the planet. Had all hell not broken loose, a manned mission to the planet would have been imminent. Adon found it difficult to envision a life there. Still, he thought it was the only logical course of action, and had slowly become committed to the refugee's plan.

Colin did not feel the same way. He was firmly in a third camp – along with the few that believed life in the underground bunkers would be sustainable. He reasoned that if nearly two-thirds of the survivors left, either to take refuge on the neighboring planet or to drift forever in space, then the remaining population would be reduced to acceptable numbers. Adon and Joyce argued with him about it. Colin's talents as an aeronautical engineer would be invaluable in designing the shuttles to get them to the neighboring planet. To stay, Adon and Joyce pleaded, would be to waste those talents. The argument fell flat. Colin would stay.

Adon and Joyce agonized over the decision they had to make. Should they stay with Colin or leave with Alek. They had hardly considered the third alternative even though it was the plan so subtly taking hold of Adon's mind. He had played a prominent role in the earlier missions to the neighboring planet, so he was not surprised when the refugee organizers had asked him to act as the flight controller. He didn't see how he and Joyce could leave their sons. He had privately agonized over it all day before broaching the subject with Joyce the previous night.

They sat in their underground cubicle so sparsely furnished with just two cots and a small table. They stared at the only decoration they had been allowed to bring into the shelter; a tabletop fountain Adon had made for Joyce when the boys were born. The fountain had a round outer bowl decorated with four statues, one a woman, one a man, and two young boys, each looking toward the sky. In the very center was a larger statue of a man gazing at the four smaller statues. Adon had intended it to represent the family being watched over by God.

He and Joyce finally decided to accept the offer and join the refugees. Adon wanted to smash the fountain. They would lose their sons forever. It made for what seemed the worst day of his life. Even so, he was struck, as he turned into the mission control reception area, with the enormity of it all; how much bigger it was than his small family. A chapter in human history had suddenly and violently ended, and a new one was dawning. For better or worse, he would be at the center of this dawning epoch.

◆CHAPTER 1◆

Clayton Jeffries found it difficult to hide his agitation when Brooke wanted to dig through the neatly packed gear waiting on the dock. "We just want to get our suits and take a swim while we wait. I didn't think we would be out here all day," Brooke said apologetically.

"Clay, what do you think could be the hold up?" Eric asked as he joined them on the dock. "Didn't the fly-in company say they would pick us up at the same time they dropped us off?" That would have been about eleven o'clock in the morning – the same time they were dropped off seven days ago. It was now nearing four o'clock, and they had all gotten a bit impatient after packing all the gear, hauling it down to the dock and cleaning the cabin. Bethany nearly drove them all crazy with repeating squeaks from the dock as she alternately paced and paused to look at the sky. Clay thought there had probably just been some mechanical problem with the old six-passenger de Havilland Otter that had brought them to this hundreds-of-miles-from-anything place in central Canada. He had told Bethany to quit worrying, but he too was quickly moving from agitated to angry.

He hadn't felt right about this little excursion from the start. Clay had done a fly-in fishing trip once before, but that had been over thirty-five years ago and with his school buddies, not his two daughters and his son-in-law. His daughters Brooke and Bethany had cooked up the idea as a way to lift Clay from his mourning. His wife had lost her battle with breast cancer nearly fourteen months ago. Caring for Kara during her illness had been rough on Clay, but not as rough as the last year had been. The girls feared that his mourning had turned into a deep depression. During their thirty-four years of marriage, Kara would have nothing to do with anything rustic so Clay only spoke of his love for camping and all things natural. A family fly-in struck the girls as a perfect way to show Clay that he still had family and that there could be life after Kara.

The plan worked. Clay had enjoyed the week, but he was anxious to get back. "The suits are in the green backpack," Clay told Brooke. "I'm going back to the cabin to fire up that emergency radio and find out what the hell is going on!" The small wooden-plank pier shook as Clay stood and marched ashore, his hidden anger unintentionally surfacing.

As he made his way up the steep path punctuated with dried pine needles and with occasional flat rocks set in as steps, Clay thought back to what their pilot had told them when they had arrived: "There's a bad storm moving in, so I need to head back quickly. I wouldn't go out with the boats right away – these lakes can get pretty rough for a small boat in a storm. But the rest of the week should be pretty nice." He included the radio in his little tour of the place with little more than, "here is a radio if there is any kind of emergency. There are directions taped on the desk."

Clay remembered that storm on their first day. They had just gotten everything unpacked and had settled in. Since they couldn't take the boats out yet to explore a little, Brooke, Bethany, and Eric had gone down to the lake for a quick swim. Clay had taunted them from the dock with descriptions of all the disgusting little creatures that lived in the water. Brooke had splashed him and told him to stop, or they would never get Bethany back in the water. When they heard the first distant roll of thunder, they got out of the water and stood on the dock watching the low black clouds move in. "Everyone loves to watch a good storm, but they are especially awesome up here," Clay had said and everyone agreed. They ran up the path to the cabin's screened-in porch as the few first rain drops turned into sheets of blowing rain.

When Clay remembered the intense calm of their first morning after that frightful storm, he once again used it to calm himself. He opened the rustic cabin's squeaky screen door and headed for the radio. It was in the utility closet along with a small water heater and a desk that was more like a built-in shelf, but there were, indeed, simple directions taped there. Clay switched the radio on, turning the dial marked frequency until it matched the frequency given on the instruction sheet. He waited for a few moments to see if anything happened, or if he could hear anyone, then he pressed the talk switch on the microphone and spoke as directed: "This is VE4XYB. Can anyone hear me? Over." He waited for ten or fifteen seconds and then repeated himself: "This is VE4XYB. Can anyone hear me? Over."

Clay jumped when a voice answered back almost immediately: "This is VE4JCS. Go ahead VE4XYB. Over."

"Ah. Hello. Is this Wilderness Fly-in Excursions? Over."

"No. I doubt if anyone is manning their radio anymore, why? Over."

"How can no one be manning their radio? This is Clayton Jeffries, and we were dropped-off at their cabin on Bigstone Lake last week. They were supposed to pick us up this morning, but we haven't seen a thing. Over"

There was a brief delay before the male voice on the other end responded. "Is this a joke? We take amateur radio very seriously pal, so this kind of joke is not at all cool! Over."

Clay shouted an answer. "Why would this be a joke? We need someone to get us out of here! Over."

Alex Lerner twisted ninety degrees from his radio set to his computer and opened the *Hamcall* call sign server. He quickly typed in 'VE4XYB' and confirmed that the call sign was, indeed, listed as Wilderness Fly-in Excursions and was on Bigstone Lake. He took a quick glance at the newspaper on the desk behind him and read the headline: "Crash Victims Identified – Cause Still Undetermined." Alex had lived in Lynn Lake, Manitoba all of his thirty-four years. He would be the first to admit it was a bit boring, but he instantly grasped that this would definitely be something exciting – he figured he would play a prominent role in tomorrow's headline.

"Give me your name and location again and how many are in your party? Over."

"My name is Clayton Jeffries. I and my two daughters and my son-in-law, four in all, are at Wilderness Fly-in Excursions' cabin on Bigstone Lake in Manitoba. We were dropped off last Saturday morning and were supposed to be picked up today. Over"

"Ah, Mr. Jeffries," there was a long pause as Alex chose his words, "something is crazy here. You and your party have been the biggest news story around Manitoba in years. The airplane you flew in on crashed last Saturday afternoon, supposedly on the way to Bigstone Lake with your party aboard. Three male and two female bodies were recovered. Dude, you're supposed to be dead! Over"

"Well I'm not dead – we're not dead," Clay shouted, "Listen; the confusion is simple. When we got to Lynn Lake last Friday, we checked into the hotel and had a message to call our pilot. He said he had another group scheduled for Saturday morning that was going to be late. He wanted to know if we could switch with them and fly out Saturday morning instead of Saturday afternoon. Which we did. It must have been that afternoon group that crashed. Over"

Alex instinctively stood with excitement as he answered. "OK, well the authorities can figure it all out. Stand by and I will contact the Mounties to get you out of there. Over."

Clayton sighed his thanks and sat back in his chair as he waited for further word from Alex. Alex knew he should just call nine-one-one, but since John, who manned the volunteer Search and Rescue radio, was a good friend he figured he could go straight to him. "This is VE4JCS calling VY2SR, you there John? Over."

"This is VY2SR, go ahead VE4JCS, Over."

The voice was not John's – it wasn't anyone familiar. "Where is John today? Over."

The operator on the other end stepped on Alex's transmission – "...not here today. What do you need?" The voice was rude. Alex was thinking twice about calling nine-one-one when his radio again demanded, "What do you need?"

***

Alex had relayed Clayton Jeffries' predicament to the man on the SAR radio who said they would get right out there and signed off without as much as a 'thank you.' Alex dialed back to Clay's frequency and told him search and rescue was on the way. "From where they are coming, it will still take some time, maybe close to two hours, so sit tight. I'll stay on your frequency, and by my radio if you need anythi..."

Alex grunted his frustration as his radio, in fact, his entire house, went black. Power failures were common, but they always picked the worst time. His computer was still up, on battery backup, so he thought to try and IM John at home, find out why he wasn't at work, and share the excitement with him. His greeting was answered with an immediate auto reply: "Sorry, I'm at work. Try me there or call me later, Eh." John thought the stereotypical 'Eh' on the end was funny since he was well-known for speaking the Queen's English flawlessly.

Alex thought about sending an email to someone at the Winnipeg newspaper or one of the TV stations, but decided he wanted to wait and call when the power came back on, which usually only took a few minutes. Instead, he decided to review the lead story in that morning's newspaper:

Winnipeg. Provincial authorities today confirmed the identities of five bodies recovered from the wreckage of last Saturday's plane crash. Forensics positively identified forty-two-year-old Thomas Young of Lynn Lake who piloted the de Havilland Otter which was caught in a storm and crashed just sixty miles South of Bigstone Lake while taking a party of four on a vacation excursion. The passengers have been identified as sixty-one-year-old Clayton Jeffries, husband and wife Eric (38) and Brooke (36) Louth, all of Bloomington, Indiana and thirty-four-year-old Bethany Jeffries of Arlington, Virginia. Brooke Louth and Bethany Jeffries were the daughters of victim Clayton Jeffries. The only surviving relative of the family, Jason Louth of Cincinnati, Ohio was notified Friday of the official identification.

Clayton Jeffries was a professor of American Studies at Indiana University where he was set to return after a twelve-month leave of absence following his wife's recent death. Eric Louth was also a professor at the university who taught Native American history.

Pilot Thomas Young moved to Lynn Lake three years ago when he acquired Wilderness Fly-In Excursions from the estate

of life-long Lynn Lake resident Peter North,
who died in a plane crash in 2002. Mr. Young
is originally from Stamford, Connecticut and
is survived by his sister Katherine Young,
also of Stamford.

Alex set the paper down and lit a cigarette. He knew it would be a huge story when he could finally tell the reporters that they had it all wrong. But, he wondered, how could the authorities have made a 'positive identification' that was clearly wrong? More than that, if Jeffries and his family were alive, who were the bodies the Mounties had recovered from the crash? He couldn't wait to talk to John. Nor could he wait for the power to come on – this failure was lasting longer than usual. He went back to reading the article:

The cause of the crash would not
likely be officially determined for several
months, but authorities are assuming the
crash was related to the strong thunder
storms that moved through northern
Manitoba last Saturday afternoon. The plane
was a six-passenger de Havilland Otter
owned by Wilderness Fly-in Excursions and
was a twin to the plane that had crashed just
three years ago, killing the company's
founder and proprietor Peter North.
Area excursion pilots staged an
airborne memorial to the victims last
Thursday while provincial authorities made

plans to mark the crash site.

Alex barely finished reading when the door burst open, and the room filled with flames. In the instant it took for the flames to focus on Alex, he caught sight of a man all in white, helmeted head and a veiled face, holding what looked like a rifle at his waist – the source of the flames. Alex would surely be in tomorrow's headline: "Gas Explosion Kills Alex Lerner."

***

Brooke, Bethany and Eric came through the door just as Clay was about to go down and update them. They were dripping wet, wrapped in towels and tracking sand on the linoleum floor as they came in. "Remember, we have to leave the cabin clean," Clay reminded Bethany.

"I'll sweep it up. So what's the word?" Eric asked.

"You're not going to believe this," Clay told them, as he recounted what Alex Lerner had told him. Bethany seemed shaken more than the others, and Clay tried to calm her with a matter of fact tone. "Anyway, it's probably going to be a little more than an hour before search and rescue gets here to take us out. In the meantime, why don't you guys get dressed while I find something for us to eat?"

They headed down the small hallway to each of the bunk rooms and Clay headed for to the gear sitting on the dock to see what he could dig up for a snack. None of them had eaten since breakfast. If everything had gone as expected Clay would just be finishing the steak he had planned for dinner in Lynn Lake. Instead, he was digging through the blue nylon backpack looking for any kind of morsel. He caught sight of a tube of Pringles – they would do for a start.

He continued digging in the food bags when he heard what he was sure was a plane landing on the far side of the island. He stood for a second and listened. It was a little less of a roar than a plane would make, but it was definitely an engine of some sort, maybe a boat. He started up to the cabin as the sound disappeared. When he opened the door, Brooke and Eric, still half dressed, poked their heads out of their doorway. "What was that?" asked Brooke. "Are they here already?"

"Can't be," Clay answered, "and it came from the far side of the island." Clay told them he was going to climb the hill at the center of the island and see what was going on. "I'll be back in forty-five minutes or so. You guys finish getting dressed and get some of the food I dug out down on the dock."

Clay had climbed up the small hill once earlier in the week. It was a rough hike, not more than a mile, but through a thick stand of small conifers with a heavy undergrowth and over rocky ground. The view from the top was spectacular. It wasn't very high, but it was just a bit higher than the surrounding landscape, and one could see most of the lake and the entire island.

As he pushed his way through the weeds and around the sapling hackberry, Clay thought of getting home. Bloomington was a fairly typical college town, not a lot of diversions. There were the usual University doings and he and Kara had frequently gone to campus events. Kara had always been a true socialite. She knew everyone. Clay, on the other hand, had plenty of acquaintances, but no real close friends. Other than work and family, there was little in Bloomington that interested him. He belonged to the men's club at church and to the local Lion's Club, but had never gotten really involved in those. He had taken the last year to figure out what he would do now that Kara was gone. The less he found to interest him, the more depressed he had gotten. This trip had cheered him up, but he hadn't figured anything out. He was going back to work simply because everyone said it was time to go back – not because he really wanted to.

He was still hoping for grandchildren. Both of the girls found reasons to wait. Brooke had gone through a first marriage to a career Marine, and they had always said they wanted to settle down before having children. In the end, he turned out to not be the father type. For that matter, he turned out to not be the husband type either. Bethany had just finished two six-year stints in the Air Force after grad school. Clay wondered if marriage, let alone children were actually in her plans at all. She was beautiful, fiercely independent and, to many, a little distant. Clay often thought she might be gay. It probably wouldn't bother him much – it sure wouldn't make him love her any less.

That empty, aimless feeling that had become so familiar to Clay over the last fourteen months was suddenly back. It occurred to him that he might like being 'positively identified' as being dead. As he had on many occasions, he wondered if he wouldn't prefer being actually dead. But Clay was not suicidal. He knew he had plenty of life ahead of him. He just didn't know what it was.

He was healthy, some might even say buff, or at least as buff as a sixty-one-year-old man can be. He was muscular, fairly tall – six-foot-two. He had dark hair that had been well salted with grey since he was in his forties, and classic features: square chin, eagle-like nose, deep brown eyes. A lot of people joked that he reminded them of the older guy in the commercial by the pool that all the young ladies ogle over as he stands up to stretch, then does a belly flop into the pool. He had a distinguished look and carriage. In fact, he was distinguished. He was a chaired professor of American Studies, which combined American history, sociology and political science; he had written a half-dozen books on U.S. social history, one of which had become a standard college text and another, about the history of sports in the U.S., that had become a popular best seller. He didn't often think about it, but he was also wealthy. He was the only child of well-to-do parents who had both died while he was still in his early fifties. Not to mention, he did pretty well on his own with the books. All he needed was something to interest him, but after fourteen months of searching, he still hadn't found anything.

He was near the top of the hill and at a point where he could look back and see the cabin and dock. He must have been pretty deep in thought as he had climbed, because when he turned to look, there was a plane tied at the dock. He had not heard it coming. There were four men in fatigues on or near the dock. One man was standing with Brooke and another with Bethany. A third was arguing with Eric. Clay was too far away to hear anything, but he became instantly suspicious – they were clearly not search and rescue. They were too early. They impressed Clay as more like thugs – smugglers, terrorists, or something like that. Clay startled when Eric's argument seemed to turn physical, and they grabbed Brooke, Bethany and Eric. They all slumped in a way Clay had seen before, during some trouble on campus; it looked like they had been tased.

Clay began to run down the hill, pushing through the brush with muscles taut with adrenaline. He had barely gotten fifty yards when he froze to a stop. A man dressed in fatigues stood before him. He was in front of what looked like a jet ski, dull black and very angular. The man was holding his left hand in the air with his palm facing Clay, like a caricature of an Indian saying 'how.' He was saying something to Clay, but he chose not to hear it. Clay was overtaken with anger, and he lunged for the man. He had taken only a step when he heard, or more precisely, felt a gunshot pass over his shoulder and strike the uniformed man. Clay watched him fall back onto the jet ski, then turned just in time to see a figure reaching for his neck. He felt a jolt, followed by pain coursing through his body for a brief second, before everything went black.

◆CHAPTER 2◆

Clay didn't want to wake up. He was semi-conscious and comfortable. More comfortable than he remembered being. The bed he was in was soft, warm and cozy. He was warm and cozy. Consciousness came back with a start. He remembered Brooke and Bethany and Eric. He remembered the strange man being shot. He remembered a figure reaching for his neck. He jerked his eyes open. He wasn't in a bed at all, but some sort of hammock. He could see the trampled ground and could smell burning pine. He heard pans clinking and jerked himself up as a woman's voice cautioned him, "Don't freak-out. I'm on your side, and I don't intend to hurt you. I want to help."

Clay threw back the thin tarp that had been

his blanket – he was ready to get up and fight. But the feel of the thin tarp was a contradiction to his senses, and it distracted him for a second. It felt like a plush blanket, and it had been warm, but it looked like a thin piece of plastic. He felt cold morning air as he tossed the tarp aside and took a moment to take in his surroundings. The hammock he had slept in was tented with a roof and three sides. The surface he was lying on was the same as the tarp that had covered him – it felt soft, but looked like plastic. The platform had rigid edges and was suspended by thin strings tied to nearby trees. He could see that there was a fourth wall folded back. The entire enclosure was a typical tent, made of the same plastic or polyester material and given shape with thin flexible poles.

Outside of the tent was a common camp site. The ground was dirt with occasional clumps of pine needles. There was a second hammock/tent hung from trees about twenty yards straight across from his. An overflowing backpack leaned against a tree to his left. To his right was a jet ski identical to the one the man in fatigues had stood in front of. The jet ski was out of place. It was too far from the water to have been carried there.

They were on a lakeshore, about thirty yards inland. The shoreline was rocky, and he could see nothing but trees surrounding what appeared to be a fairly large lake. Inland was all forest, mostly common hackberries and assorted conifers, with a heavy undergrowth of weeds. It appeared as though he was still in northern Manitoba.

A woman, maybe thirty-five, crouched over the fire in the center of the camp. The fire was straddled by a cooking grate that looked like it had been shaped out of aluminum foil. The woman was attractive, or what some might prefer to call cute. She had a classically pretty Irish face with high cheek bones, full symmetric lips, dark almond eyes with manicured eye brows. She had auburn hair worn long and flat in a pony tail. She was wearing a tight sweeping-necked tee-shirt that showed her ample cleavage and trim waist and hip-hugging fatigues with a wide belt.

"Are you OK?" the woman asked Clay.

"Just tell me who you are; why you have brought me here; and what you have done with my daughters and Eric," Clay demanded.

"*I* am Kate Young," She snapped back. "My brother was the pilot who was supposed to pick you up yesterday, but was killed in a crash after dropping you off. I didn't do anything with your daughters and the other man, nor do I know what *they* have done with them. As for why I brought you here, I'll explain over breakfast. Come get some coffee while I make us some pancakes." She sounded friendly enough. "And, for future reference, there is no need to snap at me! You don't even know yet if I am friend or foe. You don't know yet whether I am a total witch or a sweetheart. Not to mention, I might have just saved your life. So you might try a little courtesy instead of snapping and demanding things." The woman choked up very slightly as she finished.

It put Clay at ease and, besides, she was right – he had no idea what was going on. "I'm sorry, really. Some coffee sounds good. And, since you asked," the woman was nearly crying, "are you OK?"

"Well," Kate answered, "my brother has just been murdered. Nothing is making any sense to me. And yesterday I shot a person, something I would have never conceived of me doing, and I have no idea why. Yeah, I'm fine."

Clearly, she wasn't. She held back her tears and brusquely snapped open a folded disk made of the same material as his blanket and set it on the cooking grate. She poured some pancake batter on the disk and reached for a spatula as she eased herself down on the log near the fire.

Clay picked up the cup of coffee and took a sip as he sat beside her. Clay was something of a coffee aficionado, and this was exceptionally good coffee! He looked at the cup and thought he was out of his mind critiquing coffee at a time like this, but it gave him the right response to her tirade. "Well you make a great cup of coffee, so you must be all right. Why do you say your brother was murdered?"

"Because he was." She couldn't hold back the tears this time. "It is all so confusing," she said, her voice full of anguish, as she buried her head in her hands. Kate was usually very calm and strong, but right now she was tired and there was so much catching up to her.

Clay put a hand on her shoulder. "Just start at the beginning. Tell me everything." Clay thought it would be therapeutic, so he urged her to start by telling him about her brother.

She sniffled and dried her eyes as she told him, "It's a long story. You had better pour us another cup of coffee and get comfortable." She composed herself and moved to a nearby tree where she sat and leaned back. Clay poured two coffees, handing her one as he sat and leaned against a second tree.

"I visited my brother, as I do every summer, about six weeks ago," she began. "He and I inherited the excursion company when our uncle died in a crash. He had been our only living relative and Thomas was extremely close to him. We should have just sold the company, but we didn't need the money – frankly, Mr. Jeffries, Thomas and I are quite wealthy. Our father was an engineer who held several patents and owned a very successful electronics company. Even without the company, both of our parents came from what you would call 'old money' – the company was more our father's hobby. He insisted Thomas go into engineering, which he did. Strings were pulled to get him into MIT. Thomas worked as a civil engineer doing something with power grids that I never really understood. He was OK with it, but he didn't exactly love it – you wouldn't call him passionate about civil engineering. His passion was environmental issues. He gave fortunes to every environmental group that came along. He was even arrested once, doing something on a boat in Lake Michigan. So when Uncle Peter left us the excursion company, Thomas didn't think twice about moving up here. It appealed to the environmentalist, naturalist, tree-hugger in him. Plus, he thought it was a more fitting legacy from Uncle Peter than just some more money."

Kate took a long sip of her coffee and continued. "Thomas loved it up here, and I visited him every summer for a week or two. We spent every Christmas together at his cabin. Thomas was always happy, but this last visit, six weeks ago, he was downright giddy. He kept going on all week about something he had gotten into, what he said was 'a project.' He had fallen in with a small group that called themselves 'Iatros.' He said there were several Iatros working on this project and he told me, and don't ask me what this means because it lost me, but they told Thomas that he was especially lucky because he was the only 'Apoikian' they were working with. He said they called everyone an Apoikian even though he said he couldn't explain what it meant – I figured they were Polynesian or Hawaiian or something and I figured from the context that it just meant 'white person' or something like that. Anyway, I'm rambling – I do that. It's not important..."

Clay interrupted. "It might be. Like I said, tell me everything – rambling is good. Etymology is kind of a diversion for me, sounds crazy, I know, but I like it better than crossword or soduko puzzles. Both of those words are Greek. Ancient Greek, I think. 'Iatros' means savior, small 's,' not like Christ or anything religious, more like 'rescuer' or along those lines. 'Apoikiai' means 'colony,' so I assume that 'Apoikian' means something like 'colonist.'"

Kate gave Clay a glare, as if to say 'who cares.' Clay apologized and urged her to continue. "Anyway, Thomas talked all week about these guys. We went camping one night and he took me to the campsite on that jet ski – did you notice when I brought you here that it flew. Oh, that's right, you were knocked out. Thomas had a bunch of stuff that was real science fiction kind of technology. The jet ski flies, he told me, by super heating a pillow of air beneath it. I really don't understand but you have to admit, it is pretty cool and way out there. It's also stealth – see how angular it is and how it is all dull black. But I haven't figured out how to shut off the engine noise. I'm rambling again – never mind. Anyway, then when we were camping he had all of this stuff. Those hanging tents or hammocks or whatever they are called; the tarp that looks like plastic but feels like a plush blanket; the strings that are as thin as threads but hold-up the hammocks with a person on them, err...in them; the griddle I made pancakes on that looks like a piece of tin foil but acts like iron; the rods in the tent and hammocks that look like aluminum and weigh about the same as a McDonald's straw, but are still stronger than steel." Kate spoke in amazement.

Kate summed up her inventory, "Thomas set up an entire campsite: gear, food, clothes, tents and all, out of our two backpacks that together didn't weigh thirty pounds! He said it was all nothing. Little trinkets made possible by just a couple of advances the Iatros had made in alloys and nano-technology. The really big thing, he kept saying, would change the world, but he couldn't tell me what it was. I didn't take him that serious. Thomas was given to hyperbole now and then, but now I am not so sure. I started to think he might be involved in something pretty startling when I heard he was dead. Once I got here last Sunday, I really started to get the feeling that he was involved in something awfully important."

Clay asked Kate if she had any idea what it might be. She didn't. "I thought it must have something to do with airplanes –Thomas was passionate about flying. When we were young, he learned to fly our father's Beachcraft before he learned to drive. I also thought it might have something to do with the environment – as I mentioned, he was big on the environment. That's why he moved out here in the first place. I also wondered if it had something to do with his civil engineering background. It made sense as to why someone would need Thomas involved."

Kate couldn't tell anymore if she was speculating or trying to convince Clay of her theories. If she was trying to convince him, it became clear that she had failed when he commented, "Or maybe they just needed his money. Has he been spending a lot?"

"I don't know," Kate answered.

Kate paused for a second and repeated, "I don't know. That's something I'll have to look into." Kate stood and said, "We have to go. I'll finish after we get to the site."

Clay jumped up as he asked, "What site? Where are we going?"

"To the crash site," Kate answered as she strapped on a belt and holster with a Berretta nine millimeter semi-automatic. "Grab that backpack – we'll need it."

Clay took hold of the backpack, but was still focused on the pistol at Kate's side. "What's that for," he asked.

"Thomas wore it every minute I was here," she answered. "He had never been big with guns, so I found it odd. He also started collecting a bunch of spy toys, most of them in that backpack. Things like binoculars, night-vision goggles, a taser gun with which you are familiar, a listening antenna, which took me two days to figure out how to use, and a couple of things that I still haven't figured out. There is also some lunch and water in there. We will probably be gone all day." Kate was straddling the jet ski indicating to Clay to get on the back.

***

They hovered more than they flew, staying

close to the ground and below the trees when they could. The ride was not at all what Clay had expected. The lack of wind and noise gave him the impression that they were riding in some kind of invisible bubble. The four- or five-mile trip was slow going and when Clay asked why, Kate told him that a search plane had already flown over, in the distance, earlier that morning. "Don't you think they are looking for you," Kate asked condescendingly as she stopped at the base of a small hill, glanced in all directions then flew close to the hilltop. "We'll watch from here," she said as she shut down the jet ski and hopped off.

The hilltop was flat and strewn with boulders. Trampled weeds marked out a small nest near a group of large rocks. They were on yet another small island about three-quarters of a mile from the heavily wooded opposite shore of the huge lake they had just flown across. "I've been coming here every day since last Tuesday," Kate told Clay. "From here we can see the crash site and still get away pretty easily if we have to." Kate was already lying flat on her belly peeking through a gap in the rocks. "Could you give me the binoculars out of the backpack,' she asked Clay.

He dug out most of the gadgets she had mentioned earlier and handed her the binoculars as he peered over the rocks. About fifty yards ahead of them, at the far base of the hill was the edge of the island and what looked more like a river than part of the lake they had crossed – a little less than a mile wide and who knew how long. There was a channel on their left that appeared, based on the tree line, to open up into a larger lake. Straight across from them was what was obviously the crash site. The ground just off the opposite shore was burnt along with several charred tree trunks. There were small bits of metal strewn across the site, but no large pieces and certainly nothing that he could identify as part of an airplane.

"They have taken most of the large pieces, one or two or three at a time depending on how much would fit in their plane. I took a picture of every piece so far," Kate told him as she switched on the binoculars and handed them to Clay. "They are also a digital camera," she told him, "just look through them and push this button to move to the next picture."

Clay raised the binoculars to his eyes and could see a picture of the untouched crash site. He studied it closely then advanced quickly through a series of shots of a seaplane landing, men standing around the site, and close-ups of several large pieces of the crashed plane.

"There is a picture of the men carrying a wing," Kate directed. "Stop when you get to it."

"I've got it," Clay said. "What about it?"

Kate told him to notice the large hole almost centered on the wing. "Go to the next few pictures," Kate suggested.

Clay advanced the pictures and saw several close-ups of the hole. It was slightly oval with sharp metal edges pointing to the top of the wing so that it looked something like a crater on the bottom of the wing and like a king's crown on the top of the wing. "That's a missile hole!" Clay exclaimed.

"That is how I know he was murdered," Kate declared. "There's a thermos of coffee in the backpack," Kate told him. "Pour me a cup, and I'll finish telling you what I know."

Kate sat up and leaned her back against one of the rocks. Clay complied, handing her the cup of coffee and taking a seat next to her. "Go ahead," he urged her.

"When I arrived last Sunday afternoon," Kate began, "I went directly to the Lynn Lake Mounted station. They told me that they were not handling the investigation of the crash. They said CSIS had taken over. CSIS stands for Canadian Security Intelligence Service," Kate explained.

"I know," Clay told her, "I've taught several Canadian history and political science courses."

Kate went on, "They told me the team investigating the crash had just come in from the crash site and was at the excursion office. So I headed over there and when I got there several men were arranging something in a small seaplane. In hindsight, I think they were the recovered bodies or remains of my brother and the passengers. I started to head down to the dock, but as I passed the office door, a man came out and asked if I was Katherine Young. I said I was and he asked me to come inside. There was another man, dressed in fatigues, practically ransacking the office. The first man took a seat behind my brother's desk and invited me to sit. I did, but I instantly didn't like him. He was in his late forties, very fit and muscular with a close shaved head that highlighted a huge scar arching from the right side of his forehead to just behind his ear. He definitely looked and acted like a military type. He said he was Jason Randal of the CSIS and said he was sorry about my brother. I asked him what the other man was looking for, and I guess I got kind of snippy, and asked him why he was making himself so comfortable behind my brother's desk. He ignored the last comment and said they were looking for some indication of who was on the plane with my brother. I saw my brother's reservation and registrations books and told him that was easy. I looked up the reservation for last Saturday afternoon and confirmed in the registration book that the passengers were you and your party. He raised an eyebrow as if he already knew that, but thanked me and stood to leave. He called for his partner and started out the door but stopped and turned to me. This is where I started getting suspicious of him. He told me it would be several weeks before my brother's remains could be released. He said there was really no call for me to be in Lynn Lake and suggested I head back to Connecticut in the morning. It was as if he didn't want me there. He was a real jerk about it. I told him I was staying, and he told me to suit myself, but said I should stay in contact with them, letting them know where I was at all times. Like my life was any of their damn business!"

The sound of a plane rose in the distance as Kate jumped up and looked over the rocks. "That's them," she said, "but it will take them about fifteen minutes to land and taxi to the site.

Clay half watched the approaching plane, and half listened to Kate finish her story.

"As the CSIS men headed to their cars, one of the men who was working on the dock joined up with this Mr. Randal. He told Randal, 'they had secured a site well away from anything and out of sight of any usual flight patterns.' That sounded very suspicious to me. He said they had set up a tent warehouse and were 'all ready.'

I really became convinced that something was wrong when I went back through the office and into my brother's house. There were three packed duffel bags, nice ones, not military type, black leather. There was nothing interesting inside: a change of clothes, men's in two and women's clothes in the other one; toiletries; a power adapter set in one of them – typical stuff a business person would carry for an overnight. There were also four sets of dirty dishes in the sink. My brother had been entertaining, which he never did, and his guests looked like they were spending the night. I wondered if the bags were yours, but I couldn't imagine my brother having customers in his private quarters and making a meal. Then I wondered if you were part of this big discovery he had talked about when I was there six weeks ago. Whatever it was, I knew something was not making sense.

On Monday, I snooped around town. I went to Darcy's Café for breakfast that day. Darcy was a friend of my brother, and I had met her on several of my visits. Darcy came rushing over the minute I came in and hugged me all teary and said she felt terrible about Thomas. We had coffee, and I asked her if she had met the CSIS guy yet. She said he had taken over Thomas's office all day the day before and was 'summoning' just about everybody in town asking all kinds of questions about the company and Thomas and such. I asked her what kind of questions, and she said they wanted to know if Thomas had been acting strange; if he had seemed depressed lately; if he had been hanging around with strangers; that kind of stuff. I asked her the same questions. The only thing she said was that Thomas had been spending a lot of time at the library and the county recorder's office lately. She said the gossip was that he was looking at all kinds of deed records, topographic maps and weather history stuff. I confirmed that with Jill, the librarian, and the records office."

Clay turned to watch the plane as it splashed to a landing. He asked Kate to tell him more about the CSIS team.

"There were seven of them, including this Mr. Randal, who was clearly in command. I also asked Darcy about them. She said they had all been in once very early-on Sunday morning. They asked for a private room where they could talk without everyone listening. She said every time she went back to serve them, or take care of something, they would all shut up. She said they were really creepy. She also said she didn't like this Mr. Randal any more than I did when he interviewed me. Also, they all dressed in fatigues, but they didn't wear any insignia or anything, not a Canadian flag or anything, which I thought was strange.

They woke me up before dawn on Tuesday when they showed up at the excursion company's dock, loaded a bunch of gear and flew off. On an impulse, I went to a shed where my brother had kept the jet ski that he had shown me on my last visit. It was still there along with both of our still-packed back packs. I grabbed them and headed off to follow them. Of course, they were long gone, which was good because following someone in an airplane is not very subtle. However, they had told me roughly where the crash site was, and I figured that was where they were headed so that's where I went. I decided to spy on them, found this nice little perch to watch them from, and that's when I took those pictures you saw. I went back to Thomas's house that Tuesday, told them I was flying home to Connecticut, but instead packed more strategically for camping and spying. Then on Wednesday morning, I again flew back here and set up the camp you saw this morning well out of the way. I've been keeping an eye on them ever since."

The plane had anchored close to shore near the camp site, and four men were wading ashore carrying metal detectors and plastic bags. "It's been the same four every day," Kate said, "except Randal was with them for a bit on Tuesday. They're the men I saw in Lynn Lake. I don't know where the other two have been."

Clay guessed that the other two were either still in Lynn Lake or at the warehouse Kate said they had set up.

Clay thought a second, and then asked Kate if she knew where this warehouse was.

Kate answered, "I watched them leave every day and from the crash site, they always flew northwest on a heading of three hundred forty degrees. I can only assume it is somewhere in that line, but I don't know how far."

"Let's go," Clay ordered her.

She objected, "I planned on going, but only after they're done here, I don't want to miss anything."

"Even they don't look like they think they are going to find anything else. It looks like they're almost done. I think we should try to get a look at the warehouse while they are still here and not there," Clay argued. "Besides, from what you have said, it is probably where they took Bethany, Brooke and Eric."

***

Kate flew below the trees as she had earlier that morning for several miles until they were well out of the crash site area. She set a northwest heading of three hundred forty degrees and climbed as she accelerated the jet ski to its maximum speed of about eighty miles per hour. Clay kept a close watch on the landscape below, looking for any signs of the warehouse.

"You haven't quite finished your story," Clay told Kate, "How did you come to find me last night?"

"It was pretty much by accident," Kate said. "I didn't know it until I heard your radio transmission, but that is a scanner," she told Clay as she pointed to an instrument on the jet ski dashboard. "I had not heard a single transmission all week; it's only on when the jet ski is on. I was heading back to my campsite late yesterday when I suddenly heard your call. From the conversation, I figured you were probably one of the men my brother was involved with. Either way, I wanted to see whatever I could, so I headed straight for Thomas's cabin on Bigstone Lake."

Kate explained that she had gotten there a good five minutes ahead of the others and came in from the far side of the island. "I went to the top of the hill intending to watch just I had been doing at the crash site," Kate recounted, "but then you started coming up the hill, the same four men I had been watching all week landed and took the other three of you. Before I knew it you were right on top of where I was watching from, and a man was coming after you." Kate said she panicked, "I didn't think. I just reacted and shot the man. Then

I used the taser from Thomas's bag of spy stuff on you. Before I even got you back to my camp, I realized from what you had said on the radio that you couldn't possibly be involved. If you had been involved, you would have never made the radio call at all," Kate reasoned.

Clay was suddenly pointing at the ground just behind them. "There's something there!" Clay exclaimed.

Kate turned the jet ski and could make out a large blowing tarp under some trees just off shore. She cautiously moved as close as she dared and could see what appeared to be sections of a huge tent about forty yards inland. Clay stared at the tent as Kate made a wide circle to the far side of the tent and descended below the trees as she drove the jet ski across land until she was about a hundred yards from the tent's back side. She parked the jet ski next to a tree and they both jumped off.

"Damn," Kate cursed, "there has been a nice convenient hill to watch things from at every other place." Here the ground was flat and covered in tall weeds. Trees were sparse except in the small stand hiding the tent. They decided to crawl through the weeds toward the tent. They were thirty yards away when they heard a loud shrill whistle and froze.

"God damned those beavers!" they heard a voice bark, someone rustling about, and the sound of a hand slapping plastic. The whistling stopped.

Kate and Clay stared at each other for a

moment, and then continued their route to the tent. As they came to the edge of the weeds, they could see a campsite next to the huge tent with four hammock/tents, a traditional tent, and several folding bag chairs. A man was sitting in one of the chairs reading a book. Clay pointed and they both crawled just inside the weed line until they were on the side of the huge tent. "You stay here," Clay told Kate, "I'm going to have a look." Clay stood and ran toward the tent where he dropped on the ground and lifted the canvas just enough to peek inside.

The light in the tent was dim. The floor was mostly trampled weeds with dozens of tarps lined up along the far side. Airplane parts were neatly laid out on each tarp. There was a small table on the end opposite the door flaps with a folding chair. In the corner next to the table was a large pile of gear, and on the near corner next to the door flaps were eight body bags – four black and four red. No one was inside the tent, so he motioned to Kate to join him. They lifted the canvas of the tent enough to crawl inside and, without speaking they went straight to the body bags.

Clay slowly unzipped the first red bag so as not to make any noise. He saw a male who had been mangled, with his right arm detached and lying in the crook of the bag. A toe tag read 'Iatros - Unidentified' The second bag also contained a badly burnt male with a toe tag reading 'Iatros – Unidentified'. The third and fourth red bags contained females, also burned, and wearing the same toe tags.

Clay had barely moved the zipper of the first black bag when he moaned and buckled at the knees. It was Bethany. Her face was a bit puffy. Her wrists were crossed respectfully over her stomach, and she was in the same clothes she was wearing when Clay last saw her. She was ashen; no longer there. He slumped over the bag, crying uncontrollably. Kate drew her gun, certain the man outside would hear Clay and come rushing. But no one came. Suddenly, Clay stopped crying and moved to the second bag in a rage. He tore open the zipper and saw Eric, barely recognizable through the bruised and swollen face. His arms were broken and lying across his chest all cockeyed. He moved to the third bag. It was Brooke. His rage built as he tore open the fourth bag to see Thomas Young. Kate saw and dropped her head in anguish, but remained fairly composed. She joined Clay and opened the zipper further to reveal a toe tag that read 'Apoikian Thomas Young – 324-86-1222.' Clay backtracked to open each bag and read similar toe tags: 'Apoikian Brooke Louth – 458-26-9909;' 'Apoikian Eric Louth – 452-36-1920;' 'Apoikian Bethany Jeffries – 326-54-6092.'

Clay jumped to his feet and tore the gun from Kate's hand. He moved, his rage still building, and stormed from the tent and directly at the man sitting in the chair. The man turned to see Clay just as Clay pushed the chair over then kicked the man in the side with the force that comes from pure anger. He pointed the gun at the man and ordered him to get up.

Kate had come running after Clay. She grabbed a string, the type that held up the hammocks, and tied the man to the chair.

Clay didn't know where to begin, "Who are you? Why did you kill my daughters? What are you doing out here?" Clay's questions came faster than the man could answer.

As soon as Clay paused, the man answered softly, "I'm truly sorry about your daughters. I work for Jason Randal, and I don't know the why's – we just do our duty as he tells us to. We were to kill Thomas Young at all costs. We shot his plane down last Saturday thinking he was alone returning from dropping tourists off at his cabin. When we found the four other bodies in the wreckage, we were sure it was you and your party. When we intercepted your radio transmission yesterday, Mr. Randal got upset. We hustled to your cabin and were to bring you all here. Mr. Randal thought you might be involved with Young and when you shot Tim and somehow escaped the island, he became sure of it. We have been searching for you every day since with orders to bring you or your body to Mr. Randal.

"What does Apoikian and Iatros mean?" Clay asked.

"I'm Iatros," the man said, "you are Apoikian."

Clay's train of thought was interrupted by

the sound of a plane, in the distance, and coming closer. He searched the sky for a brief second then looked at Kate. Rage built in him again. He looked at the man tied to the chair then raised the gun; holding it to the man's head. Kate flinched, gasping as Clay pulled the trigger.

***

Clay and Kate crouched behind a rock. He hadn't decided on just what to do. He knew he had to confront the three men climbing out of the plane that had landed and pulled into the cove and anchored. They were covering the plane with the tarp Clay had first sighted from the air when Clay took aim with his pistol, still unsure of a strategy. Suddenly, he felt a poke in his back.

"It's nice to finally meet you, Mr. Jeffries," a voice said from behind him. "Why don't you both stand up and walk slowly to that plane? I want to introduce you to my friends."

◆CHAPTER 3◆

The sea plane that had carried Clay and Kate to this remote air field was pulling away from the dock on the water side of the airport. It was preparing to take back off as Clay glanced out the window of the luxurious Bombardier Global 5000 they had been moved to. Their guard had holstered his gun long ago and now stood in the doorway of the waiting jet. "Be respectful of those three. Two of them are this guy's daughters, and they were strictly collateral damage," the guard shouted down the stairs to the men on the tarmac loading the body bags into the rear cargo compartment. "Nobody gives a shit about the others," he said while taking a quick glance at Kate.

***

Jason Randal leaned forward in a chair facing the large desk that Whitcolm Remington sat behind. Remington was a small, trim man with a face as round as his overly round eyes. He smelled of expensive cologne and sported a two-hundred-dollar hair cut and a seventy-five dollar manicure. He was wearing a three-piece suit, perfectly tailored, and a monogrammed French cuff shirt. Each cufflink sported a large, off-center baguette diamond set into onyx. His well-shined black wingtips made an odd click as he stood and headed for the tarmac. "Alright, we're all set here," Remington said to Randal. "Keep looking for anything Young had on the batteries or the plant. I'm disappointed that you haven't found anything else yet – it's certain he had plenty."

Randal gave his assurance as he walked along and Remington continued, "Replace the team members you lost and add two more teams. Don't use any more Apoikian mercenaries either. No doubt our Iatros rebels were not the only ones willing to go this far, so expect a repeat of the plant breach soon."

"Consider it done, sir," Randal answered and asked Remington if there had been any progress on identifying the four dead Iatros.

"That is going to be tricky," Remington answered. "I would prefer to not have to include any Iatros deaths in my report to the Strategy Committee, but if I investigate their identities too aggressively, the committee will surely catch wind of it." Remington instructed Randal to let him know as soon as he found anything about Young, "and I'll get to the bottom of these two," pointing to the plane, "before we land in San Francisco."

Remington walked out the door just as it started to rain. He crossed the rain-soaked tarmac to the waiting jet flanked by two bodyguards.

***

Remington took a seat in a high-backed leather chair behind a small desk in the rear of the cabin. He had shuffled through papers, reading only a few as the plane taxied and took off. He had not spoken to Clay or Kate or even acknowledged their presence. Finally, as the plane leveled off, Remington stacked the papers neatly to one side of the desk and spoke to Clay.

"I am going to ask you both several questions. Josh here," Remington said while pointing to the man who had been keeping guard on Kate and Clay, "is going to administer a drug to you if I am not convinced that you are answering directly and honestly. The drug is actually a compound. The active ingredient is amobarbital, or what your intelligence agencies like to call truth serum. This particular compound is far more advanced than anything used in the past. Like your original drugs, it works by altering the higher cognitive functions, but it is far more effective in eliciting truth, and it does not necessarily kill you in the process the way your truth serum does. Unfortunately, it has a permanent, and very undesirable, effect on the subject's higher cognitive processes."

Clay almost wanted to chuckle. Remington was coming across so much like a mad arch-criminal from a James Bond movie. On the other hand, Clay was certain Remington would, indeed, use such tactics. More importantly, Clay thought, he had nothing to hide besides shooting the guy at the warehouse tent, and they certainly already knew he had done that. The question was, what did Kate Young have to hide?

Kate instinctively did not like the idea of cooperating in any way with this pompous fool. Even so, she also had to wonder what she had to hide, besides killing the guy when she grabbed Clay. That could hardly be at the heart of what Remington wanted to know, however. After all, she had done it, and she knew she would have to face that at some point. She was also sure, after seeing all that science fiction camping gear, that Remington was probably being accurate in his description of the truth drug. The question was, what did Clay Jeffries have to hide?

Clay and Kate both responded to Remington at the same time, with the same words: "I have nothing to hide." They looked at each and Clay had a momentary flashback to when he was a child shouting 'ditto' in such situations. He thought it showed how cunningly this Mr. Remington had put him at ease.

"That is terrific," Remington grinned, "then

instead of a flight full of nasty business, we can relax, have a good meal, and chat." Remington turned to Josh and suggested he bring them dinner. "Would either of you like a drink, before we eat? Josh makes a nice raspberry martini, Miss Young, and can measure to the drop the right amount of water to add to a glass of bourbon, Mr. Jeffries."

It didn't bother Clay in the least that Remington was making it clear that he already knew plenty. At that moment, he would have happily unloaded any and all state secrets in exchange for that drink. The point was reinforced when Josh brought out a Pittsburgh style filet with a loaded baked potato for him and a salmon filet with boiled redskins and asparagus for Kate. Josh served Remington tuna, very rare, as was his preference.

"Why don't you begin, Miss Young, by telling us of your activities over the last eight days," Remington suggested.

Kate recounted her week precisely as she had described it to Clay earlier. She told Remington of her instant dislike of Randal and of her distrust of him and his crew. She described her activities around Lynn Lake last Monday and recounted her conversation with Darcy. Kate choked a bit when she described her spying on the crew on Tuesday and seeing the wing that confirmed Thomas had been shot down. She paused and thought 'no harm in asking.' Even if there was harm in asking, she needed to know.

"Was it you, Mr. Remington, that was responsible for killing my brother?" Kate asked as she stared Remington in the eye.

"It was, Miss Young," Remington answered softly, "and I cannot tell you adequately how much I regret that it was necessary and how sorry I am for your loss." He sounded sincere, and Kate began to cry. The thought she had refused to entertain for the past eight days overwhelmed her. Perhaps Thomas was not so innocent in all of this. Clay instinctively took Kate's hand.

"Miss Young," Remington continued, "I realize that it will only intensify the pain you must feel, but you must know that your brother had become involved in things far beyond his understanding. I find it difficult to believe that he was looking for wealth, or even fame or power. I honestly think your brother became involved for what he thought was an altruistic cause. It was not. Whether he knew it or not, the consequences of your brother's actions, had he succeeded, would have been unimaginably destructive."

"My brother would have never knowingly gotten involved in anything bad," Kate told Remington, "if he did, he was tricked into it."

"I believe that is the case," Remington assured her, "and I hope it is some comfort to you."

Remington turned his attention to Clay. "Mr. Jeffries, tell me of your activities over the past forty-eight hours."

Clay was suddenly uneasy. There wasn't

much to tell, other than finding Brooke and Bethany and Eric dead, and killing a guy who was apparently working for Remington. Worse, Clay was beginning to believe this Remington was on the right side, or at least the legal side of things. He probably murdered a federal agent or something like that. He thought for a second about a possible story, or an excuse. It reminded Clay of the time he almost had an affair, and Kara confronted him. It wasn't actually an affair, but he and a woman in the school office had become very close. They flirted a lot and went to lunch a few times before the woman became direct. Clay didn't exactly say no, but he laughed her off. When Kate confronted him, he came completely clean. He even admitted that he wasn't sure that he hadn't done anything out of love for Kara, or whether he just didn't have the guts. Kara accepted his confession and never said another word about it. In the end, it had been good for them. It took their relationship to a new level of openness and honesty.

Clay decided he wasn't going to be any less honest now. He figured that his integrity was all he had left anyway. He no longer cared what this Remington or anyone else wanted to do to him. In fact, he figured they would be doing him a favor if they just killed him now. Yet, Clay still felt justified in killing one of his daughters' murderers. There was a bit of defiance in his answer: "I don't have much to add to what Kate has told you," Clay said as he sat back in his seat, "other than finding my daughters and son-in-law murdered and shooting one of the bastards that killed them."

"Mr. Jeffries," Remington sighed, "this was going so well." Remington nodded to Josh who picked up the syringe he had prepared. "I should think you have had a much more interesting time than that. Why did you run when my men came to pick you and your party up? Who tipped you off that it was us and not search and rescue? Why did you shoot my man when he caught up with you?"

Clay and Kate both jumped. "Why did *he* shoot your man?'" Kate questioned in a shocked tone. "He didn't shoot him – I did! I'm not even sure why I did. I was tired. I had been out there for four days with hardly any sleep and was convinced they were up to something. I believed they had killed my brother. I just acted on impulse."

"Miss Young," Remington looked at her, his shock and confusion showing, "Why would you even have been at Bigstone Lake?"

"I intercepted Mr. Jeffries' distress call. I assumed he was part of whatever my brother was involved in and went to see what I could learn. I got there a few minutes ahead of your men and went to the far side of the island and to the top of the hill so that I could watch, just as I had been doing at the crash site."

"And I don't know why you say I was running away." Clay added, "I heard Miss Young's jet ski and thought search and rescue had gone to the wrong side of the island. I simply went to flag them down."

"Mr. Jeffries," Remington shouted, "you can't possibly expect me to believe that fantasy." Remington glanced at Josh, who looked to the side at the lie detector sheet printing out well behind Clay and Kate. He nodded as if to say 'they are telling the truth.' Remington's voice softened. "Then explain to me why your daughter brought you to Manitoba in the first place."

Clay answered what he thought was an idiotic question. "We were on a family vacation. My daughters wanted to cheer me up after my wife's death. There was nothing mysterious about it."

"Did your daughter really find it necessary to make four advanced trips to plan this little family vacation?" Remington condescended. "She did have quite a reputation as a project manager in the Air Force, but the President of the United States doesn't do that much planning for a trip!"

Clay went instantly numb. It was his turn to be surprised and this one knocked the wind out of him. Instantly, he knew Bethany had been somehow involved in this. He always knew that she had likely gotten involved in some pretty sensitive stuff in the Air Force, not like Special Forces or anything like that, but as a project manager she might have been working on secret development projects. Whenever he had asked her about her work, she had kidded and said her role was like that of General Groves overseeing the Manhattan project. She often said the projects she had worked on were pretty cool but would then add the tired line 'I could tell you about it, but then I would have to kill you.' Suddenly, it wasn't a joke.

"Did you not know, Mr. Jeffries," Remington asked, "that your daughter Bethany had visited with Mr. Young four times over the last two months before coming on this little family vacation?"

"I did not!" Clay answered, but conceded that it was possible that she had been involved somehow. "But if she were," he thought out loud, "it wasn't because she was duped. She would have had good reasons." Clay immediately realized what he had said and took Kate's hand as if to apologize.

Remington took a long pensive pause as he stared past Kate and Clay. "The present situation is quite complex, and I must admit, a bit confusing, even for me. If your brother, Miss Young, and your daughter, Mr. Jeffries were, as you say, duped, as I now suspect they were, it would not suggest a lack of character or intelligence on their parts.

The plane had begun its approach into San Francisco as Remington continued. "There is much for all of us to sort out. There is no need to think of yourselves as prisoners, but I would like you to be my guests for a couple of days. Customs, and many other technicalities, might prove problematic for you right now anyway, Mr. Jeffries, since you are officially dead. I must return to my office and attend to several things. Josh will escort you to suitable accommodations."

As the plane came to rest in its hangar, Clay was thinking how odd it was that this Remington was beginning to seem almost likeable. He dismissed the thought as they climbed down the jet's stairs and walked a mere twenty yards to the waiting limousines. Remington turned to Clay to ask one last question. "Mr. Jeffries, your daughter also made several visits to Bar Harbor, Maine in the past few months. Might you know of a reason she would visit there so frequently?"

Clay paused a second, then answered, "My parents had a summer home there that we used to visit every summer when the girls were younger. Both of my daughters still have," Clay caught himself, "*had* long-standing friendships there."

"I see," Remington responded, "Well good night."

Clay didn't respond, but was holding his breath, grateful that Remington had not seen through the dim hanger as Clay's face went white. He needed to get to Bar Harbor.

***

"Mr. Remington keeps a tower suite here for his guests," Josh explained as the limousine pulled into the small but ornate entry drive of the Fairmont hotel. "I've never stayed here myself, but it is luxurious," Josh told Kate and Clay. "The only guests Mr. Remington puts up here are pretty important people; it's an honor."

Just as there had been no customs, there

was no check-in, no baggage handling, no annoying bellman. They crossed the marble lobby and took an elevator straight to the twenty-second floor. Josh unlocked the suite door and surprised Clay by handing him the two keys to the suite. Kate squealed a bit as she spied and went directly to the baggage she had left at her brother's house in Lynn Lake. Clay was as delighted as Kate to see the baggage he had last seen on the docks at Bigstone Lake. The backpacks were oddly incongruous with the eloquent contemporary design of the suite, but it was comforting to be reunited with some of his own things.

The feeling of being held, of being a prisoner, entirely dissipated when Josh started going on as if he were the annoying bellman. "There are two bedrooms, of course, and you only need to show the room key for anything in the hotel. There is no need to sign or anything; do not concern yourselves with gratuities. In fact, Mr. Jeffries, signing would be an obvious problem anyway. Mr. Remington has left some cash for anything else you might need from outside the hotel. Your credit cards have naturally been deactivated. There is much to see here. You might like to stroll the shops at Fisherman's Wharf or explore this area: Nob Hill." Josh looked as if he were ready to leave, much to Clay's relief, but added a final note. "Mr. Jeffries, Miss Young, you are Mr. Remington's guests, and he would like to show you every possible courtesy and hospitality.

You have been through much. I urge you to relax, put all this aside for the moment, and enjoy the evening. I will return in the morning, and we can begin the work of sorting this all out." Josh paused, then added, "Oh, we arranged for some fresh clothes to be sent up; if you need any other personal items or anything else, don't hesitate to let the concierge know."

Josh wished them a good evening as Clay closed the door behind him and turned to Kate. "Well, this looks almost as nice as that hammock thing you put me up in," Clay said sarcastically, but with a lump forming in his throat. They both slumped into overstuffed wing chairs near the large picture window that looked out over the San Francisco skyline and the bay. "I'm sorry that I suggested your brother was duped,"

"Don't be sorry," Kate demanded, "It sounds like that's exactly what happened." Kate buried her face in her hands and began to sob. "I'm so confused!"

Clay stood and crossed to Kate and sat on the arm of her chair. He put an arm around her and took her hand. "So am I," he told her, "but this Remington does not seem like the super bad guy we had imagined."

"No, he doesn't," Kate agreed. "Still, they killed my brother, and they killed your daughters and son-in-law. I have to know why! I need to know what is going on here!"

"I suspect we might get some answers in the morning when Josh comes back for us," Clay thought as he looked out the window at the falling darkness and the city lights coming to life. "Anyway, I am sure there is nothing we can do tonight. Maybe Josh had the right idea, let's try to set it aside for the evening, take a shower, change and go have a drink."

"I hope you mean separate showers," Kate laughed through her tears as Clay realized how he had phrased that. He was far too old to blush – he thought, as he grabbed the three back packs and headed for one of the bedrooms. "I'll need more than a minute," Kate said, "I've been living in the woods for four days."

"Take your time," Clay answered, "I might lay down for a minute anyway."

Clay set the backpacks on the bed. The one that had held their leftover food was empty, but he remembered digging through it hardly more than a day ago to find some Pringles. He opened the back pack Bethany and Brooke had shared. On top was a plastic bag with two swimming suits still ever so slightly damp. He took a cursory look through the bag. There was nothing there but a week's worth of clothes suitable for camping, fishing and hiking. He opened the third pack that he and Eric had shared to find the same kinds of clothes – jeans and tee-shirts – nothing fitting to wear for a drink at the Fairmont. He did dig out his shaving kit, along with the stupid looking hat that Eric had worn all week, the one that looked like it had belonged to Colonel Henry Blake on *MASH*, and that Eric seemed to think was mandatory gear for fishing. Clay held the hat reverently and thought of Eric. They were close; it was only natural for Clay to welcome a son-in-law after spending so much of his life living with three women.

It was goofy little things that Clay liked best about having another man in the family. He liked it when Eric would instinctively follow him out to fire up the grill during those frequent family cookouts, or when Eric would be right behind him grabbing a box of decorations along with Clay to carry to the tree as they readied for a family Christmas. Even so, there were deeper moments too. Clay remembered the wedding weekend. Clay came off as pretty casual about the whole affair. He had to because of what was going on in his head. Had he shown it, it would have made him look like a silly blubbering mother-of-the-bride. The memory of getting home the night of the wedding came back vividly. Clay remembered stripping off the rented tuxedo and thinking how glad he had felt that someone else loved Brooke as much as he did. He remembered his eyes filling with tears for no apparent reason. Clay's eyes were again filled with tears as he laid the hat aside, took the shaving kit, and headed for the shower.

He didn't remember how long he had taken in the shower or to put on the wool slacks and cashmere sweater he had found waiting for him in the bedroom closet, but he was surprised when he walked into the sitting room to find Kate sitting in front of a computer. He was genuinely stunned at how she had changed. Her hair was fuller, slightly curled, and hanging over her shoulder instead of in the long straight pony tail she had been wearing. She was wearing a cocktail dress hemmed just above her knees, brown with some teal trimming, tight at the waist and full in the skirt. His eyes, as they always did, went right to her crossed legs, which were perfectly shaped and looked especially feminine framed in the three-inch heels she was wearing.

"I thought I was the one that would take awhile," Kate kidded. "Did you have a good nap?"

"Actually," Clay answered, "I never really got to the nap part. The shower felt so good, I guess I lost track of time."

"Mine felt good too," Kate emphasized, "of course it wasn't an hour's worth of good."

"Sorry," Clay apologized for making her wait.

"Oh, I'm just kidding," Kate dismissed it. "Look, they have a computer in here. I thought I would Google this Whitcolm Remington and see if I could find out anything about him."

"And?" Clay urged her on.

"I'll tell you downstairs. Right now, that drink comes first," Kate said as she stood and picked up the small brown purse that had been resting by the computer.

They made their way to the lobby and the Laurel Court bar. The bar gave a sweeping view of the restaurant which featured three ornate domes each surrounded by deep beige marble pillars ribboned with dark-brown veins. The room was lively for a Sunday night, and they had to twist and push their way through the crowd to a small table in the back corner that promised some quiet. Clay figured that service would be slow so before he even sat, he asked Kate what she would like and prepared to head for the bar, but as he turned, a waitress appeared carrying a tray and set two coasters on the table. "She would like a glass of your featured chardonnay," Clay repeated Kate's order, "and I'll have a bourbon and water."

"You're in wine country, and you're ordering a bourbon and water?" Kate chided.

Clay struggled for an excuse. Kate had seemed to become quite light-hearted since they had arrived in San Francisco, especially for someone who had just lost her brother. He realized it was probably tougher to lose two daughters than to lose a brother, but her easy kidding made him a bit uneasy. He just wasn't sure whether it was because it seemed inappropriate given their circumstances, or because it seemed flirtatious, and he was ashamed that he liked it. In either case, he knew he needed to lighten up a bit too.

"Actually," he retorted, "We're near wine country, not in it. I believe I am beyond the fifty-mile mandatory wine-drinking radius and can legally order bourbon and water."

Kate flashed a brief smile before lowering her eyes. Her suddenly serious face dismissed any thoughts Clay might have that she was acting inappropriately. He could see her thoughts turning back to her brother and the improbable predicament they found themselves in.

"So tell me what you found out about this Mr. Whitcolm Remington," Clay urged Kate.

"Everything I found was interesting, but couldn't possibly be relevant," Kate started. "The first thing I found was a Forbes article on the richest twenty-five men in the world – he is number twenty-three. He started with a small manufacturing company in Italy that made office chairs. When that business started suffering, he diversified and has since built a conglomeration of companies that he owns outright or has a controlling interest in. None of the companies are very interesting; companies that make staplers, clocks, a paper company, several clothing makers, one that makes lamps, a restaurant chain. He owns a huge seed company, and he actually owns a number of large corporate farms, but they look more like a hobby than a business. A whole bunch of other companies, but nothing glamorous like weapons systems or anything even remotely like that."

"So what possible interest could he have in your brother and in us?" Clay wondered.

"He is a huge supporter of causes related to the mentally disabled," Kate added.

"I think the term now is 'other-abled," Clay corrected her, "but I still don't see a connection."

"He has given billions, not millions, billions

to causes like Special Olympics, communities for mentally retarded adults, research-related activities, all that kind of stuff. He has sat on a couple of Presidential Commissions, has testified before Congress, and even held some U.N. position – all on mental retardation issues. He comes across as something of the patron saint of other-abled people," Kate said with some admiration.

"I'm trying to think if Bethany had ever been especially involved in those kinds of organizations." Clay commented. "She was a volunteering type person, but I can't think of anything she was involved in that might be related. How about Thomas, can you think of anything that might have connected him to Remington?"

"Not a thing," Kate answered. "In fact, Thomas's insensitivity to some of those issues was kind of embarrassing sometimes. I have somewhat accepted that Thomas was involved in something, and that maybe it was something he shouldn't have been involved in. How about you, Clay? It certainly appears as though your daughter was involved as well."

"I have accepted that," Clay answered. "In fact, it makes some sense. I always pictured her working on military projects like getting an officer's club in some Podunk base refurbished, but I guess she might just as well have been project managing some fairly intriguing stuff. So, I accept that she might have been involved, but I am certainly not convinced that it was anything bad." He had his doubts even as he denied it.

Clay ordered a second drink for each of them and suggested they change the subject. The plan had been to drop this whole thing for the evening, and he still thought that a good idea. "So, tell me about yourself." Clay suddenly felt like an awkward college kid on a first date.

"I'm just a rich brat that hasn't done anything worthwhile with my life so far." Kate answered. "I try to make up for it by working for several charities; a soup kitchen that I work for two days a month; a women's shelter that helps homeless women with small children; and especially Habitat for Humanity. I'm on our local board. I love to read, love literature and own a little collectable book store in New Haven. It doesn't make any money, but I really do love that book store. I write poetry, but nobody knows that, because nobody actually reads poetry anymore, let alone *my* poetry. I just write it for fun; never shown anything to anyone."

"Well then, we're both writers," Clay jumped in. "I am technically a professor, but I have written and published several books and definitely prefer to think of myself as more of a writer than a professor." Clay was embarrassed that he had, as he often did, turned the conversation back to him. He was more embarrassed that he had made such a juvenile attempt to impress her. He determined to move the conversation back to her. "Married? I'm guessing no children?

"No!" Kate exclaimed, "No children and none of that maternal yearning I am supposed to be feeling at this age. I see too many children suffering at my charities. Plus, I guess I am more of a child myself. Never been married. I've had two serious relationships, both with men older than you," Kate sounded as if she meant to be encouraging. "Both decided that when push came to shove, they liked their wives better. As they say, the first one made a fool out of me, the second one was just plain foolish."

"I'm sorry things didn't work out," Clay said. "You obviously have much to offer.

"I don't know about that,' Kate demurred. "Besides, I have found that looks alone don't get a girl very far."

"I didn't mean your looks," Clay protested, "though forgive me for not mentioning, until now, how terrific you look."

Kate reached across the table and took Clay's hand. It alarmed him for a second until she turned his wrist and looked at his watch. "It's after ten o'clock. I imagine you want to go to bed now. Of course you want to go to bed; all men do." Kate giggled a little at her joke and realized that a mere two glasses of wine had gotten to her a bit. "We should call it a night. Today has just been too much."

They both stood to leave as the waitress appeared. Clay reached in his pocket for the room key and to search for some cash to leave the girl. The waitress seemed to cut him off as she looked at the key and said, "Have a good night, Mr. Jeffries, Miss Young."

Clay was startled that she knew their names. "Now that is customer relationship management," Clay said as they stepped on the elevator. "We have been in this hotel less than three hours and the cocktail waitress knows our name from looking at the room key!"

Kate took Clay's arm in her elbow as the elevator doors closed; she rested her head on his shoulder. "It's been quite a day," she said through a near yawn. They were silent during the ride up, and Clay thought Kate might have actually fallen asleep until she stepped off the opening elevator and through the room door Clay had unlocked. He wished her a good night and started for his room when she put a hand on his shoulder and leaned in to kiss him on the cheek. "Good night, Clay."

She was flirting, Clay thought as he stripped and fell into bed. He knew the difference between a friendly peck on the cheek and a caring good-night kiss. That had been the latter. It still made him somewhat uncomfortable, but it didn't matter; he had much more important things to think about. A picture of the family's summer home in Bar Harbor flashed in his mind as he fell asleep.

***

Bethany sat down on the deck floor with her legs dangling over the side. She laid her head in her crossed arms resting on the second rung of the deck railing. She looked up to the trees and the grassy meadows on the hill rising out of the island's center. "You know what it reminds me of, Dad?" she asked.

Clay could still picture that cute round face with expressive wide eyes and the same full eyebrows that had once gotten her picture in a local print ad. Her hair was, like Brooke's, thick bodied, but black and cut shorter, turned under at the bottom of her neck. If Brooke had taken some kidding about being skinny, Bethany took a lot about being short, she was just five-foot-two, but her muscular thighs made her powerful enough to have been one of the toughest tomboys around. She was slender, but she hated those muscular thighs. She spent most of her adolescence complaining about having to buy shorts and slacks a size too large for her waist just to accommodate her thighs. Clay was noticing how the shorts she was wearing now bunched at the small of her back. "What's that," he asked.

"Our vacation house in Bar Harbor," Bethany answered. "Remember that huge old walnut tree that Grandpa put a swing on for Brooke and I when we were kids?" Bethany asked her father.

"I certainly do," Clay answered. "I seem to remember an incident about you pushing Brooke backwards out of that swing one time and hurting her back."

"Yeah," Bethany laughed, "Brooke might be older, but I'm still tougher. Remember that pile of rocks that was pretty close to that tree? There were a lot of rock piles, cairns Grandpa called them, but remember the one near that tree?"

"Yeah, I remember it, why?" Clay asked her.

"It's just that this island reminds me so much of Bar Harbor, and the rock piles down by the beach made me think of that old cairn. You know, Brooke and I used to hide things in that little pile of rocks. Grandpa had promised us that it would be just our hiding place forever. I actually think we might still have some things hiding there. I bet that love letter Brooke got from David Ridgely that one summer when she was like nine is probably still there."

The scene seemed to play over and over as Clay slept fitfully that night.

◆CHAPTER 4◆

Three months ago, on the day Whitcolm Remington finally understood the true nature and scope of the Movement, he had committed to his brazen and brilliant plan to flush out its leaders. He had revealed Iatros society to two Apoikians. Lifting that veil had been, under Iatrosian law, an undeniable act of treason. But Remington no longer saw himself as an Iatros; he was even more than that. He hadn't chosen the role. He wasn't even sure he wanted it. But fate had chosen him, and he would do what he knew to be right. He thought of his actions as extra-legal: outside the law, yes, but undeniably necessary under the circumstances.

That treason of three months ago led to an even bigger crime. For the first time in their seven thousand year history, an Iatros had been killed by another Iatros. Had it not been for the Apoikians, the word murder would have all but disappeared from the Iatros vocabulary. Remington knew, as he finished the report that he had sat up all night to prepare, that he could easily and credibly blame the deaths on the cure experiments; the victims' status as Iatros was murky anyway. Still he could not deny the treason. He was confident in the correctness of his actions, and he would boldly go before the Strategy Committee this afternoon and admit to the act. If what he had done was a crime, then it was their crime as well.

Remington would just as boldly admit to the crime he was about to commit. Katherine Young and Clayton Jeffries had not been part of the original plan, but their sudden involvement would greatly simplify several things. He had thought through most of the past week, that things may have gone wrong; that this Clayton Jeffries was acting for some new kind of opposition who appeared to know more than they should. His relief to discover that Jeffries was no more than an innocent Apoikian was surpassed only by his delight when he realized how useful they could be.

Remington had hesitated, thinking that one more treasonous act was too much and, in the end, not really necessary. But then he realized that Clay and Kate's involvement was a gift that further proved the right of his course. He would use them. He would reveal more than just the secrets of Borden Island. And he would make no apology for it.

***

Clay and Kate had half expected Josh to show up at their room door at first light with a breakfast cart and a vague itinerary for the day. "It would have been such a cliché," Kate had joked, "But now I am wondering what the heck the deal is." It was nearly nine o'clock. They dressed, waited a bit, and then decided to go down to breakfast on their own.

They had eaten off of the buffet and lingered as long as seemed reasonable, sipping fresh-squeezed orange juice from crystal goblets. Clay was wondering what they should do now. "I hate hanging around a hotel room in the middle of the day, but we really shouldn't leave the hotel, and I don't know what else to do. I thought Josh would be here this morning."

Kate agreed that hanging around the hotel room seemed a bit weird, "But I would hardly call it the middle of the day," she had said. Both were surprised to see not Josh, but Remington enter the restaurant and have a brief word with the hostess. They also thought it a bit rude when Remington waived his hand to summon them to him, but they went dutifully.

"Forgive me," Remington seemed to read their minds, "that was rude of me, but we are in an extraordinary hurry because of my inexcusable tardiness. All that I can offer is that I have been awake all night preparing for this presentation, and another I am to make to an important body this afternoon."

"It's no problem," Kate had dismissed Remington's rudeness. "We are getting some kind of presentation?" she asked.

"Yes, Miss Young," Remington had answered. "I promised you some answers this morning, and I intend to keep my word. However, the answers I believe you need are quite complex, and I have been laboring over just how to tell you all that you need to know." At that, Remington waived them onto the elevator as if to say 'after you.' Clay assumed they were returning to their room for the presentation, but knew otherwise when Remington inserted a key and seemed to manipulate it in some kind of code. He turned it two full circles counter-clockwise, removed the key, then reinserted it and slowly moved it clockwise as the lock audibly clicked three times. Clay couldn't resist a chuckle as he asked Remington if this was an elevator or a phone booth from *Get Smart*.

Remington answered, also with a chuckle, that it was really an elevator. Clay could tell from his sudden loss of weight that they were moving downward. The elevator had accelerated as its whining became increasingly high pitched. During the ride, which lasted almost a full minute suggesting to Clay that they had traveled deep beneath the ground, Remington told them that what they were about to learn would evoke reactions much like getting the news of one's own pending mortality. "You will go through similar phases," Remington had said. "First denial; you will think me some kind of lunatic that has invented this absurd flight of fancy. Then anger; you will feel manipulated, as if your whole life has been a cruel joke. Then something like self-pity," Remington continued. "You will wonder why I have told you all this and perhaps wonder if I have some diabolical plan for you. You will finally accept what I am about to tell you and, before the morning is out, you will see the deaths of your loved ones in a whole new way. In fact, you will see the entire world in a whole new way.

Given the key shenanigans and the high talk from Remington, Clay expected the elevator doors to open to some kind of futuristic movie set, all steel and glass, with men at computer stations and analysts studying holograms or something. When the elevator finally braked to a stop and the doors opened, what Clay and Kate looked out on was anything but a futuristic movie set.

***

Clay and Kate stood behind Remington at the midpoint of an oversized corridor that stretched what Clay guessed was about seven hundred feet to his left and to his right. It was also unusually wide, maybe a hundred feet, and high, about forty feet. The corridor was lined with hundreds of dormant monitors, each ornately framed in wood carvings and flanked on either side by glass cases set into the walls. The floor, walls and ceiling were marble, and the ceiling was lined with huge circular wood carvings about thirty feet in diameter and spaced about fifteen feet apart. The floor they stood on was hardwood that interrupted the marble floors of the corridor on their left and right. They were facing a huge archway, about a hundred feet wide with a grand staircase on either side. The wood floor continued through the depth of the archway but was interrupted by a twenty-five-foot marble circle in its center. Lighting in the hallway was not visible, but pretty well mimicked daylight. Lighting in the archway, on the other hand, was much softer. It left the area rather dark, like one might see in a cathedral.

"I see you are impressed," Remington commented. "I will treat you to a full tour, but I think it will be more meaningful after we speak. My office is just this way." Remington crossed the oversized hallway and passed through the long arch and led them into the largest room Clay had ever seen. Along the end opposite the arch, at least a thousand feet away, was a raised area with ornate desks, very similar to the U.S. House of Representative's chamber that Clay had seen once from the House Gallery and hundreds of times on television. The platform and desks were, of course, much larger than those in the U.S. House. The room was clearly a legislative chamber, with long curving desks facing the platform and hundreds, maybe thousands of deep blue high-backed leather chairs arranged in rows behind the desks. There was a wide center aisle and lighting again closely simulating daylight. The floor was covered with a thick beige carpet patterned with repeating concentric circles of blue, green, red and brown.

Clay and Kate took in details of the room as they followed Remington to the first of eleven huge and ornate doors that punctuated the right wall of the chamber. The middle door, Clay noticed, was quite a bit larger and even more ornate than the others. Remington held the first door as Clay and Kate walked into an only slightly oversized room that appeared to be a corporate conference room. There was a colorful mural on the far wall and five doorways on each side of the room. Remington led them to the farthest doorway on their left.

Remington commented that it was quite a hike to his office. "Keeps me young and fit," he had said, meaning to be sarcastic, but both Clay and Kate had thought it true. Remington again held a door open for them and they all stepped into an office suite that could have been any office in the country. "Good morning, Rachel," Remington greeted the receptionist as he passed her.

"Your report has been finalized and proofed," another office worker said as he handed a computer tablet to Remington.

"Thank you Edward," Remington responded and added a request for the worker to bring coffee. They entered a typical, though huge, office that reeked of corporate excess. "Have a seat," he waived at the cordovan-colored leather couch as he sat in an armchair facing them. "I'm not sure where to begin. I've only related this story to a very few others. Let me preface it with this: the history and the story I am about to share with you will undoubtedly impress you as utterly fantastic and completely unbelievable. Once you accept it as factual, which you will eventually do, I assure you it will change your entire world view.""

Remington stopped speaking as Edward entered with a tray filled with a pot of coffee, three cups and saucers with service and a plate of breakfast pastries. He sat quietly as Edward set the tray down and served each of them a cup of coffee. He asked Remington if there was anything else he could do and left when Remington declined.

"Just less than ten thousand years ago," Remington began.

"This is going to be a long story," Clay interrupted, hoping the joke might ease some of the tension he was feeling.

Kate poked Clay in the leg and chided him to let Remington speak.

"Thank you Miss Young," Remington continued. "As I was saying, just less than ten thousand years ago the Universe was rapidly expanding. So too was our solar system. Back then, the orbit of Mars was slightly closer to the sun than it is now, by about four million miles at the furthest point in its elliptical orbit. The sun was also warmer by about seven hundred degrees. Those two facts made Mars a much warmer planet than it is now. Average temperatures on Mars then ranged from minus thirty to seventy-five degrees. Mars' orbit was also substantially closer to that of Earth. The two planets were similar in many other ways as well. They both had thick, nourishing atmospheres. Both had an abundance of water, though much of the water on Earth was, as it is now, heavily contaminated with salt, and much of the water on Mars was contaminated with iron. The magnetic field on Mars is now quite a bit weaker than that of Earth, but it was only a little weaker ten thousand years ago."

Kate was leaning forward, fascinated by the facts Remington was spewing out. Clay, on the other hand, was beginning to shift around with impatience. Yet, both instinctively knew where Remington was going, and they urged him on.

"Are you about to tell us that there was life on Mars ten thousand years ago, and that you are a Martian," Clay asked impatiently and somewhat mockingly.

"Yes Mr. Jeffries, I am," Remington responded in a matter-of-fact but gentle way, "but there is much more. Ten thousand years ago, both planets teamed with life. Life on Earth was dominated by dinosaurs and was not nearly as evolved as was life on Mars. Life on Mars was dominated by our own species. By 'ours' I mean yours and mine – I mean humans."

Clay knew Remington was serious, but he couldn't help but further mock the proposition. "So you're saying you are Martin O'Hare. I'd like to see those little antennae sprout from your head."

"*My Favorite Martian* was indeed an amusing little TV show, Mr. Jeffries; but not very realistic," Remington responded with a smile. "I realize that this all sounds ridiculous. I hope you realize it will sound just as ridiculous if you decide to repeat it at any time. I certainly wouldn't be making the claim myself, unless I could offer compelling evidence."

"Yeah, let him finish," Kate demanded as she playfully punched Clay on the thigh with the side of her fist. Clay gave her a look as if to say 'I can't believe you're buying this.'

Remington continued. "Ten thousand years ago, both planets had very similar ecologies. Human life on Mars had advanced to something very close to life on Earth today. We possessed much of the technology you are familiar with. We began space travel and nearby space exploration. Our institutions and government were highly evolved; somewhat more evolved than life today on Earth. Obviously, we had highly developed spoken and written language; understood mathematics and physics; we dwelt on questions of philosophy and religion; and we were social. In this one respect, our social organization, we were advanced far beyond what society is on Earth today."

"But then," Remington paused a second and took a sip of coffee, thinking about his next revelation, "but then a planet called Ceres, that orbited between Jupiter and Mars, exploded. It created the Asteroid belt that still orbits between Mars and Jupiter. Given the constant explosiveness and roiling of the Universe, it was really not much at all. Two larger asteroids collided; one with significant enough velocity to send thousands of asteroids pin balling and knocking hundreds of dead rocks out of their orbit. Those that left their orbit were naturally attracted to the nearest body with the strongest gravitational pull: most toward Jupiter; some toward Mars; and some toward Earth. The magnetic fields of Mars and Earth protected them from most of the projectiles. Earth's moon, not having the same protection, was pummeled."

Remington again paused, though less reflectively this time and more as a matter of catching his breath. He took a sip of coffee and looked back at Clay and Kate, now both leaning forward, anxious for him to continue.

"Note that I said the magnetic fields of Mars and Earth protected them from *most* of the projectiles." Remington said. "You know of the one large asteroid that struck Earth. It hit what is now the Caribbean and is what extinguished the dinosaurs. A much larger asteroid, about nine thousand kilometers long, struck Mars' northern hemisphere. The effect was nearly devastating.

Man survived, but in the crudest sense. Most of society was disrupted. Mars was moved into a more elliptical orbit slightly further from the sun. It became inhospitably cold. Our very atmosphere was nearly destroyed. Ninty-five percent of the human population was killed. Those that survived took refuge in large caverns with artificial temperature control and a recycled atmosphere."

"What about food and water?" Kate asked.

"There was some to last a while, and very limited production. Most crops and animal life were destroyed. Scientists asserted that the situation was not sustainable for more than one to two hundred years."

"So you came to Earth" Clay interrupted.

"*We* came to Earth," Remington corrected him, "but it was not nearly that simple. Actually, fleeing to Earth was only one of many solutions proposed and only one of the three solutions undertaken. Of the roughly six thousand survivors, about two thousand set out to build a sustainable environment on Mars. Another two thousand planned to establish an artificial environment that would basically drift through space until it came upon a suitable environment or indefinitely if necessary. The final two thousand set out for Earth. Preparing for the flight to Earth took forty-five years. Preparing an artificial environment meant to sustain itself in space took nearly a hundred and fifty years."

Remington stood with some excitement, and moved to a bookcase set in the wall behind his desk. "I have a couple of photo volumes here that document the expeditions." He opened the book and laid it on the coffee table facing Clay and Kate. Remington hovered over them like a proud grandfather sharing family pictures. "This book is about the Earth-bound expedition. This is the main craft; there were four of them," he narrated as he pointed to pictures. "Each was equally balanced in terms of knowledge stores, essential experts, medical personnel, livestock, resources, and the like." The 'ship' looked nothing like a ship, spacecraft, or any other kind of elegantly designed vehicle. It looked more like the steel frame of a high-rise building under construction, except all twisted and convoluted.

Clay and Kate leafed through the book. There was nothing particularly striking in the many pictures. Many of them could have been taken at any current event in just about any major city. There were pictures, obviously in a factory, of significant ship components being made; pictures showing a ship yard with thousands of shipping containers neatly stacked; pictures of uniformed crew members that reminded Clay of the last cruise he and Kara had taken; pictures in space similar to the types of photographs NASA puts out daily.

"They expected to reach Earth within a year," Remington commented solemnly. "Seven months into the journey, Mars lost all contact with the expedition. It was assumed that all four ships had been destroyed by some accident or some unknown space phenomenon."

Remington was silent for a second before he returned to his seat. He opened the second volume and laid it on top of the first, facing Clay and Kate. "Many of our society's elite were part of the artificial environment expedition that left Mars one hundred and five years later. You can imagine; the construction of the craft was quite a bit more complex." He turned to a page with a picture of an iron colored ball otherwise totally lacking in any descriptive features other than two bright and two faint rays of light extending to the ball's left. "Those rays are actually illustrated in," Remington commented. "The ship was driven by a large, cone shaped – I don't know what it is called – like a sail. The ship was powered by something like the solar sail popular in your science fiction; and so realistic."

***

Remington had excused himself for a moment while Clay and Kate each poured another cup of coffee and leafed through the book. "This is all very interesting," Clay said with his face still in the book, "but it's sure hard to understand what it all has to do with this guy killing your brother and my daughters."

"I'm sure he's getting to that," Kate answered, "and clearly, he thinks whatever my brother and your daughter were up to was Earth-shaking; excuse me – Mars-shaking."

They both chuckled a second before Clay

turned serious again. "Are you really believing any of this?" he asked.

"Actually, compared to all the stuff you hear about the pyramids and the Incas, or reading about Stonehenge and all that ancient mystery stuff, it doesn't even really sound that fantastic. I remember when I read Eric von Däniken, you remember that book, *Chariot of the Gods*, I took it for gospel. Subconsciously, I think I still believe most of it. So yeah, I'm buying it. I'm anxious to hear him out anyway."

"Well it's all hooey to me," Clay scoffed. "I'm trying to keep an open mind, but I still want him to get to the part where he kills my Brooke and Bethany." The returning anger was apparent when Remington returned, and Clay ordered him to return to the subject. "We were just wondering out loud what the hell all of this has to do with anything."

"Everything, Mr. Jeffries, it has to do with everything." Remington announced. "I certainly understand your focus on the horrible events of the past week, but sincerely, I couldn't possibly help you understand recent events without explaining all this to you. I had also hoped that you might become a bit absorbed in this story and enjoy a brief respite from the pain you are in."

"Well it didn't work," Clay objected. "Just get on with it."

"Unfortunately, or maybe fortunately, the artificial environment on Mars was a complete and utter failure. I'll spare you the details, but all remaining inhabitants abandoned the idea and managed to put together a fleet of shuttle vehicles in an attempt to join the expedition on Earth, if any of that expedition were left. They, in fact, had made it, but the refugees from the artificial environment were aghast and totally confounded when they arrived on Earth. What they found has shaped Earth's history, politics, culture, religion and science ever since.

✦CHAPTER 5✦

Remington had apologized profusely that he had to excuse himself to attend to matters of extreme importance. He suggested that Clay and Kate take some time to relax and tour the complex with Remington's assistant who would tell them the rest of the story along the way.

As assistants go, Edward was the perfect Costello to Remington's Abbott. The roles were reversed, of course, in terms of physical build, but Edward impressed Clay as a lackey; something of an idiot. Edward even bowed slightly when acknowledging Remington. He was lean and actually rather unnecessarily muscular. Still, his features were weak: small nose, eyes set too far apart, and a rounded chin that stuck out too far. By contrast, he wore a tailored wool suit, navy blue, that was the picture of conservative class. His white shirt was neatly starched and his winged-tip shoes brightly polished. His demeanor was completely different away from Remington. In the office, it was clear that he was in command. He barked orders to nearly everyone as he escorted Clay and Kate through the outer office and back into the oversized conference room.

"Before we begin our tour," Edward said as he waved Clay and Kate into chairs, "there's a bit more to the story Mr. Remington has been relating. I'm not sure where he left off, so if I cover some of the same material, please forgive me. As I believe Mr. Remington was saying, the artificial environment on Mars was a complete failure. After about two hundred years, that group decided to follow the first group to Earth. The earlier group was your ancestors. The latter group was mine and Mr. Remington's. When the refugees of the latter expedition first arrived on Earth, they were shocked to find that the survivors of the Earth expedition, who we still call Apoikians or colonists in English, seemed to have gone completely insane. Apoikians had only been on Earth for barely a hundred years, but they had gone through quite a transformation. First, their population had exploded to beyond anything we could have imagined. Apoikian women were reproducing, literally in many cases, every year. In our normal biology, on Mars, women reproduced three to five times, once every forty-five years at most. That was another shocking transformation.

Apoikians were, as they still do, maturing and aging at a ridiculously quick rate. Life expectancy fell to about eighty years. Normal life expectancy on Mars, as it continues to be with Iatros people, is roughly four hundred and twenty years. You might be surprised to know that Mr. Remington is two hundred and fifty years old. I am two hundred and five years old. You might also wonder how we fit in so well with Apoikians given that life span. We have developed a sophisticated system of creating identities and altering our appearance. Every eighty years or there about, each Iatros 'dies' and is 'reborn' the next morning with a completely new identity fifty years younger and playing a different Apoikian role, but the same Iatros role. Each Apoikian identity is carefully crafted, including background, past, even childhood complete with pictures, videos, and Iatros friends to verify the identity's validity."

Clay had to stop and think for a moment about the feasibility of periodically recreating oneself. It did not take him long to answer all of his own questions and realize that it was not a difficult ruse to accomplish if one had enough accomplices.

"There were several other physiological changes, all very subtle," Edward continued, "and there were sociological and cultural changes as well. Social institutions and culture had all but evaporated. Apoikians were living like herds of animals. Just as evident and shocking was that they had lost all the technology and science that had evolved on Mars over many centuries."

"What had happened to the Apoikians and why the same apparent madness never took hold of those of us who came to Earth later has remained something of a mystery ever since," Edward mused as he stood and crossed the room to the door. "But whatever happened to them, to your Apoikian ancestors, the Iatros people have since seen themselves as something of a doctor, trying to nurse the Apoikians back to health. At first, we made no attempt to hide our true identities and our technological heritage. That brief period of openness created most of what you consider myths and ancient mysteries. Apoikian reaction was, to say the least, disturbing. In some cases, they tried to kill us as demons and witches. In other cases, they elevated us to gods and played at worshiping us. They even took to calling us Iatros, which means savior in English. It was clear that we must first reintroduce our social and cultural institutions. It has taken many millenniums, but slowly we have re-educated the Apoikians in philosophy, culture and science. W have been able to reintroduce many of our social institutions and most of our technology. I think you will understand all this much better after our little tour."

***

"I guess it would be best for us to begin in the Hall of Families," Edward thought out loud as he held the conference room door and motioned

Clay and Kate back into the enormous legislative chamber they had passed through earlier. "Apoikian reaction to us has forced Iatros society to operate unseen, and as something of an undercurrent to all human societies, for the past seven thousand years. The complex we are in is the center of Iatros society and of Iatros government. I guess from an Apoikian perspective, the Iatros are something of an underground aristocracy. We have used our technology, science and high level of advancement in many, many ways to influence human affairs, always with the intent to reincorporate Apoikians into our once common way of life. It is only natural that, even within an aristocracy, some form of government is required. From our own perspective, our government is a mixed government, very much like what we tried to create for Apoikians in the United States."

"This is what we refer to as the Hall of Families," Edward began what sounded like a civics lesson. "The basic unit of Iatros society is the extended family. There are two thousand Iatros families that trace their roots back to the second expedition refugees. Family size can range from four hundred to eight hundred individuals, but, on average, include about six hundred. Our population grew from the original two thousand to one-point-two million rather quickly and has remained nearly constant since. Every twenty years or when called to order for some special reason, each Iatros family chooses a representative and sends him or her to this chamber, and they sit as a popular legislative body, similar to your House of Representatives. Our legislature is, like yours, bicameral. We have a Senate that meets formally every five years, which means pretty much continually, but it is very different than what your Senate has sadly become. Our Senate is a true and natural aristocracy. Senators are leaders in their respective and critical fields."

Edward struggled for an explanation. "I really find it difficult to explain our Senate. When we first arrived on Earth, for example, we relied heavily on our biologists to tell us what we could or could not eat; we relied on our scientists to safeguard our technology and help us establish an infrastructure here on Earth; we relied on doctors to keep us well and to try to explain what happened to the Apoikians. Those became the natural aristocrats."

"All scientists of some kind," Kate noted disapprovingly. "So your society values science above all else?"

"By no means," Edward objected. "We also needed showman, poets and artists to entertain us and inspire us; we needed philosophers to set us a direction. We value science, yes, but we equally value the arts, the humanities and, frankly, the frivolities in life. In all of these fields, those we turned to for their expertise became aristocrats. This is the concept we built our Senate on. Our definition of an aristocracy is those individuals who, through their knowledge and expertise, control the society's resources."

"That makes good sense," Clay noted. "Actually, our own Senate was supposed to be something of a meritocracy, but the people usurped the Senate through political parties and eventually through the Seventeenth Amendment."

"You are precisely correct, Mr. Jeffries," Edward noted, "and it has led to the very thing that the Constitution was convened to correct – the excess of democracy that so plagued your Articles of Confederation." Edward was tempted to dive into a discussion of American constitutionalism, but came abruptly back to the point. "Our own Senate consists of one hundred of our leading experts. The body is divided into ten equal standing committees, with ten Senators serving on each. Each of the ten doors flanking the main door on the right side of the House of Families leads to a committee's conference chamber and to the office suites of its Senators."

Edward led Clay and Kate across the wide Hall of Families to a large doorway, nearly as ornate as the largest doorway on the right side of the hall and directly across from it. They entered a chamber, second in size only to the Hall of Families. The floor was carpeted in a plush royal blue. One hundred separate desks with deep blue high back leather chairs faced an elaborate raised desk; something like a judge's bench. As one would expect of a judge's bench, there was what appeared to be a witness stand to the right of the bench, though this looked more like a pulpit, similar to those in old European cathedrals.

"This is our Senate chamber," Edward narrated. "The objects that line the walls on either side represent some of the greatest leaders to serve in this chamber over the centuries. Because most Iatros must change their appearance regularly, portraits don't hold the same meaning to us as they do in your own culture. As an alternate, Iatros have come to identify individuals through objects that played a significant role in their lives. This, for example," Edward said as he pointed to a reverently mounted and framed quill, "was once guided by an Iatros hand to create one of the most important documents in Apoikian history, and some might say one of our most valuable gifts to Apoikian civilization."

Clay's eyes lingered on the quill that he assumed had drafted the United States Constitution as he wondered, almost out loud, if Thomas Jefferson had been an Iatros. "Bear in mind," Edward contradicted Clay's thoughts, "that from our different perspectives what we see as 'most important' might be something other than what you consider important."

Edward moved on with his tour guide monologue. "The chamber is heavy with symbolism. The circles on the carpet represent the colors of Earth and Mars – blue and green for Earth and red and brown for Mars. Most of the symbolism would be meaningless to you until you have had some time to spend in the Gallery of

Iatros History. I will show you that next, then we can look in on the royal court and throne room. Our government is headed by a king, descended from the leader of the Mars-based environment. Senate proceedings are closed to everyone not a Senator except to our King, who presides over the Senate. Other than that, there is not much to tell you of this chamber." With that Edward turned and went back out the door they had come in. He motioned Clay and Kate to follow him once again through the Hall of Families.

They again crossed the Hall of Families and passed through the dark long archway into the oversized hallway they had first entered through. "This is the Gallery of Iatros History," Edward continued. "It is something like your Library of Congress, Smithsonian Museum, and national monuments all rolled into one." Edward went on to explain that the monitors in the walls and pillars (actually holographic projectors) flanking each monitor, were programmed to offer dynamic displays that depicted the treasures and memories of Iatros life on Earth.

"We will not have much time to explore right now," Edward apologized. "But there might be an opportunity later for you to spend some time here alone if you like. Just so you get the idea, and so that I can show you how to work the displays, we can quickly look at one gallery."

Edward walked to one of the blank monitors and casually waved his hand just slightly over his head. The monitor flickered to life and displayed a menu which Edward scrolled through simply by lowering an outstretched hand. He selected an item, titled United States Populism, by making a subtle poking motion with his finger. The screen ran a documentary that depicted populism as an anti-capitalist movement that threatened to undermine the United States constitution by promoting debt relief through bimetallism and usurping aristocratic power through popular election of Senators. As the documentary continued, the holographs suddenly appeared atop the pillars alongside the monitor. One held gold and silver coins that looked real enough for Clay to slip into his pockets. He felt a bit silly trying it, but chuckled with amusement when he discovered he could, to a degree, manipulate the ghostly coins. The other pillar sprouted the figure of a man dressed in an 1890's business suit as the narrator commented on Iatros policy to thwart populism that was so brilliantly executed by, Clay assumed, the man depicted atop the pillar.

"There is nearly ten thousand years of history preserved in this hall. Iatros most often access it remotely, but still crowd the hall during events in the Capitol. I guess it's the difference between watching midnight Mass on TV or actually being at the Vatican for that annual event," Edward commented. "I'm sorry," Edward added, "we will need to move through the rest of the tour quickly. We are due at a committee meeting very soon."

Clay started to ask Edward about this committee meeting, but found Edward was walking briskly away and already saying something to them. "You will find the Throne Room most inspiring," Edward had said as he guided them back to one of the grand staircases.

"I didn't notice these when we first came in," Kate commented as they began to climb the stairs leading to an upper floor. "What is at the bottom of the stairs that go down?" she asked.

"I'm afraid I won't have time to show you now, nor am I sure you would be that interested," Edward answered, "but the lower levels contain the more practical elements of the capitol. It is like the largest mall you have ever seen, but about a hundred times larger."

"Malls are my thing," Kate joked. "I would rather see that than some king's chair."

"It is not exactly a mall," Edward corrected himself. "It is more like a whole city. There are accommodations, like hotels, for tens of thousands. There are also food services, stores, and other necessary facilities to care for the many that attend Iatros legislative sessions. Unfortunately," Edward added addressing himself to Kate, "there is nothing in operation, nothing opened, when there is no legislature in session. It is like I was giving you a tour of Yankee Stadium during the off season. Imagine how different things might be if there was a World Series game in progress."

"So you're saying this place really comes to

life once every twenty years or so," Clay commented, "otherwise it's much like the catacombs it now feels like."

"Exactly so, Mr. Jeffries, although there is some measure of life every five years when the Senate is in session," Edward answered. "I hope you someday get to see all this when it is really active and in all of its glory."

They left the top of the stairway and crossed through an archway similar to the one just below it and just as oversized. "Speaking of Yankee Stadium," Clay commented, "this looks like a suitable upper-deck even if a bit too plush." They were now walking along a wide walkway behind an even wider tier of over-stuffed balcony seats overlooking the Hall of Families.

"Family members that are not acting as representatives often attend the legislative sessions," Edward instructed. "They watch the proceedings from this gallery."

They turned ninety degrees to their left and continued along a balustrade that ran above the ten doors on the right side of the Hall of Families. On this level, there were twenty arched doorways, less ornate than those below, but still flanking two larger archways in the center of the balustrade. There was an elaborately fashioned bronze railing running along the outer edge of the balustrade, interrupted every two hundred feet or so by three-foot diameter marble pillars that reached the fiftyish feet to the ceiling. On the interior walls were hung huge brass plaques that divided the twenty doors into ten sets of doorways, each set framing one of the ten large plaques. Both Clay and Kate found their eyes drawn toward the center set of doors framing what could only be described as an absurdly over-sized plaque. Each plaque was engraved with a committee name followed by a rather poetic description of the committee's function and mission and concluded with a listing of members' names.

Clay and Kate's eyes had been drawn to the center set of archways, not only because they were larger than the others, but because they were their obvious destination. Once there, Edward ushered them through the closer archway with a wave of his arm. They were again atop a wide, subtly sloping, and very plush gallery. Below was what impressed Clay as a caricature of a royal throne room. Facing them, at the opposite end of the room, was the most elaborately carved chair Clay had ever seen, padded in satin and sitting atop a large raised platform. Running from one side wall to the other was a railing reminiscent of communion railings found in some older Catholic churches. There was a similar railing running perpendicular to each side wall that created pens about a hundred feet wide and running the length of the room. The pens were filled with rows of tables, standing height, facing the raised platform. The room was made entirely of marble, including the railings and tables, except for the wooden carved chair and a ribbon of red carpet that ran the length of the one hundred foot wide center aisle. The whole thing looked something like a stark cathedral of some kind. Kate thought it very cold.

"The whole king idea seems kind of unenlightened for a society so advanced," Clay commented.

"The Apoikian view of royalty, Mr. Jeffries, is a classic example of why we find the Apoikian mind so seemingly confused at times," Edward answered with some exasperation. "Whoever came up with the notion of a blue-blood; of some inherent superiority in royal blood?" Edward asked rhetorically. "The overwhelming advantage of an inherited monarchy is not some divine differentiator, but that society is given the leadership figure it needs, and the individual filling that role is prepared for it from birth. A royal is a regular person in every conceivable way except that their entire existence is focused on the role of leadership they will likely someday fill. What about that do you find so unenlightened, Mr. Jeffries?" Edward was clearly offended by Clay's remark.

"I'm sorry," Clay quickly apologized. "I meant no offense."

"None taken. It's just that our monarchy is quite an emotional subject for me, Mr. Jeffries. Anyway, we must hurry along," Edward said as he turned back toward the door and led them along the balustrade to a doorway that Clay deduced led to a gallery overlooking the conference room into which Remington had first taken them.

Clay was correct, but that didn't prevent the surprise confronting Clay and Kate as they entered.

***

The gallery overlooking the Strategy Committee meeting was about half full of men and women dressed in business suits and taking notes. Television cameras on either side of the gallery were manned by two men wearing identical knit shirts, apparently some kind of uniform. Edward motioned Clay and Kate to two seats in the front row as he sat and turned his attention to Remington addressing the committee below.

It was clear that Clay and Kate were only a few minutes late and that the meeting had just begun. Four committee members sat on either side of the conference table. A gentleman who appeared to be chairing the meeting sat at one end while Remington sat at the other. Young, professional-looking assistants sat closely packed along either wall, each holding a tablet device, some stacked on top of a traditional book or two. A long desk at the far end was lined with stenographers. The meeting looked like any low-level committee meeting one might see in Washington, D.C. As Clay and Kate settled, the chairman recognized Remington for a report.

"Thank you Mr. Chairman," Remington began. "As I reported to this committee just over four weeks ago, the events that have unfolded since this committee recommended, and the Legislature adopted, the policy to maintain the proprietary status of Borden Island technology have shaken the Iatros community throughout the world. For the first time in our seven thousand year history on Earth, a movement actually willing to act in defiance of Iatros' proper government has emerged. Iatros society has always valued opposition, but it has always been understood that unlawful opposition could bear no positive fruit. Unlawful opposition to the acts of this cordial government has, until now, been a line no Iatros would cross, and it is now my sad duty to report to this committee the pains such actions have already caused."

Remington paused and panned the faces of his fellow committee members to heighten the drama. When he continued, his voice was noticeably softer. "Nine days ago an intrusion was detected at Borden Island. A plane was tracked from the island, and security forces were prepared to take the intruders into custody as soon as the plane landed. Approximately two hours after the plane had departed from Borden Island, however, it was discovered that vital information was being transmitted from the plane and downloaded to an as yet undiscovered system. To prevent further transmission of sensitive data and acting on my authority as director of security, I ordered the plane shot down. Five Apoikian bodies were recovered including the pilot Thomas Young. Mr. Young was an electrical engineer known to have been recruited by the Movement to reverse engineer the power generator at Borden Island. We have evidence that he was very close to completing a patentable schematic of the generator."

There was a slight gasp from several of the committee members that left Clay with the impression that a completed schematic equated to some kind of mega-disaster.

"The other four Apoikians aboard,'" Remington continued, "were originally assumed to be Bethany Jeffries, who was known to be the Apoikian recruited by the Movement to act as project manager in revealing Borden Island technology to Apoikian society, and her family. Just two days ago, however, it was discovered that Bethany Jeffries was alive and operating from a remote island in the area of the crash. Security dispatched to take Miss Jeffries into custody was met with deadly resistance. One member of the security force was attacked, and an officer sustained what would have been a fatal gunshot had he not been revived only yesterday by Iatros physicians.

Miss Jeffries and her party were taken into custody and, given the magnitude of the issues at stake, I authorized aggressive interrogation. At the time, the interrogation seemed especially justified since one member of her party, her father, remained at large. Nonetheless, the interrogation failed to yield the status of the

Movement's project or the identities and roles of the four Apoikian corpses recovered with Mr. Young."

Jeffries almost thought to correct Remington: the four recovered with Thomas had been Iatros. He had seen their toe tags.

"To my personal shame," Remington continued, "neither Miss Jeffries nor any of her party survived the interrogation." Remington, choking up a bit, reached for a glass of water and took a drink.

The chairman noted Remington's distress and interjected, "I believe I speak for every member of this body when I assure you, Senator, that your actions were both necessary and courageous. You are to be complimented, not castigated, for what you have done."

"I thank you for that Mr. Chairman," Remington responded. "But to make matters worse, we have since determined that, while Bethany Jeffries was deeply involved in the project, albeit through deception, none of the other members of her party had any involvement. They were complete innocents." Remington's voice became firm. "Mr. Clayton Jeffries, Bethany Jeffries father, is with us today. Consider the tragedy from his perspective: Though innocent of any wrongdoing, his entire family, his two daughters and his son-in-law, have been taken from him. He himself, for a short time, was forced to run under an unfair cloud of suspicion instead of being given the time to mourn his profound loss." Remington motioned for Clay to stand.

Clay stood and raised his arm in a subtle wave. The entire room turned to him and erupted into a somber applause that continued for what seemed an eternity. Clay completely broke down, not from anger as he had before, but this time in a true and deep sorrow. Kate held his hand as Remington continued.

"Mr. Jeffries is accompanied here by Katherine Young, Thomas Young's sister, who has been similarly victimized by this unprecedented and egocentric opposition to a policy..." Remington was interrupted by additional applause for Kate as she waved her gratitude. Edward rose from his seat and began to escort Clay and Kate from the gallery where they might compose themselves in private. As they made their way to the exit, Clay could hear Remington ramping up.

"As I was saying," Remington continued, "Policies of this government are only enacted through the consent of a majority of Iatros citizens along with the support of our aristocratic Senate and our Most Benevolent King. Loyal opposition, not unlawful opposition, has always been the cornerstone of a government that has, at every turn, exemplified the utmost respect for each individual and has been, until now, rewarded with the unwavering respect and loyalty of every citizen." Remington's words were beginning to fade as Clay and Kate left the gallery, but they clearly heard his final booming declaration: "Mark my words well. The pain so far caused is only a beginning. No good shall come from this unlawful opposition! It must be stopped! It will be stopped; no matter how high the cost. And it will surely be high!"

***

The rest of the committee meeting had gone pretty much as Remington had planned. The committee had signaled support for whatever measures he needed to take to stop the Movement. The committee had been entirely willing to overlook his transgression in revealing Iatros society to Clay and Kate. That was a pretty good indication of how far he might be able to go before the committee's resolve might weaken. He was a bit disturbed, actually more like disgusted, that the idea of revisiting the decision to maintain Borden Island's proprietary status had even been raised. The idea of revealing Borden Island to the Apoikian world was, of course, dismissed out of hand. No, the Movement would not have its way. He was free to deal with the band of outlaws as he saw fit.

Edward broke Remington's thoughts as soon as Remington entered the office suite. "Mr. Jeffries and Miss Young are waiting on you in your office sir," Edward said.

"Very good, Edward. Have arrangements been made along the lines I requested?" Remington asked.

"They have sir," Edward answered as he

held out two tablet devices to Remington. "All the details and necessary documents have been loaded, and all support personnel are in place, or will be in place, by this evening."

"Thank you Edward," Remington answered as he took the devices and tucked them under his arm. "I am not sure what their preference will be, but I suggest you be prepared if they choose to leave immediately. Also, make sure that one of our security agents is among the support personnel. We will need to keep an eye on them as well. I have a troublesome feeling that Mr. Jeffries is still more foe than friend."

***

Remington apologized for the ambush of the committee hearing. He explained to Clay and Kate that he needed to drive home the point that stopping the Movement was no longer so much about Borden Island as it was about the very idea of opposition in and of itself. "There was a time very recently in your own history," Remington had explained, "that you celebrated 'civil disobedience'. You correctly made heroes of the likes of Martin Luther King, Gandhi and Russell Means, but they chose to oppose governments that were not sincere. The sincerity of Iatros government has gone unquestioned for thousands of years." Remington genuinely seemed to get a bit emotional as he spoke. "Neither revealing nor keeping the secrets of Borden Island could possibly be as damaging to our society...and yours, now that I think of it...as doubting the sincerity of this government."

Clay felt uneasy. He knew there was a good reason to question Remington's sincerity. He knew for a fact that Remington had just lied to the committee about the other four recovered bodies. He thought for a second about confronting him directly, but was interrupted when Edward entered the office and announced Remington's next appointment. Remington apologized and explained that his meeting was with a prominent doctor and was quite urgent. They parted, both with the feeling that they were not through.

◆CHAPTER 6◆

Clay had elected to stay in San Francisco for a couple of days as Remington's people finalized his new identity. He was a bit surprised but delighted that Kate had elected to wait with him. He was even more delighted that Kate had agreed to have his new identity interwoven with her. He was to play the part of an old friend of Kate's father who had surfaced when he heard of Thomas's death. The story would be that he contacted Kate and met up with her in Lynn Lake. He had been of indispensable help in arranging a service for Thomas, and Kate had become quite attached to him. He returned to Connecticut with Kate to help get family affairs in order. He had been recently widowed, retired, and was looking for a fresh start himself. He would, at the appropriate time, announce to all of Kate's friends that he had decided to move to Connecticut where he could 'keep an eye' on Kate. His new name would be Clifford Eastman. Only Kate would know him as Clay. To the rest of the world Clayton Jeffries had died in that plane crash just as had been originally reported.

For two days, Clay studied his new life. He memorized bits of information about his past and about his friendship with Kate's father. To give the story credibility, two Iatros residents of Connecticut would play the part of mutual friends of Clifford Eastman and Kate's father. A third Iatros would play the role of an old school friend of Clifford's. Other than all of the studying, Clay thought the time was more like a vacation. They toured all the sites around San Francisco: Fisherman's Wharf, Alcatraz, the Golden Gate. They had even taken a day to drive up to Sonoma to experience the wine country. It had given him time to get to know Kate and his new life.

Preparing for that new life had taken so much time that Clay had had no chance to absorb all that Remington had told them of Borden Island. He hadn't even glanced at the documents on the tablet Remington had given him on the promise that Clay would delete them after he and Kate had looked them over. He briefly glanced at the tablet sitting on the night stand but decided tomorrow's long flight to Connecticut would be a better chance to catch up. Right now, sleep was probably the wiser idea.

Clay hadn't seen Kate much during the few days he had to study, but they had still had dinner together each of those evenings. Under the guise of preparing for his new role, they had talked for hours about Kate, her family, her growing up, her relationships, her aspirations and a few secrets she had thought she would never tell anyone. She even recited one of her poems to him. It was titled Ice Cream and was about a rich young girl whose father takes her to Rupplemeyers, and a social worker who takes a small group of children to Dairy Queen during an outing. It alternated stanzas showing how the girl was delighted to get some attention from her father, and how the group of poor children was happy to get some ice cream. In the later stanzas, the girl fights back tears when her father makes a phone call and the social worker fights back sobs for the impoverished children. The last stanza reveals the social worker in place of the rich girl at Rupplemeyers, still sobbing, and replaces the father with one of the poverty-stricken children asking the young woman what is wrong. The poem still haunted Clay.

As something of a way to put his past to rest, Clay also told Kate the many details of his life. Earlier that evening, Clay talked in detail of his daughters, especially his special relationship with Bethany. He had been surprised at how comforting it was to have Kate listen. Even now, as he reached to turn out the light and pull up the covers the thought of Kate, her beauty, her passion, her light-hearted disposition, all pleased him.

At first, he thought there was something wrong with the switch as the lights turned off, but then came back on. He understood when he saw Kate closing his bedroom door behind her. The green satin pajamas she was wearing added to the sensuality of her long red hair. "I was trying to think of some plausible excuse to come see you," Kate had said as she crossed the room and crawled into his bed, "but I couldn't think of anything except being direct." Kate rolled on her side, her back to Clay, wrapped herself in his arm, and guided his hand to her breast. Clay felt her hardened nipple only for a second before he rolled her back toward him and kissed her for what seemed half the night.

***

The morning had been normal and comfortable as he and Kate readied for the flight to Connecticut. Little had been said about their lovemaking or about the relationship that had clearly changed. Any meaningful conversation was preempted by the scurry of getting through the airport, the security check and boarding. Now that they were comfortably seated in first class, had climbed to a suitable altitude, and everyone else was booting their laptops or powering on their iPods, Clay reached for the tablet containing documents about Borden Island.

"We should take a look at these," Clay

suggested as he held his eye still over the tablet for the boot-up security scan.

"I guess we should," Kate responded, "but I also think we should talk about last night. I'm not sorry. Whatever you feel last night was, whether a wonderful one-night thing or, as the movies say, 'the start of something big, kid,' I'm glad it happened."

"I don't know what it was, Kate. But I know what I hope it was." Clay said softly. "Jumping into a relationship now, especially with someone half my age and so far out of my league, is probably the dumbest idea since I married Kara."

"What do you mean 'out of your league? Are you saying you think I'm hot?" Kate asked with a giggle. "And have you looked in a mirror lately? I don't know any girl out of your league." Kate paused a second as she turned serious. "Tell me about Kara. Why was it dumb to marry her?"

"Kara and I met during our senior year in college. It was late on a Tuesday night in the library. We were both studying. I had just been dumped by the girl I had been dating since high school and had been engaged to for the last two years. I decided the best way to recover was to start dating. So, when I saw Kara, who looked like a goddess to me, I went straight over to her and boldly asked her for a date. We went out that Friday, saw each other that Saturday and Sunday, then, since mid-terms were coming up, we ended up spending every evening of the next week together in the library. We talked a ton and studied not one lick. That next Friday I told her that I 'intended' to ask her to marry me. She said she 'intended' to say yes. We were married five months later and only waited that long because we felt we should finish school. For the next thirty-five years, we jokingly kept telling each other how dumb we had been to rush into things so fast."

"I take it that it was a good marriage." Kate said tearing up a bit for Clay.

"The best in the history of humankind!" Clay declared. "But what I am saying, Kate, is that it sounds dumb, but my instincts have served me well, even when on the rebound, and my instincts are that I want to throw caution to the wind and just see what happens with you and me. What do you think?"

"I think we should go shopping tomorrow and pick out a China pattern," Kate laughed through her tears. "Seeing what happens sounds perfect to me," she said as she laid her head on his shoulder and hugged his arm. "But first I want to know why you are still so interested in Borden Island. It all seems sensible to me. Remington is a good guy. I understand why Iatros people might have reservations about sharing Borden Island technology. Thomas and Bethany got duped into helping some Iatros people who disagree. I am sad about it all, but I understand."

"There is just one thing that keeps nagging at me," Clay said pensively. "During his report to the committee, Remington said that five Apoikians were recovered from the plane he shot down."

"OK," Kate responded, not sure where Clay was going.

"Well, we saw the bodies, remember?" Clay reminded Kate, "at the make-shift morgue, or tent, or whatever it was. There were eight bodies: Brooke, Bethany, Eric, and Thomas, plus two male and two female bags marked 'unidentified Iatros.' Remington lied to the committee. The other bodies were not Apoikian. They were Iatros. And besides, Remington mentioned that the man you shot was revived two days later. So if they can do that, why couldn't they revive the four Iatros who were on the plane?"

"Remington said that an Iatros had not killed another Iatros in over seven thousand years," Kate speculated, "maybe it was just too shocking for Remington to admit to."

"That's hard to believe," Clay rejected Kate's theory. "Seems clear that Remington didn't want them revived. He preferred them dead. And he could only prefer them dead, it seems to me, if he knew them. I was also curious as to why he never mentioned the man I shot at their temporary morgue. That seems like a pretty big detail to leave out."

Clay tapped on the tablet he had been holding. "The other thing," Clay added as an afterthought, "Is that I don't quite get why Remington has taken so much of an interest in us. Why has he been taking such care of us?"

"I think he feels guilty," Kate responded.

"I think he wants or needs us for something." Clay countered. "I can just feel it. Anyway, I was hoping there might be a clue in here." He glanced at the listing of documents and leaned toward Kate so they could both look over the first page.

The first document was a fact sheet about Borden Island. As Clay and Kate read, they began to understand that Borden Island was an energy generation plant. The plant consists of a series of strange antennas that attract electricity directly from Earth's magnetic field and stores it in huge batteries, about the size of semi trailers. One battery is enough to provide all of New York City's energy (electricity and fuel) needs for a day! That shocked Clay, but he was staggered when the report suggested that the plant could, if run at full capacity, produce thirty-six hundred batteries per day!

Iatros used Borden Island to satisfy the high-energy demands of their own technology. Those demands surpassed the demands of many Western European industrial countries yet used less than one percent of what Borden Island was capable of producing. Clay was dumb-struck. Borden Island could solve most of Earth's environmental problems. No wonder Bethany wanted it to be shared. But what possible reason could the Iatros have for keeping it secret?

Clay posed that question out loud to Kate. She, of course, had no idea but added that it was no wonder that Thomas would want to do everything possible to open this kind of technology to everyone. "This is exactly the kind of thing he was passionate about," she said, "and it was right up his professional alley."

"From Remington's report and from the way the Iatros seem to work," Clay mused, "I guess if the Movement had its way, Thomas would have been known in history as the inventor of this. He would have saved the world and been remembered in history as another Einstein. That's a lot to tempt a person with!"

"No kidding," Kate exclaimed. "I myself can't fathom why anyone would want to keep this secret and why others would do just about anything to reveal it."

"The rest of the documents are all related to Iatros discussions in committees, their Senate and their House of Families about Borden Island," Clay responded. "They should give us a good idea of what the Iatros are thinking. My neck is getting stiff leaning over so we can both read. You haven't lost your tablet, have you?" Clay sounded alarmed.

"Of course not," Kate objected, playing offended at the suggestion. "I just liked leaning over you. But fine, I'll boot my own device."

The argument was well framed within the first fifty or so pages. At an initial committee hearing, one side argued that Borden Island needed to be revealed. They argue the obvious case that Apoikian reliance on fossil fuels was destroying the Earth's environment; an environment that the Iatros were just as dependent on as the Apoikians. They felt the issue was extremely time sensitive and argued convincingly that the destruction of Earth's ecology was imminent.

Timing was also the critical issue to those on the other side. They argued that Apoikian society was very close to being 'cured.' Within the next two reigns they argued. Sharing Borden Island technology with an Apoikian society in its still 'insane' state would surely lead to someone abusing the technology.

Those in favor of revealing Borden Island challenged both the premise that Apoikians were close to being cured and the premise that the technology could or would be abused. The next two committee hearing transcripts explored the validity of those premises.

Almost all the discussion about Apoikians being cured was deleted. Remington had warned Clay and Kate when he handed them the tablets that several sections had been deleted because they were just too sensitive and highly classified. All that was left were bits of a report from an Iatros doctor who had discovered two cases of spontaneous recovery. Both cases involved Apoikians, who had somehow 'mutated' back to an Iatros physiology while battling a rare Apoikian disease known as Guillain-Barre. The Iatros doctor and his team had a special interest in Guillain-Barre because the disease destroys and rebuilds the nerve sheaths in Apoikians, and nerve sheathss are one of the most fundamental physiological differences in Iatros and Apoikians.

A fairly detailed description of Guillain-Barre horrified Kate. "You just lay there in a sort of coma; completely paralyzed and unable to communicate, but your mind is perfectly clear," Kate had gasped. "That sounds absolutely unbearable!"

"The mind has a defense," Clay told her. "I know from first-hand experience. Bethany had to leave the Air Force because she had Guillain-Barre. It used to be pretty rare but it is becoming much more common. Most patients get it from getting a flu shot. Bethany had it for eighteen months, and we all imagined it must be like a living hell, but when she recovered she had no memory of it."

As they read on, it became clear that the Doctor believed transforming the nerve linings was a key to 'curing' Apoikians, and from the fragments of the report left in, Clay inferred that the Doctor felt he could develop some kind of anecdote for Apoikians by studying Guillain-Barre.

The sections of the report dealing with weaponizing Borden Island were much meatier. The argument was that Apoikians had never developed a weapon that had not been used. The report listed dozens of political and religious figures that might use the weapon. Many of the names were familiar to Clay, and many were the leaders one would expect to find on such a list: leaders of terrorist groups, rogue nations, fanatics, etc. Some of the names, however, were unexpected, including the front-runner in the upcoming U.S. presidential election.

The report detailed a half-dozen scenarios that all logically ended with one side or the other using Borden Island technology. The scenarios were so convincing that Clay thought he might use the technology himself if put in some of the same situations.

The only other part of the report deleted was an actual description of a Borden Island derived weapon. Clay was, nonetheless, able to draw a picture of a weapon that made the A-bomb look like a firecracker. It was the ultimate smart bomb that could define boundaries anyway the user liked, from a single square foot to an entire continent, and then literally scrambles the brains of every Apoikian in that area; all in the blink of an eye. They had finished the bulk of the reports just as the plane landed. Clay wasn't going to bother looking at the after matter and footnotes, and was about to shut down the tablet when a name among the contributors' signatures jumped out at him. There couldn't possibly be two Dr. Ezekiel Rothlensbergers. At least not two in Bethesda, Maryland!

***

The flight to New Haven had gone quickly compared to the drive to Noank where Kate's family home sat overlooking Beebe Cove. The house was massive and screamed of established wealth. To the right side of the property was a two-story Tudor style guard house that was clearly large enough to be a guest house. To the left of the guard house was a brick and iron fence that turned to the rear of the property almost a city block away. On the left was a wide gate blocking a straight and narrow cobblestone driveway. It was flanked on the right by a tall and perfectly manicured hedgerow and to the left by the brick and iron fence.

Kate pushed a button on the console of her bright blue Mercedes SLK-Class, and the gate swung slowly open. Clay didn't see the house until they were halfway down the half-mile driveway. It was also a Tudor-style house: stone on the first floor and exposed framing members on the upper floors. The complex and steep roofline finished the classic look. The drive forked just in front of the house, one fork leading to a garage area and another to the front entry of the house. The drive leading to the front of the house ended in front of four wide stone stairs that led to the house's large front portico.

Once inside, Clay was struck by the absurdity of one person living alone in such a massive home. More, he was struck by the incongruence of the conservative décor and Kate's impish personality. As if reading his mind, Kate said, "I feel ridiculous living here alone but the house has been in the family for four generations, and I hate the thought of selling it. After all, I grew up in this house. I took an apartment in New

Haven for a while, but it seemed even more ridiculous to keep this house solely for the housekeeping staff, and none of them are live-in anymore!

"How big of a staff does it take to run a house like this?" Clay asked.

"Right now there are six," Kate answered, "an upstairs maid, a butler, a morning cook, a chef, and two maintenance men. They all work regular nine to five hours except the cook who works five to two and the chef who works twelve to nine. The butler is the main supervisor, and I sent him a text that we would be here tonight. He texted back that the chef would have dinner ready, but it is almost ten o'clock local time, and I don't know if he stayed. Why don't we check the kitchen and see what we can find? I'm hungry."

As if on cue, a man in a chef's jacket and hat appeared from the far end of the entry hall. "Hello Kate," he said in a surprisingly informal manner. "We are all so glad you are back. I didn't get a chance to see you before you left. I'm so sorry about Thomas."

"Thank you, Louis," Kate answered. "Things will never be the same, will they? Oh, Louis, this is Clifford Eastman. He was a close friend of my father's. He called me when he heard about Thomas then flew out to Lynn Lake and helped me get Thomas's affairs settled. He is going to be staying with me awhile."

"Yes, Jonathan said you would have a second for dinner," Louis confirmed as he looked

Clay over.

"Jonathan is head of the household," Kate explained as Louis shook Clay's hand and seemed genuine when he expressed gratitude that someone would be looking out for Kate. "The name is Clifford, but all my friends call me Clay," referring to the one concession his new identity made to his former self. Clay almost felt like a teenager meeting his girlfriend's father.

"He also asked me to give you these messages and to warn you that he was letting everyone know you were returning. You can expect callers non-stop tomorrow," Louis added turning to Kate and handing her a small pile of pink slips. "He said he held out the earlier expressions of sympathy and routine matters for later, but wanted you to have these."

"Thank you Louis," Kate sounded less than sincere. "We're going to have dinner on the breakfast patio."

"It will be ready in ten minutes," Louis answered as he turned back toward the kitchen.

"Let's get the bags up to my room," Kate turned to Clay. She had emphasized her room as if there were any doubt where he would be staying, given last night and their conversation on the plane. He was caught confused when she added, "There are several guest rooms right down the hall; you can have your pick." Clay stammered a bit as Kate giggled, "Of course, it is just for appearances for now, and because I don't have any room in my closets for your stuff. Plus, the house is haunted, and I will need you to sleep with me and protect me from all the ghouls."

"At your service," Clay responded.

"Good. That's just how I like it," Kate answered as they started up the steps, bags in hand.

Kate's room was a large suite on the southeast corner of the house. Clay played at shopping the guest rooms, four in all, as she gave him a tour. He settled on the room across from Kate. It was also a spacious suite, and it was convenient to her room. He also preferred it because it was the only room decorated in a more masculine style, and it was on the northeast corner, exposed to plenty of morning sun. He tried to change his mind when he found out that it was Thomas's boyhood room, but Kate insisted.

Between the rooms was a back stair that they descended. The stairs exited into a long hallway that ran along the back of the house. To the right, on the front side of the house was a large formal dining room. To the left was a screened porch.

"We call this the breakfast patio because this is where we always ate. Especially in the morning," Kate explained.

The patio was more of a sun room. The ceiling was a white plaster molding with a simple chandelier. The walls were wainscoted with a natural dark oak paneling along the bottom third and continuous large windows along the upper two-thirds. There was a simple white buffet alongside the doorway on the interior wall. The wall was decorated with a painting of a seascape at sunset framed in a thin dark oak frame. In the center of the room was a dinette set with a blue oval table and six blue and gold padded swivel chairs. The view was spectacular. A large lawn, framed on either side by heavy woods, swept downhill to meet Beebe Cove. It was barely a mile to the far shore of the cove, but Clay could see only blackness beyond the water.

They no more than sat down when Louis entered with a tray. Dinner was a simple spinach salad, fresh baked Italian bread and lobster ravioli in a cream sauce served with a pinot grigio. Clay found it surprisingly light – perfect for a late dinner. Kate sent Louis home promising to take care of the dishes herself. After they had eaten, Clay followed Kate into the kitchen, Kate carrying the dishes and Clay carrying the last two glasses of wine. They drank the wine, rinsed and stacked the dishes and planned the following morning. They decided they would need to spend the next day planning some type of gathering in Thomas's honor, but Kate did not want it to be like a funeral or anything like that. She just needed to give the family's friends a chance to gather, share their sympathy and, as a bonus, meet Clay.

For a moment, as Kate dried her hands, Clay felt oddly comfortable, as if he were at home. He kissed Kate softly, then passionately. She stopped him and said she wanted to take a shower. "My place in half an hour, OK?" Kate spoke softly. Clay went to his room to shower and change. He had gone through Kate's open bedroom door and was about to turn down the bed when Kate emerged from the bathroom. Last night had just happened. It was much like any other couple making love for the first time. Tonight was planned. They made love several times through the night. They were both, in moments, sharing; and both, in moments, selfish. As the sun rose, they had barely slept and were both exhausted. They had, it seemed, just fallen asleep when Kate's phone rang. As she answered it, Clay glanced at the clock. He was shocked to see it was ten-thirty. Kate hung up the phone and crawled out of bed. "Jonathan says there is a friend of yours downstairs who needs to see us."

"OK," Clay said, "but I don't have any friends. At least not ones that know I am alive, let alone staying with you."

"An emissary from Mr. Remington," Kate suggested.

***

Clay had dressed quickly and gone down to meet the guest while Kate took a leisurely shower. Jason Randal looked vaguely familiar to Clay as he introduced himself, but Clay couldn't place him. "We met briefly when you were taken into custody," Randal explained as saw Clay struggle. "I work for Mr. Remington. The Iatros members of my team will act as old friends of yours to help establish your new identity. They will also act as a security force to protect you and Miss Young, though there is not likely going to be much need for protection."

"And to keep tabs on us for Mr. Remington, I assume," Clay added with some disdain.

"Yes Mr. Jeffries," Randal answered directly, "But there is nothing nefarious about it. Think of it as a caring father sending someone to look after a son while he is away at school. Mr. Remington has taken a genuine interest in you and Miss Young and simply wants to be assured of your well being."

"Well thanks," Clay responded curtly, "But I am not a college kid, and I don't need anyone to look after me."

Randal ignored Clay's rejection and held up one of the tablets that Clay and Kate had been reviewing on the plane. "I must remind you to be cautious with Iatros information," Randal scolded Clay. "This was left sticking out of your bag in plain sight. Devices such as this containing highly sensitive and 'for your eyes only' material must be treated with great care."

"I apologize," Clay said. "We seem to have gotten off on the wrong foot for two who are supposed to be life-long friends according to my new identity. Sit down Jason and tell me what brings you here this morning."

"I will want to introduce you and Kate to the rest of my team as soon as possible," Randal said as he sunk into the couch. "I know you and Kate are planning some type of memorial service for her brother. We need to be sure everyone understands each other's role before then."

"It's not really a memorial service," Clay corrected him. "It's just an informal chance for friends to get together. We were thinking about Saturday evening."

"That only gives us three days so we should meet today," Randal said as he was thinking. "Could we plan on having dinner here tonight with the team? There are four of us. Tell Jonathan that we are all old friends of yours come to welcome you back to Connecticut. We can also use the occasion to plan the gathering. Would that work?"

"That would be fine," Kate said before Clay could answer as she came down the stairs. "Hello, Mr. Randal."

"Good morning, Miss Young," Randal said as he rose from the couch. "It is good to see you again."

"Is it?" Kate asked sarcastically, "I spent nearly a week spying on you, shot you, was hunted by you, and you say it is good to see me again."

"Well," Randal said smiling. "I certainly have a much better understanding of your situation than I had during those early encounters, and I trust Mr. Remington has told you enough about mine that we might be friends."

"He has and we can be friends," Kate said, "It's just that you must admit that the situation is a bit odd."

"I play, as you will discover as you get to know me better, primarily a political role for Mr. Remington. And you know what they say – 'politics makes strange bedfellows.'" Randal paused then invited Kate to join the conversation. "We were discussing your plans for a gathering of your family's friends."

"I overheard you to say you would like us to meet your team before we do that," Kate answered. "Tonight would be fine. I will let Jonathan know that old friends of Clay's will be here tonight, and I will have him extend invitations for a gathering this Saturday."

"Perfect," Randal said. "Just one other thing, would you please have him include Dr. Ezekiel Rothlensberger on the guest list? If Jonathan asks, tell him he is one of Mr. Jeffries' old friends.

Clay was stunned, but Randal was half out the door, making it clear he could not answer any questions. "I'll explain later, Clay," Randal said as he left.

◆CHAPTER 7◆

Jason Randal thought fast as he drove back to Hartford. If Remington found out about the meeting, he would just write it off to Jeffries insisting on it after seeing Rothlensberger's name in the report. But Randal was not supposed to have seen the report, so Remington was sure to ask why Randal didn't get suspicious when Jeffries brought up Dr. Rothlensberger. He would say that he didn't know about Rothlensberger being on the guest list until he saw him at the gathering. That would probably satisfy Remington. Besides, it was all mute if Randal's hunch proved correct. If that was the case, surely Rothlensberger would want to join forces, and Remington would never know he had met Jeffries.

Randal pulled into the parking garage at

Blue Back Square and headed to the office complex where they had agreed to meet in John's office. John Morley had been on Randal's team for thirty-two years. He was young by Iatros standards. He had done well in school and when he entered Iatros service at the required age of seventy-five, he was given the prestigious assignment of Royal Family Service. John only had eighteen years left on his mandatory service and Randal often wondered if he might make a career of the service as Randal had.

John's current Apoikian cover was as a tax attorney. His clients included some of New England's wealthiest families. It provided for the luxurious lifestyle that all Iatros enjoyed while also giving him significant influence over Apoikian affairs. His office, of course, reflected his upper-class status, situated on the top floor of the exclusive office complex attached to Blue Back Square Mall in one of Hartford's most affluent areas west of downtown.

By the time Randal entered the office everyone had arrived and the four of them went directly into the conference room. It was a typical executive conference room with a highly polished mahogany table and eight oversized burgundy executive leather chairs. The recessed wall lighting was dim and no one had bothered to flip on the overhead light. The dim lighting gave the meeting a sinister air about it that seemed even more so when Randal took a seat at the center of the table, and all three team members sat across from him.

John sat to one side, next to Tom Benton. Randal didn't have to wonder if Tom might make a career of the Royal Service; Tom made no secret of his intentions to stay as long as the service would have him. He was the gung-ho type; fiercely loyal to the Royal family and the service. Even his Apoikian cover reflected his rigid core; he served as a security consultant to governments and wealthy individuals. Randal thought Tom might be a problem if his growing suspicions about Remington proved justified.

The final member of Randal's team hardly seemed a likely candidate for field service. Evan Mills was bookish, and he was not at all happy about the duty he had been assigned for his mandatory service. He was passionate about his Apoikian cover as a historian and author of Medieval Europe. He often published 'theories' on the Knights Templar and Freemasonry as suited the agenda of the Iatros Senate. Other than that, he was a natural skeptic; not especially patriotic or passionate about anything. He was the kind of Iatros citizen whom Randal thought might prove very useful.

Randal spread several papers in front of him and looked through them as he began to speak. "Our assignment, as you know, has shifted from Thomas Young to his sister Katherine Young. The team that had been assigned to Bethany Jeffries has been deactivated, and our assignment will now include Clayton Jeffries as well. Both

Miss Young and Mr. Jeffries, as you also know, have been fully briefed on Iatros history and current affairs. They were briefed by Mr. Remington himself with the full approval of the Iatros Senate. It makes our assignment rather unique; for the first time in all the Service's history our targets will be aware of us and of Iatros existence. In that sense, Miss Young and Mr. Jeffries will be our clients as much as our subjects."

Randal still leafed through the papers spread in front of him as he continued. "Mr. Remington is certain that neither Mr. Jeffries, nor Miss Young is involved in the Movement in any way as Bethany Jeffries and Thomas Young were, but frankly, they are Mr. Remington's only remaining thread connected to the Movement. He is hoping that our subjects might come across something, what we do not know, that will provide further leads into the Movement."

Randal finally looked up and glanced at each of his team members before continuing. "Our assignment lacks any concrete definition, gentlemen. We are on a fishing trip and we are simply to keep an eye on Mr. Jeffries and Miss Young to see if they come up with anything relevant to the Movement."

The team members' dissatisfaction was palpable as they shifted in their chairs.

"It's not the kind of assignment one would like to receive," Randal added quickly. "But Mr. Remington's instincts seem to be serving him well. Miss Young will be holding a reception this Saturday which we will attend. I have checked the guest list and discovered that Dr. Rothlensberger, the Iatros physician well known for his work on an Apoikian cure, was included. Both Thomas Young and Bethany Jeffries were among the Apoikians that Dr. Rothlensberger had so famously cured."

The team sat up straight; they almost gasped. Two completely separate and distinct connections to Iatros affairs, the infamous Movement and the famous Rothlensberger cures, was an inconceivable coincidence.

"Obviously," Tom Benton almost shouted, "that connects Dr. Rothlensberger to the Movement and makes him a major suspect. It seems like *he* should be our assignment. Have you briefed Remington yet?"

"No," Randal insisted, "and I want to question Rothlensberger before I do."

"That's crazy," John Morley objected. "You might tip him off and drive him underground."

"That's what?" Randal demanded with the voice of rank in a way to put Morley in his place.

"My apologies, sir," Morley responded as he remembered he was talking to his superior. "But it seems obvious that the invitation is something that Remington should know."

"It is," Randal said in a lower voice. "I am scheduled to debrief with Remington's assistant, Edward, Sunday morning. I need something concrete before I talk to him, so I simply want to wait until I have had an opportunity to question the Doctor."

"We will meet our subjects this evening. We are joining them for dinner at Miss Young's estate," Randal addressed all three of the team members. "I want no discussion of Dr. Rothlensberger tonight or Saturday until I have had an opportunity to question him. Is that clear?"

They muttered agreement as they were dismissed and filed out of the room. Randal gathered his papers as he wondered if his gamble was worth it or if one of his team members would contact Remington on his own.

***

Dinner that evening went well. They had exchanged pleasantries and shared small talk over drinks before sitting down to a late dinner in the formal dining room. Louis pulled all the stops, using the full complement of fine china, linens and silver service to serve his beef tenderloin aux poivre with a complex brandied mushroom sauce and potato pancakes. They all looked a bit surprised when Louis followed dessert with a silver tray of Davidoff Presidential cigars, clippers, glasses of Janneau Seven-Year-Old VSOP Armagnac brandy and crystal ash trays. Kate put them at ease by pointing out that the dining room held nearly a hundred years of cigar smoke and, if she had learned correctly from the many meetings her father had held in this same room, it was time to talk business.

As Clay dipped the tip of his cigar in the brandy, Kate pointed out the irony of having such a fine and enjoyable dinner with the four of them just weeks after lying on a hilltop in the wilderness of central Canada and spying on them. Randal had explained that their primary role now was to help Clay establish his new identity. Randal also discussed the possibility that members of the Movement might attempt to contact them to learn what they knew and see if they might be some kind of asset to the Movement.

"So we are the bait on the end of Mr. Remington's fishing pole?" Clay asked. "Is that it? Is that why we are so valuable to him?"

"That is exactly correct, Clay," Randal answered. "But be assured, you will not be placed in the slightest danger."

It made sense. If Movement members were going to contact them either way, it might be nice to have a team of servicemen protecting them. Kate felt the same way and said so after the team had left and she, Clay and Jason Randal had moved to the den. She admitted that she felt guilty for liking the men who had shot down Thomas's plane. She did like them, but she realized that even though these men had killed her brother, it was really the Movement that caused his death. Clay admitted to the same kinds of feelings. He felt anger toward the Movement, not toward these men. He also felt guilty. He felt guilty for sitting at dinner with them. He felt guilty for laughing with them. He felt guilty for actually enjoying the evening.

Clay produced two more Davidoff's and offered one to Jason. They had gone outside to smoke them, and Randal took the opportunity to explain Dr. Rothlensberger's invitation. Just as Randal's own team had instantly recognized, it was too much of a coincidence that both Thomas and Bethany had been involved in not one, but two critical Iatros operations – the Movement and Dr. Rothlensberger's cure research. It cast the Doctor as suspect number one.

What Randal did not tell Clay was that he wanted to interview the Doctor, off the record. He didn't tell Clay, nor his own team, for that matter, that Dr. Rothlensberger was simply not a viable suspect. The Movement had caused the death of at least two of the Doctor's most prized subjects and Rothlensberger would not have done that to himself. What the coincidence meant was that the Movement was being led by someone who knew a great deal about both the investigation into the Movement and Dr. Rothlensberger's work; someone who knew each operation in detail; someone very close to the next king of Iatros society, or even the next King himself.

Clay echoed what Randal had been thinking. "I remember Dr. Rothlensberger well. When he was treating Bethany for the Guillain-Barre, he impressed me as far more sensitive than most doctors. He was more personally invested in curing her than a doctor should be. It is hard to imagine he would turn around and kill her."

"Maybe there is more to his experiments than we know," Randal suggested. "Perhaps he is not so anxious for the results to be fully known."

"I spent most of my life working at a major university," Clay chuckled. "You don't have to explain that phenomenon to me."

"No, I imagine not," Randal answered. "So you can see why Dr. Rothlensberger is of some interest to me. Even if he is not involved in the Movement directly, he most definitely knows someone who is."

The tone of the conversation gave Clay the confidence to ask Randal about the four Iatros that had been with Thomas when they were shot down. "Jason," he asked after some hesitation, "who were the four Iatros with Thomas? Why weren't they revived? And why did Remington lie to the committee and report that they were Apoikians?"

"He didn't lie," Jason answered with a degree of firmness in his voice. "The four were all subjects of Dr. Rothlensberger's cure experiments. All of them were, at least officially, Apoikians. I identified them as Iatros based on their physiology. To put it simply, they were Apoikians who had been cured. As I understand it, the cure does not fully take for several months, so I am not sure they could have been recovered. Still, I did call Edward in Mr. Remington's office to get an EMT team out there which might have been able to revive them. However, there was some sort of screw-up and the team was sent halfway around the world to an Iatros facility in Siberia. What can I say? Iatros are far more advanced than our Apoikian brothers, but we are no less capable of occasional human errors. After all, it was an Iatros that coined the term *snafu* during World War II."

The answer seemed to satisfy Clay except for Remington's lack of an explanation to the committee. Before he could raise the question however, Jason continued.

"Mr. Remington just didn't want to open that whole can of worms to the committee until he had investigated the error in his own office." Jason added that Remington was even now still investigating the snafu with unusual vigor.

***

After a busy Saturday afternoon making final preparations, Clay and Kate were both dressed and ready well before the first guests arrived. A portrait of Thomas sat on a gold decorative tripod surrounded by arrangements of carnations, Gerbera daisies, lilies and daisy pomes. Photo albums were laid out on several tables and much of Thomas's cherished memorabilia was displayed throughout the room. Many of the PhotoShopped pictures featured Clay with Kate and Thomas as kids, with their father, and with Thomas in Lynn Lake. Clay still felt uneasy about the ruse and said so as he fixed Kate a drink. "These are your friends, and tonight is supposed to be about your loss. They have no idea who I am, and I doubt if they care."

"That's just the point. Thomas was not big on funerals and mourning and all that. He would want tonight to be upbeat and, personally, I would like it to be as much about what I have gained as what I have lost. Tonight is as more a debutante's ball than a funeral – and you, Mr. Jeffries, I mean Mr. Eastman, are the debutant." Kate embraced Clay playfully as she added, "and before the night is over, I plan to claim you as my own."

"How could I resist," Clay conceded as he bent to kiss Kate only to be interrupted by the doorbell.

Jonathan showed Jason Randal into the living room. Kate barely had time to hug Randal before the door bell rang again. Within thirty minutes nearly two hundred guests arrived. Kate and Clay circulated and spoke briefly to old friends of Kate's family, to friends of Thomas's, to business associates and to a few distant relatives. Each offered sympathy and bemoaned Thomas's tragic death. Kate was gracious with each, but turned each conversation to an introduction of Clay. She told the bogus story of his long friendship with her father and the invaluable help he had been in Lynn Lake. She pointed to pictures of a younger Clay with her father, with her mother, and with her and Thomas as children.

Jason Randal joined several banal conversations and made a point of saying hello to the two Iatros guests not part of his team. They were long time business associates of Kate's father. They had heard through Iatros news that

Thomas Young had somehow gotten involved in the Movement and were anxious to ask Jason how the investigation was going. "I understand Mr. Eastman and Miss Young are now on the inside of Iatros society," commented one.

"That is correct," Jason answered. "They were briefed by Mr. Remington himself."

"So, are they fully Iatros," asked the other.

"No, not at all," Jason answered. "They are still, of course, fully Apoikian. They would not recognize you as Iatros unless you told them."

"It raises an interesting question," commented the first. "With that can of worms opened, we are going to need to promulgate some rules about how Iatros are to handle dealing with informed Apoikians. I really don't know if we should or should not mention that we are Iatros."

"It does indeed raise a lot of questions," conceded the other. "A subject for our next Assembly of Families to take up, I suppose."

The two Iatros had left long before Dr. Rothlensberger had arrived. An arrangement Jason was grateful for, lest they raise dozens of other difficult questions about Dr. Rothlensberger's attendance. Jason saw the Doctor enter and scan the room clearly uncomfortable about seeing no one familiar. Jason twisted his way through the crowd of guests making his way to the Doctor and had nearly reached him when Rothlensberger spotted Clay and greeted him warmly.

"Mr. Jeffries," the Doctor half shouted then

lowered his tone as he came next to Clay. "I know this is a service in Thomas Young's memory, but it appears I am one of the few in attendance that can express to you how sorry I am for your loss as well. Bethany Jeffries will always hold a place of great honor in Iatros society as the first truly 'recovered' Apoikian. She filled the role with dignity and courage. I hope that is some comfort to you."

Clay was literally dumb struck. For one, the Doctor caught him off guard referring to his real identity. But of course, the Doctor was Iatros and would know of Clay's plight. Of greater implication was whatever the Doctor had meant of Bethany's 'recovery' and the role she played. It gave rise to dozens of questions which Clay was only beginning to formulate when Jason interrupted them.

"Dr. Rothlensberger," Jason said as he held out his hand. "It is an honor to meet you."

"What are you saying, Doctor?" Clay asked brusquely, ignoring Jason. "What do you mean by Bethany's recovery?"

"Clay, Doctor," Jason insisted, "we clearly have much to talk about. Let's find a quiet corner where we can talk."

As they moved toward the door to a back patio, the Doctor turned to Clay with an answer to Clay's questions. "I was referring to her recovery from Guillain-Barre."

"Oh," Clay deflated, "You made it sound like you were referring to a recovery in the Apoikian sense. Like she had become Iatros."

The Doctor paused and gave Clay a puzzled look. "I was," the Doctor replied, "and she had become Iatros, Mr. Jeffries. You didn't know?"

**

"Doctor," Jason began the discussion, "it would be most helpful to Mr. Jeffries, and to my investigation, if you could update us on your research."

The Doctor looked confused. "The bulk of my research has been published, Mr. Randal. If you feel it is somehow relevant to your investigation and to the Movement, I would think you would have studied those reports in some depth."

"I have," Randal responded somewhat apologetically. "But as you can see, Mr. Jeffries knows nothing of your work."

"Then I shall consent to a full briefing for Mr. Jeffries' benefit," the Doctor responded with a note of defiance, "but you will be most disappointed if you are hoping that interrogating me will help in your investigation."

"My apologies Doctor," Randal offered, "I perhaps should have been more direct, but two of the most notable subjects in your research have emerged as prominent players in the Movement. Even you must see the connection as beyond coincidence."

"I do," Rothlensberger answered with a bit of a chuckle. "But a simple and innocent explanation is just as obvious. I assume they were both recruited by the Movement *because* of their cure. Surely, you can see what a valuable asset they were to the Movement as a result of their cure."

"I do see that," Randal said somberly. "The problem I have is that very few would have known about their cure at the time they were recruited to the Movement. It creates a very disturbing suspect pool."

Rothlensberger looked aghast. "I see your point," the Doctor said before taking a long thoughtful pause. "Well," he finally said, "let me brief you on the work I have done."

"Please do, Doctor," Clay urged him impatiently.

"I came upon the suspicion that Guillain-Barre might hold the answer to curing Apoikians. It is not important how I stumbled into that suspicion, suffice it to say that the hypothesis has proven correct. I have treated dozens of Guillain-Barre patients and have nearly perfected a treatment that results in recovery from the disease and often results in a fully cured Iatros. The treatment involves intentionally infecting the patient with a small tumor at the base of the Medulla as the Guillain-Barre destroys the body's nerve sheaths. Very quickly after the nerve sheaths are restored, the tumor is removed. Once removed, the patient recovers over a period of several months into a full Iatros state, mentally and biologically. The difficulty is that I have now applied the regimen of treatment to eighteen Apoikians. Six of them, including Miss Jeffries and Mr. Young, thrived. The other twelve quickly developed additional tumors that proved fatal within days." He didn't mention the other two he had wanted to cure in San Francisco.

"That hardy seems to be what you called an effective treatment," Clay scoffed.

"The key," Rothlensberger countered, "is to isolate the critical difference between our six survivors and our twelve fatalities. That is a fairly simple, though a time-consuming process, which we are now working on."

"Why do you say that it is a simple process?" Randal asked.

"The critical differentiator can only exist in one of three realms: post-infection environment, pre-infection environment or genetically. We can safely eliminate post-infection environment since all the subjects existed in identical environments after treatment. They ate the same foods, slept at the same times, maintained identical regimens. Pre-infection environment could prove difficult to isolate but my instincts are, in fact I feel nearly certain, that the key is genetic and genetic isolation will, as I said, prove simple, though time-consuming."

Both Randal and Clay were taking several minutes to absorb what Rothlensberger had said. As if thinking out loud, Randal asked the Doctor if Thomas and Bethany had spent much time at the medical facility at Borden Island.

Clay interrupted. "I thought Borden Island was an energy facility."

"It is." Randal answered. "But it is much more like a city. Power generation is one of its more important aspects, like auto manufacturing is in Detroit. Borden Island also houses a major medical research facility among many other things. It is even a popular resort among Iatros. Remember, we have a lower body temperature and prefer things a bit colder than Apoikians."

Clay nodded his understanding while Rothlensberger returned to the original question. "Yes, both Mr. Young and Miss Jeffries maintained regular quarters at Borden Island. I know it is not yet in any of Mr. Remington's reports because he has been trying to discover what the Movement was looking for, and if they found it, but I should think you would have known: both of their apartments were ransacked during the intrusion."

◆CHAPTER 8◆

Clay and Kate spent the next couple of weeks learning about Iatros society. Clay had wanted to go to Bar Harbor, but Jason had told him they would have to wait a bit until he made the necessary arrangements. They spent the weeks talking with Jason about Iatros culture, institutions, history and life in general. All Iatros were, at least by Apoikian standards, wealthy. Class was determined more by age than by economic status. Each Iatros citizen was required to fulfill certain roles at various points during their lives based on their age. "For example," Jason had told them, "the Iatros hotel staff you met in San Francisco would be very young, fulfilling their servitude requirements." Jason explained that Iatros children spent their first thirty years in school, then spend thirty-eight years in what they call servitude duty. "Burger flipping, if you will," he joked. Then there is thirty-two years of staff duty. All of this is necessary before entering one's chosen profession. All through that first hundred years, the Iatros youth fulfills only an Iatros role. After that, everyone must mesh an Iatros role with an Apoikian cover. That way, the demands of an Iatros life are met while Apoikian society is cared for. "I, for example," Jason further illustrated, "chose the Royal Service as my Iatros career, while at the same time I fill an Apoikian role as a senior official in the Canadian Security Intelligence Service."

Jason had explained so much about history, how so many of the ancient mysteries, even many myths and legends could be explained by the presence of the Iatros. "At first, we didn't make any effort to hide ourselves and our technology. We built transportation, communications, industrial, and energy infrastructure all over the world. We built the Pyramids, but the Apoikians reacted to us so weirdly!"

"*You* built the Pyramids?" Clay asked, urging him to give details.

"We did," Jason answered proudly. "Have you ever heard about a guy named Christopher Dunn? He wrote a book titled *The Giza Power Plant.* You should read it; it's right on the money. The Pyramids were just a big power plant."

"So explain Stonehenge," Kate teased.

"Stonehenge was actually a large musical

instrument that we call, not ironically, a *henge,*" Jason obliged her. "Sound is created when wind passes through the gaps between the rocks. Each gap produces a different note based on the direction of the wind passing through. A henge concert is very much like an opera. There are two dancers for each gap. The dancers each hold a long pole vertically and there is a cloth stretched between and attached to their poles, like a sail. The dancers cover their gap with the sail until that note needs to be played. The whole henge takes dozens of dancers to play, and they are carefully choreographed to make music to accompany their dance," Jason had apologized for the lack of exact detail explaining that he didn't know how to play. "But that gives you a rough idea," he added. "Iatros still hold henge concerts in different places. I will make a note to take you sometime."

Clay had immediately grasped how so many of the ancient mysteries, myths, and legends could have grown out of Apoikian encounters with Iatros. He had enjoyed several of these types of explanations from Jason over those weeks.

Clay and Kate also took the time to deepen their relationship. Clay read some of Kate's poetry, and Kate read two of Clay's history books. They spent several days lounging around Kate's massive house, Kate usually curled on a couch with a cup of tea, and Clay sat somewhat askew in an overstuffed chair he seemed to have adopted as his own. They talked about Kara, Thomas, Bethany, and Brooke. When all was said and done,

Kate had a pretty good idea of what life was like for an upper-middle class Midwestern family. Clay had also gained significant insight into what it was like to grow up wealthy, among old money and Eastern establishment pompousness.

Jason had sat in on one or two of those long, rambling conversations and had even given some insight into what it was like growing up in Iatros society. His father had always been political. The old man served as the head of state for several different countries in his Apoikian cover roles. He was an Iatros Senator and had played a major role in foiling the Nazi's research into nuclear weapons during World War II. Iatros were not perfect and Jason pointed to that piece of history as a monument to Iatros mismanagement of Apoikian affairs. His father's political leanings are what led Jason to a career in the Royal Service. He liked the politics, but was more a man of direct action than his father had been.

It was during one of those late-night conversations, after Kate had gone to bed, that Jason brought the idea of Bar Harbor back up. "Why are you so anxious to go?" he asked Clay bluntly.

"Bethany left her journal there," Clay answered. "I am certain I know exactly where it is."

Jason was stunned. He stood silent for at least a minute, appearing to be thinking, before speaking. "Well then, we need to get to Bar

Harbor...now," Jason said as he turned away from the bookshelf he had been mindlessly staring at as they talked. "Be ready to leave within fifteen minutes. I'll be back for you and Kate after I make some arrangements," he said and just as abruptly went out the front door.

"OK," Clay said to the already absent Jason as he shrugged and started up the stairs to get Kate then suddenly stopped. He was struck by the thought that it might be dangerous. He could not risk losing her by putting her in danger, but he knew she would insist. He decided instead to leave her sleep and left a note on the table at the bottom of the stairs: *Jason and I went to Bar Harbor. We should be back by morning. I will call you if there is any delay.* He hesitated only a second, looking at the note, then walked out the front door to wait for Jason.

***

Kate stirred from her light sleep and was trying to remember what she had been dreaming about. It took her a moment to come fully awake and realize that she had just heard the front door and that Clay was not beside her. She jumped from bed, unable to imagine why he might have gone out. Her panic subsided when she read the note. It didn't anger her; she liked the protectiveness. Neither did it lessen her desire to go along. What did anger her was the ringing phone on the mantle when she dialed Clay's cell number. She became furious when Jason did not answer his phone. She hesitated for only a second before running up the stairs, throwing on some jeans and a sweat shirt, grabbing the keys to her Mercedes SLK, and racing to the garage.

Kate had always been a fast driver but had never really tested the limits of her little sports car. She was surprised, and a little thrilled, when she stomped on the gas pedal. The car accelerated so fast that she was nearing the gate before it was fully opened. Even when she slowed down a bit, she worried that it would be a tight squeeze to get through the gate panels as they rolled open. She was glad she had slowed down once she realized how sharp a right turn onto the street she needed to make. She was pressed so hard against the door that she was sure the car would flip over, but it held the turn with little more than a squeal of the tires.

She assumed if they were going to Bar Harbor and planning to be back by morning, that they would be flying. And if they were flying, they would be heading for Westerly State Airport. It was only fifteen minutes if they used Interstate 95, so they were probably already there. She hoped all the pre-flight rigmarole would give her time to catch them. At least she could really open it up on the interstate, even though passing a couple of semis got a little hairy. The exit on to Liberty Street was a long curving ramp that allowed her to keep the car almost wide open. She was still doing about a hundred forty miles per hour when the sharp left turn onto the Westerly

Bypass came up much quicker than Kate expected.

The blood must have gone right to her head because there was no rush of adrenaline; no moment of panic, no scream. The car rolled onto its side once before becoming airborne then tumbled side over side before landing in a mangled heap in a field. The driver of a semi on the northbound side saw the whole thing. He screeched his rig to a stop and ran to the field even though he knew there was no urgency. No one could have survived that crash.

***

Jason had called Evan Mills and asked him to take over surveillance an hour earlier than he had been scheduled. Evan was just arriving at the Young estate when he saw Kate race out of the driveway. He struggled to keep up with her. Now he was one of the first at the scene and had already worked his way up on the phone to Mr. Remington, who had him on hold for the past ten minutes. When the line finally came to life again, Remington instructed Evan to accompany the body to the morgue where a team would meet him.

Evan had never been really big on the Service, but he was in awe of the team that took over. They had replaced Kate's body with the body of a drug crazed woman who had a week earlier jumped bail in Georgia. They had slipped in a stolen car report from Kate Young that appeared to have been filed three days ago. They carefully prepared Kate's body and took it to the airport. All of this was done without anyone other than Evan ever knowing they were there.

Remington had ordered Evan to stay with the body until it was turned over to Dr. Rothlensberger at Borden Island. As instructed, Evan followed pre-revival procedures during the long flight, keeping the body as warm as possible, administering the artificial coagulant, and attaching the baseball-sized heart and lung machine. Kate once again had a pulse, but was far from being revived.

***

A call directly from Chairman Remington was unusual enough for Dr. Rothlensberger, let alone a call in the middle of the night. He was not fully awake when Remington cut right to the point. "Kate Young has been killed in a car accident. I am having her body sent to you now. It is critical that she be revived."

It took Rothlensberger a good ten seconds to place Kate Young. It was beyond him as to why revival would be so critical, but it didn't matter. "She's an Apoikian. An Apoikian can't be revived," he reminded the Chairman.

"She *has* to be revived," Remington barked. "It is becoming clear that without her, there is no hope of recovering her brother's journal and without her brother's journal, there is little hope of exposing the Movement." The Doctor was not very political and didn't quite follow what

Remington was saying. It didn't matter – she was Apoikian and Apoikians could not be recovered.

"Doctor," Remington had turned to pleading, "Can't you keep her stable long enough to administer your cure, then revive her?"

"No! I'm sorry sir, but that is crazy. It's like asking me to do brain surgery and a heart transplant simultaneously. It just can't be done," the Doctor insisted.

"Nonetheless, you are to try. A team with Miss Young is enroute to you from Connecticut. I will be a few hours before they get there. You will get a call when she arrives." With that Remington hung up abruptly.

***

It was really not necessary, but Dr. Rothlensberger had driven to the hospital, as soon as he was informed of Kate's arrival. The hospital staff was plenty competent in initial procedures, but his medical instincts dictated that he be with his patient. Besides, the staff had never initiated recovery procedures on an Apoikian; no one had because it was not possible.

Rothlensberger had supervised the young intern's application of the accelerated healing gauze over the traumatized areas of the body. He watched as nurses inserted the PICC line that would supplement the blood flow. He personally connected the four transmitters to the back of Kate's head that would keep her brain visually, aurally, kinetically, and internally stimulated.

Medicine had long ago learned that brain cells could be inactive for only a brief time before they died. Keeping them active was the key to revival. The transmitters were designed to send pictures, sounds, feelings and internal data about the body's condition directly to critical brain areas and thus keep them active.

Once Kate was stable, Rothlensberger administered a virus that he hoped would infect Kate with Guillain-Barre even though it was far more likely to end his efforts to bring her back to life. Now there was nothing left to do but wait. It would be two days at the most. On the slight chance the virus worked, and on the even slighter chance they could keep this young Apoikian woman stable, the Doctor would prepare to administer the isotope that would not only save Kate Young's life, but would cure her.

***

The images and sounds flashing in Kate's brain had no obvious connection to each other. They would have been considered random by anyone else. To Kate, though, each image and each sound brought Clay to mind. There was a picture of a little girl on a swing. Would she and Clay ever marry and have children? How many? Would they be boys or girls? Did she have a preference? Did Clay have a preference? Would he finally want a son?

There was a picture of a factory billowing smoke. Would Clay work or would he be a stay at home dad? What kind of work? Would he go back to teaching? Would he like to write? Would she work? How could she even think about it?

There was the sound of a crowd at a baseball game; the crack of the bat hitting the ball was distinctive. What would they as a family do for fun? Would they travel? Would they like baseball games and going to the movies? Or would they like more 'cultured' entertainment? Would they go to museums and operas?

There was the sound of crickets. It was late at night. Would she be able to share in Clay's love of nature? Would they keep the fly-in company? Would they stay in Connecticut? Would they move to Canada? Kate laughed to herself. Maybe they would buy a modest house in Bloomington?

There was a picture of a train, the caboose in the foreground, and the sound of its whistle growing fainter. Was Clay on that train? Was he leaving? Kate felt panic. She needed to catch that train. She needed to be with Clay.

There was a picture of a merry-go-round and the sound of its organ. She noticed the small boy high on a horse at the right edge of the picture. His back was to her. She imagined him coming around to where she could see his face. She was sure Clay would come back. She needed Clay to come back.

Clay was her life. It's not like she didn't already know it, but for the first time she could actually say it. She loved him.

Everything seemed to be out-of-body, but

when she thought about it, she realized that she was comfortable; warm and relaxed. Her hands and feet were tingling a bit, enough to be a little annoying, but she was still comfortable. It was just that she missed Clay.

◆CHAPTER 9◆

It was just before midnight when Jason Randal piloted the small Piper Cub toward the only runway at Hancock County Airport outside of Bar Harbor. During the flight, Clay had once again brought up the news that Bethany and Thomas had been 'cured,' even as Jason continued to insist that he thought Remington had told them. "We had talked enough about Rothlensberger's cures that we all just assumed you knew," Jason pleaded. He had tried to change the subject several times by suggesting that it had been a mistake to leave her behind. "She is going to be mad as hell, and you are going to be one unhappy human," he chided.

Clay dismissed the warning. "That's my problem. I am not going to put her in even the slightest danger, whether she likes it or not." Still, Clay knew Jason was right. He wasn't looking forward to that inevitable first argument.

They had finally dropped both subjects by the time they landed and drove the 'borrowed' car across the short bridge onto the island. As they veered toward the left onto Eden Street, Jason reminded Clay that the trip needed to be strictly clandestine. No one, Iatros or Apoikian, was to know of it. Even though he knew it was necessary, Clay was worried that he had even told Kate where they were going.

Jason turned off the car's headlights and slipped on a pair of special glasses as they approached the Jeffries' family cottage. He backed into the unpaved driveway and turned the engine off. Clay hesitated before putting on the glasses Jason held out for him. They were an Iatros version of night-vision goggles that emitted sixteen million beams of distilled light energy. As the beam bounced off an object, it returned to the glasses and reunited with its particulate counterpart producing a somewhat narrow but almost daylight view in full color, depth and detail.

Clay was disoriented for only a moment before he adjusted to the glasses. Clay followed Jason out of the car without a word and headed down the driveway. The ground was sandy and covered in pine needles. It was windy enough that Clay could hear the waves coming off of Frenchman's Bay. The salty smell from the water was invigorating. Jason took a crouched position behind a small bush on the inside corner where the drive made a sharp right turn about thirty yards from the road. Clay jogged the last twenty yards to the front porch of the house.

It had been nearly three years since he had been to the cottage. It was modest by comparison with its neighbors. Dark brown wood siding rose to a steep shingled roof. The ornamentation was architecturally unremarkable. Clay couldn't help but notice the crumbling mortar between the rocks of the chimney as he circled around the north side of the cabin. Even though the house was not far from the road, it was completely hidden by the heavy woods. It was covered enough that Clay was comfortable taking a quick look through one of the windows flanking the chimney. He knew the layout well. The window looked into the great room that made up the bulk of the main floor. Opposite the window was an open staircase that led to four bedrooms. To the side of the staircase at the front of the house was a generous kitchen. To the other side was a narrow sun room with French doors that led to the large covered porch at the back. Clay vividly remembered the small powder room with the odd sloping ceiling that was tucked beneath that staircase. The house was furnished with the same rustic pieces his father had commissioned well before he had been born. The classic white Adirondack chairs that lined the large back porch came to mind, and he took the few steps necessary to look – they were still there.

Clay had climbed on those chairs, and on to his father's lap when he was a young boy. He sat in those same chairs, holding Brooke and Bethany as a young father. He remembered the day only a couple of years ago that Kara had sat on his knees and wrapped her arms around his neck as they both cried, finally accepting the inevitable outcome of her illness. He was tearing up again. The memories of a whole life came back in that moment. A life he would never again know. He sat on the ground, head in hands, and for the first time he truly mourned the long list of losses he had suffered. He would have been content to sit there for an eternity, but he suddenly sensed a presence. He looked up and was startled by Jason's understanding gaze.

"I knew we should have used radios," Jason said. "We have to get moving."

Clay did not know how long he had sat there, but he climbed to his feet and headed for the large tree just off the porch. "I'll be right there," he whispered to Jason as he brushed aside a growth of weeds covering the cairn his father had given over to Brooke and Bethany so many years ago. The rocks were smaller than he remembered them; easy for two little girls to move. Beneath them was a single item, a blue leather bound journal, about letter size and stuffed with loose papers. Clay felt around as if disappointed that there was nothing else, then replaced the rock and headed back around the house where Jason waited for him.

They were about to climb the steps onto the back porch when Clay suddenly stiffened and grabbed Jason's arm. "There was a light!"

"What?" Jason asked.

"There was a small green light in the kitchen, an LED on the old dishwasher," Clay repeated. "It was so common to see that light on that I didn't even notice it at first. It signifies that the dishwasher is running. Someone is here."

Jason stood still for a moment as he considered the possibilities. "OK, let's get back to the car. I have an idea."

When they got into the car, Jason told Clay to head toward town and look for a restaurant. It was now after one o'clock in the morning, but there was still plenty of activity in the touristy village. Clay turned left on West Street then pulled into the parking lot of the Fish House Grill, an odd-looking clapboard building that actually looked like several buildings because of its many and complex roof lines. They declined an outdoor table on the pier in favor of a large corner booth made of dark heavy timbers gouged and scratched from years of use. The absurdly high seat backs were more like a wall that made the booth quiet and private.

"We can take some time to look through the journal," Jason explained. "Then you can go back and just walk through the front door since it seems you have been expected. You can say you're putting loose ends together and wanted a few days alone to put your old life behind you. I'll hold onto the journal and stay hidden outside to cover you in case anything funny happens. That way everything appears normal and we can see who has been watching the place and why. Sound like a plan?"

Clay agreed as he reached for the journal he had recovered from the rock cairn, anxious to look inside. He was forced to wait one more second as the waitress appeared with order pad in hand. Jason ordered a bowl of the corn chowder with lobster meat and some garlic bread. Clay quickly ordered a lobster roll then turned his attention back to the journal.

***

The first page was nearly blank, but of heavier paper than the rest; clearly meant to act as a section divider or title page. The only words included were a long and convoluted title: *Project One: the Introduction and Global Adoption of Universal Energy Supply (UES) Technology to Apoikian Society.*

The second page began the first section and was labeled 'Project Charter and Scope.' They skimmed the four-page section, but saw little they didn't already know. There were a few paragraphs about replacing the current battery distribution method with technology that would allow for the transmission of electricity over the air; like a radio signal. Jason noted Clay lingering over the section and interjected. "Iatros had begun to use the technology when we first arrived on earth. It's like that Christopher Dunn book I was telling you about; pyramids and obelisks that are found all over the world were part of such a system. The idea is correct, but in the end, it could not be done covertly, so we went to a battery system instead." Jason leaned forward a bit as if he were about to reveal a secret. "Nikola Tesla's experiments a century ago were actually one of the very few technological advances made without Iatros guidance. That guy was one smart Apoikian! In fact, I was part of a team assigned to slow him down."

The second section was more interesting. It was titled 'Project Team' and included a list of names and contact information. The first name listed was Whitcolm Remington's assistant, Edward. Thomas Young was listed second. Neither Clay nor Jason recognized any of the other half-dozen names. Jason looked his part as a detective as he copied the names by hand into a small notebook. Each name was followed by a brief description of the team member's role. Clay read Thomas's role description out loud, "Responsible for revealing energy capture and storage technology. Mr. Young will serve as Apoikian inventor. He will also assist Mr. Boyle with research on the wireless transmission of energy."

As he finished, Jason took the journal and read the role descriptions following each of the other names. They revealed little, but the last description, under the name of Karen Howell, struck Jason as odd or incongruent. It read simply, "Assistant researcher on the transmission of alternate isotopes."

As Jason made a few more brief notes in his notebook, Clay leafed quickly through the third section titled 'Work Breakdown Structure and Master Schedule.' Just before he reached a second heavier sheet or divider, Clay noted that the project schedule called for complete implementation within four years.

The pages following the second divider followed the same pattern as the pages in the first half of the journal. The divider page included a simpler title: 'Piggy-backing Various Isotopes with The Wireless Transmission of UES.' The title seemed self-explanatory but was, nonetheless, followed by a three-page charter and scope statement. Jason went straight to the Project Team page. Again, the first name listed was Whitcolm Remington's assistant, Edward. Karen Howell was listed second as Jason expected, but it was a name further down the list that made him curse. It was Tom Benton, the gung-ho member of his own team. Bethany and Thomas Young might have been duped, but not Tom Benton. "So Benton is a member of the Movement," Jason thought, "but clearly not one of the leaders."

"So what does this journal tell us?" Clay asked Jason.

"It tells us everything," Jason responded. "I had a suspicion before, but now it is clear who is behind the Movement."

"I don't understand," Clay barely had time to get the words out.

"I'll explain on the way to the airport," Jason promised as he put two bills into the small black guest check folder and stood to leave. The waitress thanked them and wished them a good night.

"I thought we were going back to the cabin," Clay objected.

"Not after seeing this," Jason retorted. "We need to pick up Kate and get to San Francisco."

***

Clay reached for his phone to call Kate and tell her to get ready. He panicked for a second when he realized he had left it at home. Jason pulled his phone out instead and held it for Clay to see. "The phone was off and I missed a call from her just after we left. Bet you're in trouble, buddy," Jason teased as he dialed her number and handed the phone to Clay.

Clay was surprised when her voice mail answered. "Must not be in that much trouble," He answered Jason. "She's still asleep" He handed the phone back to Jason, not sure why he felt troubled by the failed call attempt.

They pulled up to the parked Piper Cub until the headlights fully lit the plane. They exited the car and walked the few steps to the cabin door. Clay shuddered from the cold as he thought about the scene seeming a bit eerie and foreboding. The late-night air was chilly, and it was late enough in the year that they could see their breath. Jason barely began his preflight inspection when a voice behind them sounded. "Can I help you gentlemen?"

Jason recognized the security agent as Iatros as soon as he turned to face him. He paused a second before declaring, "I am Colonel Jason Randal of the Royal Security Service. You can help by telling me who the hell you are."

The security agent looked flustered for a moment before a voice spoke up from inside the plane's cabin. "He is with me, Colonel," Tom Benton said in a clearly defiant tone.

Jason was flustered for a moment before regaining his authoritative voice. "Tom, aren't you supposed to be in Hartford helping to establish Clay Eastman's identity," Jason pretended to be surprised then added with some emphasis, "As I ordered you to do?"

"I don't take orders from treasonous bastards," Benton growled. "You must be tired after your long trip Mr. Eastman. I wish we could stay and enjoy your cabin a while and I hate to rush you, but I must insist you give me what you came here for."

"I don't know what you are talking about. We came to say good-bye to my former life and do some fishing for a few days," Clay answered.

"Then why, exactly, have you decided to leave in the middle of the night just a few hours after arriving?" Benton asked smugly.

"It's alright, Clay," Jason said calmly as he

steered Clay's eyes to the gun held out by the security agent.

Clay stared for a moment then stepped forward and leaned into the cabin of the plane. He grudgingly handed the journal over to Tom Benton. "Thank you Mr. Jeffries," Tom said sincerely as he exited the Piper Cub and turned to face Jason. "Colonel Randal, you are under arrest for high treason and for the murders of Thomas Young, Bethany Jeffries and several others."

"Tom, you have this wrong," Jason objected.

"Save it," Benton barked as he turned Randal toward the airport's only hanger. "If you don't mind Mr. Jeffries, we have a plane waiting to take Mr. Randal into custody and return him to Borden Island. Mr. Remington has asked if you would be so kind as to come along."

The four of them walked through the hanger door where a jet was waiting. The plane looked similar to the plane that had taken them to San Francisco and where they had first met Mr. Remington. As they climbed the stairs and through the plane's doorway, Clay could see it was furnished with the same high leather chairs with small emblems embroidered into each headrest. He thought it must part of some type of fleet – the Royal fleet he assumed.

Clay took a seat on a small couch parallel to the windows while Tom Benton took Jason to a seat in the rear of the plane. He handcuffed Jason and placed a lock on the latch of his seatbelt. The other security agent sat in a jump seat in the galley toward the front of the plane and told the pilot they were ready. The plane began moving slowly out of the hangar and taxied toward the runway.

No one spoke as they climbed to a cruising altitude when the silence was finally broken by Benton. "As I am sure Mr. Randal has explained to you, this journal proves that the Movement is being led by someone quite high in the Royal court."

"How does it prove that?" Clay asked.

"Well," Benton explained, "since your daughter was reporting each project team's progress to the Crown, and since those reports included several very critical deceptions, it is clear that the reports were falsified between the time Bethany wrote them and the time Mr. Remington received them. As we explained to you when we first met over dinner at your home in New Haven, our security team was assigned to you to help establish Mr. Jeffries' new identity; to help you and Miss Young assimilate into Iatros society; and as you correctly assumed, to keep tabs on both of you. Bethany and Mr. Young were also assigned a security team. Bethany would give her reports to just one person, the leader of her security team. That team leader would then submit the reports to the Crown."

"So clearly that team leader was responsible for falsifying the reports," Clay interjected. "Why don't you arrest that person?"

"Exactly Mr. Jeffries," Tom Benton said with a smirk as he glanced toward the rear of the plane where Jason Randal sat shackled.

***

Clay sat silently for over two hours. His questions were coming too fast. Tom Benton and Jason Randal had exchanged a few words during the flight, but Clay hadn't processed any of what they had said. He thought he might have dozed off a bit, but mostly he worried about Kate. It was past dawn, and she would soon be out of bed. He would insist on calling her as soon as they landed. Before they did, Clay needed to ask his many questions since he didn't know when he might see Tom Benton again.

"How well did you get to know Bethany while you were 'handling' her," Clay asked Tom softly.

"Not well at all," Tom answered. "Our team was divided into two halves during the assignment. Half of us were assigned to Thomas Young, and half to Bethany. I spent most of my time with Thomas's team. I met with her on many occasions, especially when she would come to Lynn Lake. She was a commanding and impressive presence, even among Iatros."

"So you knew Thomas well," Clay urged him.

"I knew Mr. Young very well" Tom said. "He also was an impressive man: intelligent, energetic, committed, and caring. I was shocked when it came to light, just a week before he was killed, that he was involved with the Movement. I never accepted the notion that he had become involved knowingly."

"Who were the four Iatros that were killed with Thomas?" Clay asked.

"They were all patients of Dr. Rothlensberger. After their cure," Benton explained, "they were assigned as quasi-members of a security team. That way, we could both put them to use and keep an eye on them. Just like Thomas and Bethany, they were duped into assisting the Movement. Karen Howell was a physicist who had worked at Oak Ridge. Jill and Steven Heire both did high level programming for the U.S. military, and Allen Kopeski was a marine."

Clay returned to Benton's earlier comment. "Then you too are convinced that Bethany and Thomas were duped into cooperating with the Movement?"

"I have no doubt, Mr. Jeffries. Just think how close you and Miss Young came to being sucked in yourselves." Benton answered as he again glanced at Jason Randal.

Clay let the thought sink in as he turned his gaze out the window, looking at nothing in particular. In reality, there was nothing to look at anyway. Just endless snow and ice until a jolting bolt of lightning made Clay jump as it struck the tip of the only break in the uninterrupted white landscape, a small grey tower not more than thirty feet high.

Seconds later the plane touched down. Jason Randal had stared at Clay as the plane taxied to a non-descript spot that turned out to be an elevator. As the entire plane was lowered below the snow, Benton released the lock holding Jason to his seat. They all stood to exit but paused as Jason looked Clay in the eye and said, "I am not a member of the Movement. I am certain that I will be dead before the matter is ever tried and before that happens, I want you to know that I have been completely honest and sincere with you."

Clay had started out of the plane, but now he stopped and turned to face Jason Randal. "You've been completely honest you say. Then what of your role as Bethany's handler? When exactly were you planning to mention that?" Clay paused and glared at Jason before adding, "Go to hell."

Clay was greeted at the bottom of the stairs by a familiar face, Edward, whom he recognized from the tour in San Francisco. "Welcome to Borden Island, Mr. Jeffries. It is good to see you again. I will need to get some statements from you, and I would like to chat a bit, but let me show you to your bungalow first. We can get that nasty business out of the way after you have had a chance to freshen up. I do have some news for you, but I do not want you to be alarmed. We can discuss it in the levcar." Clay recoiled when Edward reached for his elbow. He didn't know why, but he decided to not like the man.

***

Jason led Clay to an odd-looking vehicle. It had no wheels, so Clay assumed it operated like the jet ski he and Kate had used around Bigstone Lake, but it was enclosed. And it was luxurious, shaped more like a rickshaw than an automobile with traditional leather seats that one would expect to find in a limousine. As they rode, Clay was struck by the high artificial sky that gave the impression that they were outside instead of under a frozen wilderness. Tom Benton stayed behind to debrief and file a report. He watched the two men board the plane and emerge several minutes later struggling with the bag that held Jason Randal's lifeless body.

◆CHAPTER 10◆

"Where are you taking me?" Clay asked.

"We need to stop at the hospital before we go to your bungalow. We'll talk there," Clay took Edward's words to mean 'no more questions right now', but the tone was sympathetic. The answer was confusing enough that Clay sat silently until they turned into the hospital parking lot. He expected a large research hospital complex. He was picturing Massachusetts General with a confusing array of buildings connected with ad-hoc walkways and laced with a scribble of long, un-navigable corridors, like any big-city hospital. Instead, they pulled up to a fairly plain two-story brick building. It looked like the offices of a typical mid-sized company. A nice lawn between the building and the hundred or so parking spaces on either side of a center walkway done in stone pavers framing a large sculpture about a hundred feet before the main entry.

The lobby added to the illusion of an office building. There were seating areas on either side of the main door with modern style furniture that didn't fit with the ornate rugs laid on the marble floor. Opposite the door was a reception desk manned by a uniformed security guard who immediately buzzed them through a doorway behind the desk's right side. Once through the door, Clay noticed a couple of offices on either side of the long corridor, but other than that, the corridor now looked like a typical hospital with occasional carts of equipment parked in the hall. There was a long flat handrail running down the corridor, and a small array of lights above each doorway.

"The few patients here are experiencing different stages of Guillain-Barre," Edward explained. "Since we now have a treatment that will either restore an Apoikian patient to Iatros physiology or result in death, they are winding down their research on actual patients. Dr. Rothlensberger can explain all of that a lot better than I can. What little I know is from reports on Apoikians the Doctor has cured. It has probably occurred to you that Thomas and Bethany once occupied rooms here." It had not occurred to Clay, but it gave him an uneasy feeling to think of it as they passed through the corridor.

They rode an elevator to Rothlensberger's

second-floor office. It was spacious; it reminded Clay of the University President's office. Two side walls were lined with overstuffed bookcases. The doorway was framed by a wall full of plaques and citations. The huge desk they faced was lined with small figurines and sculptures. There was a row of windows behind the desk with a large statue on either. They sat on facing couches in the center of the room.

"I expected the facility to be more like a large hospital," Clay said to Dr. Rothlensberger as if expecting an explanation.

The Doctor obliged, "It is rare for an Iatros to require hospitalization. Birthing is done almost exclusively at home. At birth, Iatros infants are given an oral application of nano-sensors that monitor their health for the remainder of their lives. The sensors defeat most viruses and bacteria almost immediately. What they can't defeat, they warn the individual's physician at the earliest possible stage, and the physician can treat most of those maladies remotely or, at worst, on an outpatient basis."

"But have you found a cure for the common cold," Clay said sarcastically.

"Actually no," the Doctor surprised him. "The cold is really not an illness as you assume. It is a necessary maintenance device the human body, Iatros and Apoikian, requires. It is more like menstruation than a sickness. Uncomfortable as a cold can be, they still afflict us all."

"What of your elderly?" Clay asked. "Surely

they require ongoing care."

Dr. Rothlensberger answered after some hesitation as if the answer was going to be complicated. "Our health sciences are very successful at maintaining the human body's structures for well over four hundred years. The one structure that cannot be maintained beyond that is the brain. Once cell structures within the brain begin to fail, quality of life is unrecoverable. It is the custom of Iatros society to euthanize the patient once dementia is confirmed. That almost always occurs at about four hundred and twenty years of age.

The concept clearly disturbed Clay, but he was in no mood to get into a complicated moral and ethical debate. Dr. Rothlensberger sensed his reaction and dismissed the subject: "It is a practice deep in the culture of Iatros society."

"Hospitals are really only needed by Iatros," Rothlensberger returned to the subject, "in some cases of trauma."

"Which brings us to why we have brought you here," Edward interrupted. "Mr. Jeffries, Miss Young apparently tried to follow you to Bar Harbor last night. She was driving very fast, probably trying to catch you before your plane took off."

Clay could see where this was heading and was instantly alarmed. "Where is she? Is she OK? I want to see her!"

"Mr. Jeffries, her car rolled several times while trying to make a sharp left turn at high speed."

"You did this!" Clay shouted.

Edward held out the palms of his hands toward Clay and spoke softly. "This is the last thing we would have wanted to happen. Miss Young is our only hope of finding Thomas Young's notes, which is our best hope of exposing the Movement. We are taking every possible measure to try to save Kate's life, but her condition is confusing. I want the Doctor to explain it to you, and I need you to listen very carefully."

Clay glared at Edward for a moment before sitting back in his chair, though he didn't relax. His grip on the arms of the chair even tightened a bit as he turned and tried to focus on Dr. Rothlensberger.

"By Apoikian standards Miss Young was killed instantly in the crash," the Doctor started. "Now, Iatros medicine is not capable of reviving an Apoikian. To revive her, I first need to administer my cure which you know is still experimental and fails more often than it works. The revival procedure is usually pretty straight forward, but it is tremendously complicated by the fact that we must administer it and my cure procedure simultaneously. I need you to understand that Kate's chances of surviving are very slim. If she does survive, however, she will emerge as an Iatros. Do you understand, Mr. Jeffries?"

Clay sat silent and considered his only two options. He calculated all the possibilities. He really didn't care if the outcome, whatever it was, was the same for both of them. But, what if she lived, and he died? What if she died, and he lived? Either possibility sent a shudder through him. It didn't matter anyway. Rational or not he knew what he would do. He finally spoke, his voice calm. "I understand. I would like to see Kate and then, Doctor, I would like you to initiate your cure procedure on me."

"We suspected as much," Edward conceded then turned toward the Doctor and nodded.

Kate's room was just down the corridor. Clay had put on the blue gown and mask as instructed and washed his hands with the foam from the dispenser that hung on the wall. There were still signs of trauma; her face was swollen and there were bruises everywhere. He was careful of the cuts on her hand as he held her fingers. He spoke to her softly. "I don't know why I couldn't have just dropped this whole thing. I'm sorry Kate. I love you." He gazed at her for a minute before turning and resolutely walking out.

***

There was a picture of a door and murmured sounds from behind it. She needed to open it, but was afraid. She stretched out her arm behind her, without looking back, offering her hand and hoping Clay would take it.

***

Edward had left, but Dr. Rothlensberger

was still waiting in the hall when Clay closed the door to Kate's room behind him. The Doctor took Clay into the next room, nearly identical to Kate's. A nurse was waiting there with another gown and a pair of slippers. She told Clay to change and get into bed. She made some notes on a clipboard then left.

A few minutes later she returned with Dr. Rothlensberger. Clay expected carts full of equipment and monitors. Instead, the Doctor gave him a shot that he was told would put him to sleep. Then, there was nothing.

***

When Clay awoke, four days later, the room seemed full of people. Dr. Rothlensberger was there, standing by a window, along with his nurse who was fussing with one of Clay's arms. Tom Benton was standing by the door, holding a folio full of papers. And Kate was there, standing over him and holding his hand. She was dressed and looked like herself. There were no cuts or bruises; no swelling. "Hi," she said caringly.

"Hi," he answered. "How are you?"

"I'm fine. More to the point, how are you?"

"Hungry," Clay decided after thinking a second. The others all chuckled and began filing out of the room leaving only Kate. "So is that it? He yelled after the Doctor.

The Doctor turned back and paused. "That's it, Mr. Jeffries. You have been asleep for four days. The cure procedures were successful in both of your cases. Miss Young was revived last night, and she has been sitting here ever since." The nurse promised to bring some breakfast and told Clay he could get dressed if he felt up to it.

Kate laid her head on Clay's chest and began to cry. "I'm so, so sorry," she sobbed.

"Kate! No. I'm the one that is sorry. I should have never gone to Bar Harbor without you. I was just trying to protect you. In fact, I should have never gone to Bar Harbor at all. I should have just dropped this whole thing."

Clay held her tightly for a long moment. She finally stopped crying and laughed as she wiped her eyes and said, "So, we're Iatros now. Do you feel any different?"

"No, not one bit," Clay was surprised. "I thought there would be something. How about you?"

"No. I feel exactly the same. Some things don't seem quite as important as they once did, but I think that has more to do with almost losing you. From now on, we stay together," she insisted.

"Trust me Kate; I don't plan on ever leaving you again."

Clay had gotten dressed, and the nurse brought breakfast for both of them. As they ate, Clay brought Kate up to speed on everything that had happened in Bar Harbor. After they had eaten, Tom Benton came in waving some papers. "You are liberated!" he declared. "Edward has asked that you stay here in Borden Island for a few days. He has arranged a nice vacation bungalow for you." Clay and Kate's bungalow was luxurious. It looked like one of those high-end time share condos that Clay had more than once been suckered into touring in return for a 'free' vacation.

The entry was wide with a marble floor and a very subtle textured wall paper. An ornate bench with coat hooks sat along one wall opposite a doorway into the kitchen. The countertops in the kitchen matched the entry's marble floor, and the kitchen walls were the same rusty color as the entry wallpaper's subtle pattern.

The far wall of the living room was shaped like a three-way mirror that one might see in a tailor's shop. The center section held a fifty-inch plasma TV and stereo equipment. To the near side was an angled china cabinet and on the far side was a symmetrically angled fire place. Next to the fireplace, opposite the dining area, were a set of French doors that opened to a well landscaped patio. The wall on the other side of the doors was also slightly angled to accommodate a leather recliner and end table that sat facing the TV. The angles gave the entire area an almost octagonal shape. To Clay's left as he stood at the end of the entry hall was another hallway that their driver explained led to a powder room and two large bedrooms.

The only downside to the bungalow was that it was frigid. Just as he was leaving, Kate quickly asked their driver if there was some way to turn up the heat. "I am so sorry,'" the driver said clearly embarrassed. "Of course, you are Apoikian and would prefer a warmer temperature."

"Actually we are not," Kate corrected him. "We are Iatros. We have been cured."

"I am aware," the driver said. "I work for Dr. Rothlensberger and have met all of his cured patients. I can tell you it takes about a month for the cure to take hold. So, while the room is a normal temperature for an Iatros, it might still feel a bit chilly for you." He crossed the living room to a phone and asked the operator to raise the temperature in the bungalow to seventy-two degrees. "You should be comfortable within five minutes," the driver said as he hung up the phone. "If you need anything else, the operator will be more than happy to accommodate you."

As promised, the bungalow was comfortable within a few minutes. Kate went immediately to one of the bedrooms and Clay followed. Neither was surprised to find the closets well supplied with appropriate clothing. Kate went to take a shower, and Clay, just as he had in San Francisco, laid on the bed intending to take a short nap. He was disoriented for just a moment as the door bell shook him out of the deep sleep into which he had fallen. By the time he turned into the living room, Kate was already seated on the patio with Edward, drinking a cup of coffee and picking at some cookies that Edward had apparently brought along. Kate turned to say hi, and Clay was once again struck by her beauty, just as he had been after their showers in San Francisco. She was wearing an obscenely short light-green skirt and a sheer white blouse with an open, shapeless jacket that was just an inch or two shorter than her skirt and the same shade of green that Clay thought looked so perfect with her long red hair. Suddenly, he felt more like a tourist relaxing in Cabo San Lucas than a hapless victim of this surreal Iatros intrigue. At least for the moment, the tourist thing was by far his preference.

"Good morning Mr. Jeffries," Edward greeted him. "I can almost tell what you are thinking. Borden Island is THE vacation spot, and we want you to have the time to relax and enjoy it."

"That is not *almost* what I was thinking," Clay said impishly as he impulsively caressed Kate's shoulder, "That is exactly what I was thinking. Now that you have your Movement leader in custody, perhaps we can all put this whole thing behind us. Case closed, right?"

"Almost," Edward said somberly. "There is one matter still to be resolved. Miss Young, your brother would have kept a journal similar to that kept by Bethany Jeffries. We were unable to locate that journal in Lynn Lake, and I am afraid we will not be able to conclude the matter until it is located. It contains information that is vital for us to recover."

"I know nothing of it," Kate protested, "and I have no idea where it might be."

"We understand, Miss Young," Edward said, "but it is our hope that if you take a few days to relax and think about it, that you might come up with some idea of where he might have hidden it."

"I will try," Kate was sincere.

"Good," Edward said with a sigh. "I will let the Security Service know, and you have no other obligations while you are here. My job then is to again act as your guide. Would you like me to show you around or would you prefer to explore the island on your own a bit?"

"I think we would enjoy just spending some carefree time on our own," Clay interjected, "if that is alright with you."

"I suspected as much," Edward said, "and that is not a problem at all. I will just tell you that there are some spectacular restaurants, mostly on the north end of the complex. Make certain the servers understand that you were Apoikian. There are some Iatros dishes that are unsuitable for Apoikian consumption, and the Doctor thinks you should wait. Such a pity for you! The east end is dominated by art shops. Iatros are passionate about art and sports. You might be interested to know that all the major sports in Apoikian culture were a gift from Iatros. Football, baseball, basketball, hockey, especially hockey, all were played in ancient times on Mars." Edward babbled on. "We find it odd that hockey has caught on the least among your societies. Iatros have always assumed that it takes a special Apoikian to appreciate hockey."

Before he left, Edward gave Clay and Kate each a bracelet that he promised would keep them comfortable as they were out in the cold Iatros resort, cautioned them to avoid any areas signed as restricted, and again urged Kate to think of the journal her brother had hidden somewhere. He also explained to them that Apoikian visitors were an uncommon occurrence at Borden Island. He advised them to avoid questions by simply saying they were guests of Mr. Remington.

"Oh," Edward turned in the doorway, "that reminds me. I lied. You do have one obligation while you are here. Mr. Remington wondered if you would like to join him for a round of golf tomorrow morning. It is not strictly an obligation, but given his high office I would advise against declining."

"I think I would actually enjoy a round of golf," Clay said enthusiastically. "Do you golf?" he asked Kate.

"Six handicap," Kate gloated.

"The same, with a very wide streak of competitiveness" Clay offered, "this might be interesting."

"Careful you two," Edward interjected. "Mr. Remington thinks he is better than he actually is. I have been playing boss golf with him for more than a hundred years. That takes a lot of motivation if you know what I mean, but he *is* the heir-apparent"

◆CHAPTER 11◆

The revelation that Mr. Remington would be the next king had come as less than a shock. What did interest Kate was that he would be the six-hundred-sixty-sixth king. Edward had explained away the significance of that number by explaining that Iatros scientists had long ago calculated roughly how long it would take to develop an Apoikian cure. Since the reign of Iatros kings was for a fixed period, and since Iatros tended to measure time by the reigns of kings, they had predicted that a cure would be implemented during the reign of the six-hundred-sixty-sixth king. "That is where the number's significance had originated. It simply leached into Apoikian legends from there," Edward had said, "and been assigned all kinds of crazy meanings."

Something about the whole revelation and the six-six-six thing bothered Clay, but he really didn't know what. It had been fixed in his head the whole morning as he and Kate had explored the art shops along the main hall. Everyone seemed to know who they were and treated them as something like celebrities. At one shop, where Kate had greatly admired a handmade necklace, the shop owner had even insisted she take it as his gift. The morning had been relaxing and relatively carefree. It felt like any other shopping stroll in a high-end touristy location. There were jewelry shops, art galleries, expensive clothing shops, even a couple of something like coffee shops, though the fare was not coffee but some type of latte looking drink that Clay and Kate had been advised to avoid.

The café they chose for lunch was bustling to say the least. There were at least a dozen couples crowded around the entrance waiting for a table. Again, Clay and Kate were greeted as celebrities and shown to a small table near the edge of the 'outdoor' terrace. The table's steel meshed top fit in perfectly with the red decorative concrete floor and the low wrought-iron rail that surrounded the terrace. Just as the waiter emerged from the archway passage between the terrace and the indoor dining area Clay and Kate each felt a hand on their shoulder and heard a gleeful greeting. "Mr. Jeffries, Miss Young, how do you do? My name is Brian Flaherty. I was a friend of your brother's, and I just couldn't resist introducing myself."

"Mr. Flaherty," Clay said as he extended a hand to shake. "It is nice to meet you. Please join us. Kate would surely enjoy talking with a friend of her brother's."

"I wouldn't want to spoil your lunch," he apologized. "I saw you come in and just had to meet you. Are you enjoying Borden Island?"

"We insist," Kate interjected as she looked to the waiter for a chair. "We would be delighted."

"I see you have discovered Radford jewelry," Flaherty said as he sat. "He is one of our true jewelry design masters. The necklace is lovely on its own, Miss Young. It is spectacular on you."

"Well thank you," Kate bowed her head graciously. "To answer your question, yes, we are enjoying Borden Island very much so far."

"All it is missing," Clay added, "is a long white sandy beach, or it would be all the great Caribbean resorts rolled into one."

"Apoikians enjoy ocean side resorts so much because of the salty air; it is comforting to them," Flaherty said as the scientist in him slipped out. "The brisk air of Borden Island has the same effect on Iatros."

"So you are vacationing, Mr. Flaherty?" Kate asked politely.

"Oh no," Flaherty frowned. "I am fortunate to call Borden Island home. I am the director of research at the power-generation plant. That is how I met your brother. He was fascinated by our power production capabilities, and a tour had been arranged just after his cure. We became friends after that. Perhaps you would like a demonstration? We have a facility nearby just for that purpose.

"That would be terrific," Clay answered. "We have nothing planned for this afternoon."

***

Mr. Flaherty gave them an overview of his research over lunch then led them to one of the funny little rickshaw-type vehicles, Clay had heard several Iatros refer to them as levcar's, and drove the two miles to a tourist-looking theater. He led them through a lobby where a crowd was filtering through doors into an amphitheater. They climbed a flight of stairs and entered what was obviously some kind of VIP box with windows looking over the crowd below and facing a large manicured field. He pointed to two plush chairs in the front row for them to sit in then took a seat himself immediately behind Clay and Kate.

"As I was mentioning, and as I think you already know, Iatros draw power from the Earth's magnetic field. The power-generation plant is like a giant lightning rod that captures energy and stores it in batteries. That is nothing new to Iatros, but this is," Flaherty stopped speaking as an announcer began.

"When man first arrived on Earth, energy was transmitted and readily available to whatever device needed it, wherever it needed it," the announcer began. "Energy transmission is a technology that has been dormant for thousands of years as was necessary for interaction with our Apoikian brothers and sisters. Today, the time is near when this awe-inspiring technology once again plays a critical role in our everyday lives. No longer will energy consumption be the adversary of our environment. We wish to welcome you to this demonstration. Please remove the batteries from any devices you may be carrying and prepare to be amazed!"

The lights dimmed as the announcer exited the field with a flourish. The crowd began to remove batteries from cell phones, tablets, mp3 players, and especially flash lights. The flash lights must have been handed out at the door because they were all the same and nearly everyone had one.

"Do you have cell phones on you?" Flaherty asked as Clay and Kate shook their heads. "No matter," he said as he handed them each a flashlight. Clay checked; there were no batteries in the flashlights.

The theatre went dark as a glowing obelisk slowly rose out of the middle of the field. "They don't really glow," Flaherty whispered. "That's just for effect." Laser lights began to flash lightning bolts all over the theater as music rose.

Suddenly, the music and lasers stopped. The glow from the obelisk softened. There was silence then rising murmurs from the crowd as flashlights began to turn on. By the time Clay tried his flashlight, the crowd's murmurs had erupted into applause. Kate couldn't help joining in as she was amazed to see her flashlight turn on.

The announcer was back at center stage as the applause trailed off. "Imagine a world," he said, "that is immersed in energy." Two levcar's circled the field, stopping on either side of the announcer who opened a trunk lid with each hand. Out of one trunk, where the batteries would normally be, climbed a koala bear; out of the other leaped a snow leopard. They were greeted with 'awes' and cheers from the crowd.

"Imagine no depleting resources; no pollution," the announcer challenged the audience. A juggler juggled laptop computers, while they were booted up, then tossed them like Frisbees. "See how light they are?" Flaherty whispered.

Similar acts followed in quick succession for a half-hour. Kate was impressed. She could easily understand how Thomas would want to be involved with technology like this.

Clay had questions. "Do the obelisks capture the energy?

"No," Flaherty explained. "Energy is captured and converted by a pyramid type structure and then transmitted to the obelisks. The obelisks are like cell towers; they receive the energy than re-broadcast it to the immediate vicinity."

"How do devices receive the energy?"

"Two thin wires joined by a tiny receiver

connect to the positive and negative terminals in the device," Flaherty handed Clay a sample. "The flashlights were pre-installed with the antennae."

As they thanked Flaherty and were about to leave, Clay asked him one last question. "I have heard of experiments on broadcasting isotopes in a similar manner. Is that possible?"

"It might be possible, yes," Flaherty answered. "But why would anyone want to? What's the practical application?"

Clay just shrugged. "I don't know."

***

Clay hadn't swung a club in better than a year, and it showed. He had bogeyed three of the first four holes and only a lucky bounce back to the fairway had saved his par on the second hole. Kate was faring a bit better. She had par on the first three and just missed a twenty-five-foot putt and took a bogey on four. Remington's ego was intact after birdies on one and four and pars on two and three. The fifth hole of the Tom Fazio inspired course was characteristically long and narrow with a slight dog-leg to the left.

Led by Remington, talk through the first four holes was all golf. He was clearly an enthusiast. The trend continued as Remington placed his tee on five. "This green can be reached in two," Remington advised as he boasted that he had eagled the hole twice in years past. "But you have to place it just perfectly," he added as he stepped up to the ball. "Miss and you're in a lot of trouble – like that!" Remington gently tapped his driver on the ground and looked disgusted as his ball disappeared in a large clump of something that looked like saw grass.

Kate played a safe shot down the middle of the fairway, but Clay had gone to school on Remington's shot and figured he had a bad round going anyway. Why not go for it? He followed his perfect drive with a four-iron shot that none of them would ever forget. He knew he needed to be long with just enough back-spin to start the ball back down the steep slope of the green. Too much spin and the ball would surely roll off the front; not enough and he would likely be off behind the green. His first thought after striking the ball was that he was going to fly the green, but the ball seemed to die and dive into the back of the green where it completely stopped for a moment before beginning its long slow roll back toward the hole. Clay wasn't breathing. Kate and Remington stared in disbelief. The ball seemed drawn to the hole like it was a magnet, accelerating as it rolled. Clay had hit two aces before, both when he was playing in college, but he didn't remember either of them feeling quite like this double eagle shot. It and Remington's double bogey framed Kate's par nicely. Remington's only other comment, after congratulating Clay, was to insist that the score was actually called an 'albatross'. "A double-eagle would be four under par," he said in a snooty kind of way, but he was clearly excited by the shot.

After six, they were all even. Everyone had

proven themselves, and they all relaxed a bit. Heading into seven Clay wondered if he was now obligated to buy a round once they got back to the clubhouse. He knew the tradition on aces, but did it extend to a deuce on a par five? He asked Remington, who brushed him off with a laugh. "Kate's fortune would not be enough to buy a round at this club," he exaggerated. "Besides, it's not about the money. Why is everything with you Apoikians about the money?"

"Money is power," Clay retorted. "I should think no one would understand that better than a politician."

"Oh, I understand it well," Remington answered, "but I operate in a very different political and economic system than any you know of. You are correct, to Apoikians money is power, but it shouldn't be. Money should be a medium of exchange; nothing more and nothing less. It confounds me that you would go through all the machinations of a constitution, a legal code, and a justice system to control and properly channel the accumulation of power, then negate it all by allowing the unbridled misuse of money by some to exercise power over others."

"And what is the alternative?" Clay asked. "The relationship between money and power seems natural and inseparable."

"It is not natural and it is very easily separated if you just adjust your paradigm a bit," Remington answered with some fervor in his voice. Clay had clearly struck a nerve. "Look, if money is used strictly as a medium of exchange as intended, to buy goods and services, then why should any one person have more money than needed to buy all the goods and services one could possibly consume in a lifetime?"

"Are you suggesting some form of socialism," Kate asked.

"Absolutely not! Iatros are decidedly capitalist," Remington objected. "Even Apoikian society recognized early in the twentieth century that capitalism required a bottom; a safety net that provided all people with at least subsistence. You have not organized it well, but at least in theory your society concedes that there must be a bottom. What you have yet to realize is that capitalism also requires a top. If a man earns, say, fifty billion dollars, what is his incentive to earn another fifty billion dollars? What can he buy with the second fifty billion that he couldn't afford with the first fifty billion? The answer is power. But it is uncontrolled, unbridled power. Ideally, there should be a top. It should be outrageously high, something like three or four percent of gross domestic product. Let's say for the argument's sake it is fifty billion dollars. After that the individual should be taxed at one hundred percent. However, the individual should be compensated with the very thing that drives him to earn the second fifty billion dollars: power. That would be an ideal Senate, composed of the ultra wealthy who have reached the top of the ladder. That way, the power would be controlled with limits determined by society at large."

"You're saying just tax the ultra wealthy at one hundred percent but give them a Senate seat in return," Clay asked as if the idea was absurd.

"Exactly!" Remington exclaimed. "Not only is the power controlled and defined, but then your Senate would be truly aristocratic and a perfect balance to a democratic House."

"Edward sang the same kind of praises over a 'balanced' government when we were with him in San Francisco," Kate added impatiently.

"Well," Remington sighed, "I love talking economics, politics, religion and the like, but don't get me started on Edward. He is a subject all his own."

Kate puzzled over the comment but forced a change in subject with a troublesome drive into the trees lining the left side of the number eight fairway. Remington insisted that a flattened long iron would put her back in good shape. She tried just as he instructed and was delighted with a second shot that rolled and rolled and rolled just to the front fringe of the green.

At the green, Clay solidified the change in subject by asking Remington about the power-generation plant and the breach that had led to Bethany's death. "I haven't seen anything that looks top-secret or anything," he wondered.

"The power-generation plant is not actually on Borden Island," Remington explained. "It is about thirty miles offshore to the north of the island and it is strictly off limits."

"Well, I'll bet you're glad to finally have this Movement thing behind you," Clay said.

"You can't imagine," Remington exclaimed. "Exposing the Movement forced me into a plan so diabolical that it still disgusts me. I curse history for choosing me for the role. I have had to break laws; something of far greater significance to Iatros than to Apoikians, I assure you. For God's sake! The Movement forced me to commit murder! Surely, you can begin to understand the burden the whole affair placed on me. Thankfully, my own contemporaries have exonerated me. I suspect history will as well though it is little comfort to a conscience that now tortures me."

"Was it really worth it then?" Clay had to ask. "Would exposing the power-generation secrets of Borden Island really have been so devastating?"

"The Movement was about much more than electricity, Clay," Remington said somberly. "The Movement's aims were darker than the darkest, most misguided ambitions by which man has ever been victimized."

***

The clubhouse was relaxing despite the stiffness and fatigue that was setting into Clay's body. It was a dark barroom with a thick, though short pile, green carpet. The small tables were all walnut. Opposite the long bar was a row of floor-to-ceiling windows that looked out over the eighteenth hole. The Maximo rum with ginger beer that Remington recommended added to the relaxed atmosphere. Clay thought the hi-ball glass felt especially comforting to hold. Kate and Remington seemed to enjoy the cherry garnishes. Clay had set his aside. The drink along with the soft leather captain's chair that he sank into inspired thoughts of a nap. An idea nixed only by his aching feet.

Remington was gloating a bit about scoring birdies on each of the last three holes with a detailed recounting of each. Clay worried he might yet fall asleep in the dim light of the club's bar, but Edward's exuberant entrance and near gallop over to their table shook Clay alert.

"Sir, I am sorry to disturb you," Edward apologized, "but I have an important dispatch that you should see immediately."

"What is it, Edward?" Remington asked with a tone of disinterest.

"Perhaps we might step outside," Edward suggested.

"Of course," Remington apologized to Clay and Kate as he rose.

While Kate was switching subjects back and forth between commenting on the ornate walnut bar and the huge etched mirror right out of the early twentieth century and making dinner plans, Clay was only thinking of that nap. Neither was especially interested in the hushed conversation Edward and Remington were having near the doorway. Clay knew it was serious by Remington's stiffened posture.

Once Remington and Edward had concluded their conversation, and Remington returned to the table, he immediately excused himself. "I just received a bit of bad news," he said, "and I must return to my office in San Francisco at once." Edward waited calmly at the door as Remington explained.

Clay and Kate had no idea that suicide, though still not common, was more frequent in Iatros culture than it was in the Apoikian world. This despite the fact that Iatros technology, with its immediate response sensors implanted in the blood, also made it very difficult under normal circumstances. It should have been nearly impossible for a prisoner. Even if they had known all this, Edward's news that Jason Randal had supposedly committed suicide in his cell in San Francisco would still have left them both shaken; and more than a little bit saddened.

◆CHAPTER 12◆

Clay and Kate had sat in the clubroom silently stunned for several minutes, when suddenly something seemed to strike Clay. He bolted from his chair and grabbed Kate's arm, rushing his way to the door. "We need to catch Remington before he leaves," Clay urged Kate.

"What is it Clay?" Kate asked.

"I know who really leads the Movement" Clay blurted excitedly. "That was the last piece that narrowed the suspects to one. I even know the 'why'. It's just a question now of the 'how'. One thing is for sure: this isn't over."

They ran into the street and chased after Remington's speeding car or sled or whatever those things were called. They looked like a couple of groupies trying to get a Hollywood starlet's attention as they waived their arms and shouted. It was to no avail. Remington's car turned the corner, and they were gone.

Clay paused only a second before he reached into his pocket for a cell phone and dialed Remington's number. Edward answered just as Clay managed to calm himself enough to sound casual. "Edward," Clay asked, "Kate and I were wondering if it would be possible to accompany Mr. Remington to San Francisco."

There was a long pause before Edward answered. "That would be quite difficult, but I will see what I can do. Let me see if I can arrange that or at least arrange an alternative, and I will get right back to you."

"What was that?" Remington asked as the call ended.

"Oh, nothing sir," Edward brushed it aside, "Just one of my administrators needing some unexpected time off."

Remington only nodded and returned to the brief he was reading. Edward looked out the window and wondered what prompted Clay's request. Had they gotten that close to Jason Randal that they wanted to be involved or was there more to it? Either way, he was not about to grant them time with Mr. Remington right now. They would be waiting a long time for that return call. He would blame it on the flurry of briefs coming in about the suicide and the attention they demanded from him. Clay and Kate would surely accept his apology.

Clay had thought about calling Dr. Rothlensberger but thought the better of it. He just couldn't be sure. He and Kate had gone back to their bungalow, certain that they would not be hearing from Edward. Clay was pacing at a furious clip, poking his forehead as he tried to think of something to do. It was making Kate nervous as she also tried to think.

It had hit her as they were running back to the room. She blurted out at nearly the same instant that the thought came to her. "It's Edward, isn't it!"

"Yes!" Clay had answered as if Kate had just solved a puzzling round of charades. "Remember, Jason had told us that night in Bar Harbor that Bethany's journal did not match official reports; that reports, even his own reports, were being altered somewhere along the chain. He looked to everyone whom those reports went to, knowing it had to be someone who had access to all of them. Think about it; it is a pretty short chain from Jason to Remington. Jason must have narrowed the possibilities to just two: Edward and Remington.

Jason didn't commit suicide. He was murdered. He tried to tell me that he would be as we left the plane. If Remington were leading the Movement, he would have known that there was no suicide. Clearly, it's all a ruse for his benefit. That leaves only Edward. And it's not about solving the world's energy problems either," Clay insisted, "Just as Remington suggested. It's about much more than that. I think he may be planning to weaponize Borden Island technology. "

They had no choice but to act. They had to do something, but what? The question kept pounding Clay as he paced. He had figured out what the Movement planned to do, but he was not sure how they would do it. Bethany's journal had given a clue as had Dr. Rothlensberger. There were still many pieces missing; pieces that only Thomas Young could provide. Clay stopped in mid-pace and turned to Kate. "Surely Thomas kept some kind of records or journal just as Bethany had. Can you think of any place he might have kept it?"

"I have been thinking about it since you told me about Bar Harbor," Kate voiced her frustration. "I have it narrowed down to Manitoba."

"There was no special place at the fly-in company? Maybe at one of the cabins or a favorite camp site," Clay kept urging Kate to think. "Was he especially close to anyone in Lynn Lake?"

"Oh my God! That's it," Kate exclaimed. "Darcy at the diner in Lynn Lake!"

"You think they were close enough that he left something with her?" Clay pushed for more.

"No," Kate answered as she thought it through glaring past Clay. Yeah, she thought, that had to be it. "Clay, Darcy told me that Thomas had been spending a lot of time at the library. That is just like Thomas. If he wanted to hide a book, he was the type to hide it in a library; in plain sight!"

"Perfect," Clay said, "we need to get to Lynn Lake. Will you know where to look once we get there?"

"I certainly do!" Kate was now proud of having figured it out. "Thomas gave me an autographed first edition of Taylor Caldwell's *'Captains and the Kings'* last Christmas. I liked having the autograph because I am a Caldwell fan, but that was by far my least favorite of her works. It was an odd choice. What do you want to bet that the Lynn Lake library has a copy?"

***

The attendant at the airport was adamant. Flying restrictions were in place and neither a return to Connecticut nor a visit to San Francisco would be possible for at least several days. The attendant either couldn't or wouldn't explain why, but Borden Island was basically on lock down. The order came directly from Remington.

Clay had been fascinated by the sporting goods store during their leisurely shopping trip the day before. Now he and Kate were on a mission. Lynn Lake was over a thousand miles to the south, on the far side of a vast wilderness. Nevertheless, Clay was determined. The lock down made him even more convinced that the Movement was not finished; that something far worse than revealing Borden Island's energy secret was afoot, and that time was critical. Thomas's journal would reveal the greater aims and explain the 'how' of the Movement's plan, but that was in Lynn Lake, and this was the only way Clay could think of to get there.

Kate acted disinterested as Clay casually inspected one of the latest models of equipped camping sleds. The sled itself looked like a sleeker version of the flying jet ski they had used months earlier. It seated two, and one of the three compartments under the seat was packed with gear similar to the backpacks Kate had taken from Thomas's home. A sign standing near the display listed the items included and boasted that the assortment of tools, gear and gadgets included everything one could need or want while camping. A second compartment was clearly for personal items: toiletries, clothing, and the like. The third compartment was filled by a prepackaged food pack. The display unit was a dummy, of course, but it focused Clay's attention to the couple at a nearby counter.

The clerk was informing the couple that their new sled came with an initial food pack of their choosing and suggested the "Continental" package because it offered the greatest variety of meals. The clerk told the couple that the only decision left then was color. There were several versions of the "Sport" paint scheme that included colored swirling pinstripes on a white base. The couple did not like any of them. There were also several 'Touring' schemes with contrasting colors on the top and bottom halves of the sled. The couple liked the Teal and Navy version, but settled on a third 'Camo' scheme. The husband seemed to like the desert tan version, but she liked the forest green. They chose the forest green.

The couple signed several papers before the clerk told them that prep would take about forty-five minutes. "Just show these papers and the receipt to the attendant at customer pick up located behind the store," the clerk said as he reached to shake the husband's hand. The couple walked out looking very excited as the clerk approached Kate and Clay. "Beautiful, isn't it?" the clerk asked, sounding as if he had just been trained at a local Chevy dealership.

"I'll make this easy," Clay answered confidently. "We would like the same as that other couple ordered. This one in forest camo with the continental food pack."

The clerk looked a bit stunned as Clay handed him his Iatros credit account card. The clerk hesitated in a way that let Clay know he was about to hear a line of BS. "Ah, very good Mr. Jeffries," the clerk recognized Clay. "The only thing is," the clerk continued, "is that as a first-time buyer I will need to set up licensing, registration and such for you. You will not be able to take delivery for a few days if that is OK."

Clay sighed. "Well, in that case we might as well take a day and think about it. Even so, I do love these camping clothes. I think we will just get a few things in the meantime then." Kate followed Clay's lead and they took about thirty minutes shopping for clothes, personal items kits and a couple of cool camping gadgets not included with the sled. The clerk was glad to see them go since it was coming up on closing time.

They exited and rounded the corner of the store just a few minutes before the couple that had purchased a sled. Clay had planned to stop them through some clever maneuver, but it proved unnecessary. As they caught sight of each other, the couple approached them. "Miss Young, Mr. Jeffries, it is an honor to meet you in person," the wife said as they both stuck out their hands.

"I didn't realize that we were famous," Kate exclaimed.

"Oh, you are," the husband corrected Kate. "We have heard a great deal about you on Iatros evening news. This must all be something for you to see."

"To be honest, it's all a bit confusing," Kate said as her bracelet seemed to break and fall to the man's feet. "Darn," Kate exclaimed as she begged the man's pardon and bent to pick it up. "Honey, I'm going to dash in a second and fix this. Would you wait here for me? Maybe this nice gentleman can give you some camping tips."

"You bet I can," The man interjected enthusiastically. He began sharing tips, from one car enthusiast to another, sounding very expert.

Kate was back in less than ten minutes, but not through the door she had gone in. She pulled up in a new camo green sled. "Honey, I saw the sled was ready and picked it up. Hop in," she motioned to Clay.

"We bought the same model," the man

exclaimed as he reached toward his back pocket to show Clay and Kate the papers. He looked confused as Clay and Kate abruptly flew off, and he searched for his papers.

***

It was surprisingly easy to board the elevator and make their way to the surface. The only other man on the elevator had made some small talk about camping and told them to have fun. With a top speed of nearly eighty miles per hour, the sled had taken them almost a hundred miles south before investigators at the store had pieced everything together and reported to Edward. Then, by the time Edward had issued orders and had a team in pursuit, Clay and Kate were nearly two hundred miles away from Borden Island. The thick winter snow had given way to some sparse vegetation, and Clay thought it a good time to stop and collect themselves.

They figured it would take about twelve hours to make Lynn Lake. That time would probably double if they stayed low, below any radar Edward might be using. Kate was also concerned there might be some kind of tracking system on the sled, but Clay reminded her that Iatros used a system that tracked the individual. The system sounded an alarm if an individual was in biological distress and could be keyed to locate a subject. There was, therefore, no need to track something like a sled.

Adrenalin had carried them this far, but it

had worn off and the long day of golf, drinks, sled hijacking and traveling left them exhausted. Nonetheless, stopping did not seem an option. Clay suggested they take shifts driving. Kate dozed off leaning against his back once already, so sleep while flying was possible. They agreed that Edward would surely have a team waiting for them in Lynn Lake. Even more likely, Clay suggested, Edward would assume they were racing to meet with Remington in San Francisco and would focus more of his resources to prevent them from reaching that goal. On that point Clay was correct. Edward had already mounted a massive search effort along the route from Borden Island to San Francisco.

Clay took the lead shift. The first two hours were ok, but for the past hours, he struggled against drowsiness that had actually become painful. Kate's head on his shoulder and her dead weight against his back did not help. Neither did the flat, featureless landscape nor the cozy warm bubble that surrounded the sled. Clay thought some cool air might help him stay awake and had looked for a control to turn down the heat, but hadn't found any. He tried to formulate plans beyond just retrieving Thomas's notebook, but his mind continually wandered to the immediate need for some comfort. A bed would be nice, but he would happily settle for just a moment to close his eyes, or a second to stretch out.

He decided he could take no more. He brought the sled into a soft landing and slowed to a stop. He opted to close his eyes for a moment before waking Kate. Her stirring and the dawning of the sun's brief appearance woke him nearly a half hour later. Kate lifted the panel on the rear left side of the sled's body and rummaged through the food compartment. Between the printed checklist of contents and the recipe-slash-instruction booklet, she managed to find a coffee packet. She unrolled the three inch packet and pulled the small string at the top as instructed and a small flap fell back to open the containers mouth. She was amazed at how fast the little plastic tube became hot and rigid. She began adding handfuls of snow to the now thermos shaped container; once it melted she added another handful until the thermos was full and she could replace the flap that adhered to form a nice lid; drinking hole and all.

Clay had discovered a stowed back rest (actually two thin poles connected by what seemed a piece of plastic) and had fitted it into the two mounting holes on the back of the sled. He had also discovered that the back rest could be adjusted to a near prone position. Kate offered him some of the coffee, but he declined, preferring to lie back on the sled and get some sleep.

"Well then," Kate said in an almost cheery voice that Clay wanted no part of, "looks like you are all set to go." Kate handed him a four-inch bundle of plastic. "That backrest comes with a blanket and pillow," she said as she hopped behind the controls of the sled. Clay did not struggle long with the blanket as he unfolded the small packet into a blanket-sized and plush-feeling sheet. It took him a few seconds to figure out the pillow, but once he had pulled the small string the tiny little bag blew up into what felt like a fine down pillow wrapped in a satin pillow case. He maneuvered into a comfortable position as he cautioned Kate to keep the driving shifts short. The four-hour stint he had just completed was too long.

"A few of two-hour stints each, and we'll be there," was the last thing Clay remembered saying before falling into a deep sleep.

The first two hours went by quickly. Kate had been thinking about Thomas the whole way. She wondered why she hadn't just dropped this whole thing, satisfied that Thomas had been duped into taking part. She did want to know more, but wasn't quite as driven as Clay had been. The quest for answers seemed to be the only thing keeping him going. She was along mostly because Clay was about the only thing keeping her going. Thomas would have liked Clay. He would have definitely loved this adventure. He would have been an asset too. He may have been duped into playing his part, but she was sure he figured it all out eventually. That is probably what got him killed. She liked Remington well enough, but Clay was right; Edward is the bad guy in all this, and he has been doing some fancy manipulating. She came to think of Edward as Thomas's real killer. Soon enough she and Clay would also know the whole story, and Thomas would have his justice. They only needed to get to Lynn Lake then to San Francisco with proof in hand.

Kate had been so deep in thought and really not very tired that she hadn't realized how long beyond the two hours she had been driving. Nor had she noticed the faint cluster of lights she was headed straight toward. The explosion certainly brought her back to the here and now with a start that caused her to swerve in no particular direction. Had he not been belted in, Clay would have been tossed into a free fall from the sled. He bolted awake with a 'what the hell!'

"I hadn't noticed it until now," Kate apologized, "but we are coming up on some little town or hamlet or work camp or something. Something exploded on the ground just outside that cluster of lights."

"You had better land," Clay ordered, "but avoid the town. There is no way we avoid giving an explanation if we show up in some small Nunavut village."

Kate glided to a landing several miles from the town. There were still very few trees, but some grass was poking through the snow. Clay was both thrilled and furious that Kate had been driving four hours. He felt guilty that he had slept so long, but he was delighted that they were now nearly half way to Lynn Lake.

It took him a second to realize that the town had to be either Baker Lake or one of the small hamlets along Hudson Bay. He hoped it was

Baker Lake, because, even if it was they were a little bit too far east. If they were along Hudson Bay at all, they were way too far east.

"The explosion was probably a planned blast at a mine," Clay assured Kate. He stretched as he climbed off the sled, then shuddered at the frigid cold. "I'm going to duck behind that little bit of tall grass for a second," he told Kate. "Why don't you see if we can find something to eat in that mess compartment?"

"OK," Kate said as he walked away, "but hurry; I need to take a turn too; badly!"

They both ate their beef with green peppers and rice sitting on the sled inside its bubble of warmth. "This food is far better than any Army MRE," Clay seemed impressed. "There doesn't happen to be any wine, is there?"

He had been kidding so was shocked when Kate produced a packet that read 'Pinot Noir'. "I just figured it would put us both asleep for about twelve hours," Kate said seriously.

"You're probably right," Clay agreed, "though I feel ready to go." With that they both buckled onto the sled, and Clay took hold of the handlebars. "By the way," When we get to Lynn Lake I don't want you doing anything on your own. You scared me once, Kate, and I am not going to let you get hurt again."

Kate did not respond. She thought for a second, then smiled. She pulled the plastic-looking, plush-feeling blanket over her as she laid back in the seat. It didn't matter how plush the blanket felt. The best silk sheets and the softest down comforter could not have made her feel any warmer, nor any safer than she felt with Clay. She wanted to enjoy the feeling a bit before falling asleep. But sleep overcame her quickly.

***

The landscape turned to thick forest a couple of hours before Kate spotted the early-morning lights of what she recognized as Lynn Lake. They had each taken a couple of turns at driving since they had stopped near the mine explosion. Kate did not sleep at all during Clay's last turn. Instead, they talked, mostly about their childhoods, past relationships, their careers, favorite books. She could feel their relationship strengthening and reached to her stomach where Clay's arms wrapped around her. She held his hand, promising herself never to let go.

Kate had only been at the wheel for about forty-five minutes when she brought the sled to a landing along a beach just out of sight of a large, clearly occupied cabin. Clay was alarmed. "What are you doing? We don't want to be spotted!" They hadn't worked out any kind of plan to get to the library, but they were sure Edward would have agents waiting for them anywhere they might show up, including Lynn Lake.

"I'm pretty sure this is Darcy's house," Kate said calmly. "She has a restaurant in Lynn Lake and was a close friend of Thomas's. I told you about her when we first met. We were out here a couple of times for dinner during some of my visits. Darcy and I got fairly close, so I think she will help us get the book."

"Good plan!" Clay was surprised. He had been thinking about a way to get past Edward's agents and into the library. The more a plan eluded him, the more worried he had become. He was relieved and surprised that Kate had it covered. They hid the sled in some nearby brush and headed for Darcy's house. The walk turned out to be a difficult hike as they stepped over, and sometimes on, rough rocks along the shore. They were forced to wade into the lake's edge a couple of times by thick, low hanging branches. Still, it felt good to be off the sled. They paused as they came to the edge of the clearing where Darcy's house sat, both looking at the back door. The thought of just walking up seemed oddly awkward. So uncomfortable that they both jumped back into the woods when Darcy came through the door, sat on one of the white Adirondack chairs, lit a cigarette, and opened the evening newspaper. Even from a distance Clay could make out the huge one-word headline: *Pandemic!*

◆CHAPTER 13◆

Darcy literally fell backwards in the chair with a start when Kate stood upright, stepped into the clearing and called Darcy's name.

Darcy stared at Kate for a good ten seconds before raising her hand to her mouth and exclaiming, "Kate?" She took another long pause. "My lord! What are you doing here?"

"We need your help, Darcy," Kate said softly. "Thomas's plane crash was not an accident. He had gotten involved with some bad people, and we are still trying to figure everything out." Kate preempted many of Darcy's questions by explaining that they did not yet know very much. That seemed to satisfy her as she scurried Clay and Kate into the house and sat them down at the kitchen table while she poured coffee.

Clay was amused as he took in the room while Kate and Darcy seemed to go off track into some discussion about her restaurant. The kitchen décor was consistent with the cabin's aged exterior, white painted wood siding and all. The floor and counters were speckled linoleum as was the table they sat at with its steel legs and edging. The matching chairs were upholstered in red vinyl. The appliances were all white and, Clay thought, a little newer, maybe the nineteen-fifties. They were fashioned with the rounded edges characteristic of the fifties, and the refrigerator was nearly half the height of the more modern versions – plenty of room for the porcelain clown-shaped cookie jar that sat atop it. Even the coffee pot Darcy was reaching for to pour refills seemed ancient; a percolator actually, with the little plastic bubble at the center of the lid. None of the décor amused Clay as much as the mismatched coffee mugs Darcy set in front of them. Each had some odd graphic and slogan. He had drawn the 'World's Best Mom' mug decorated with hearts. He was about to crack another smile when he realized that Kate and Darcy's conversation was anything but banal.

"Darcy!" Kate interrupted her, "What on earth are you talking about? Clay and I have been out of touch for the past week or so. Has something happened that we don't know about?"

"Good lord, Kate," Darcy looked stunned. "You don't know about the virus?"

"I'm afraid not," Clay interjected. "You'll

have to fill us in completely."

"Well," Darcy wasn't sure where to start. "It just started two days ago in Finland, they think. A virus hit so suddenly that it has mystified all the experts. Two days ago, thousands of people in Finland became very sick. They became paralyzed, even their diaphragm, and they suffocated within hours of the first symptoms. The initial wave hit during the night so most died in their sleep. By yesterday, it had spread to all of Scandinavia, Iceland and Greenland. They seem to think this is the big pandemic that everybody has speculated about for years. Last night they announced that the whole world is on lock down. Businesses are closed; traveling is suspended; everyone is just staying home watching the news."

Kate's hand instinctively covered her mouth in horror. Clay knew instantly that it was Edward's work. He was suddenly filled with determination, tempted to jump up and find a way to get to Remington.

"That is why I am home. The restaurant is closed. Fortunately, they think they have it contained. There have been no new cases today and everything is reopening tonight. Kate, almost eighty percent of the area's population has died! Something in the neighborhood of seventeen million people! Can you imagine what it must be like?"

"Darcy," Clay switched to something of a pleading voice, "This may seem petty in light of all that, but it's not. In fact, it might be somehow related." Clay wanted to avoid questions but had to drudge forward. "Thomas may have left something for Kate in a book at the library. We need you to check it out and bring it to us as soon as possible." Darcy just stared at Clay in silence. "I can't explain," he said apologetically.

Darcy turned to Kate and asked, "What book do you need?"

"*The Captains and the Kings* by Taylor Caldwell," Kate openly pleaded. "It's really important Darcy."

"OK. I'll pick it up on my way to the restaurant and bring it back when I get a break" Darcy gathered command. "You two stay here, make yourselves at home. I should be back within a few hours."

"Darcy," Clay added urgently, "We also have to find a way to get to San Francisco."

Darcy again just stared at him in silence for a moment. "I'll try to think of something before I get back. Just sit tight."

***

Before heading out, Darcy turned on the television so Clay and Kate could catch up. They remained glued to reports that struck Clay as completely inappropriate. Of course, the reporters were talking soberly of the millions that had died; they talked of the grief overwhelming the region; they talked of the massive implications of a population so reduced. Overall, however, the reporters focused more on how deftly the world was dealing with the crisis. They spoke proudly, almost boastfully, of how quickly and effectively world governments were reacting and successfully containing the pandemic. They spoke with certainty that scientists would soon find a vaccine. The entire coverage came off with something of a 'better them than us' and 'we're too good to have that happen to us' attitude. Clay and Kate were equally disgusted and alarmed.

***

The stranger in the diner was making Darcy very nervous. That nervousness had turned to near panic when the stranger left moments after her, and she caught sight of him in the car behind her as she left the parking lot. She was convinced he was following her and decided not to head directly to the library. She needed gas anyway, so decided to stop at the only gas station in Lynn Lake. "Actually, there was one other," Darcy imagined saying to no one in particular, "but it's technically about two miles outside of town. It's where I usually gas up. They're cheaper, far more modern and have a nice convenience store attached. The gas station in town is old and instead of a store, it has two bays where most Lynn Lake residents get their repair work done." Darcy's mind worked that way. The more nervous she got, the more her mind would wander on to non-sensible subjects.

The unscheduled stop for gas turned out to be a huge stroke of luck. Carl Stanford had just started filling his ridiculously oversized 1972 sage green Cadillac. "Carl, I was about to call you," Darcy exclaimed, omitting the normal pleasantries. "I desperately need your help."

Carl was Thomas's best friend in Lynn Lake. They were nearly always together, and people rarely mentioned one without mentioning the other. Carl was what one might consider one of Lynn Lake's leading citizens. He owned the hardware store, Lynn Lake Cabins and Lodge, and the small airport just outside of town with the only land-based runway for a hundred miles in any direction. Carl was a major investor in dozens of area businesses. Residents often called him the National Bank of Carl because he seemed to lend more money to local business people than the real bank did. He was also an avid conservation activist. That's how he and Thomas became so close. Carl even went to Ottawa twice to lobby for building restrictions on the surrounding lakes. He was also the only pilot in town that could get Clay and Kate to San Francisco.

Darcy thought all morning of how to approach Carl. Now she just charged forward. She told him Thomas's sister was at her house, that Thomas's plane crash might not have been an accident and that Kate was trying to figure it out. She had come back to Lynn Lake secretly to look for some notes she thought Thomas might have hidden and needed to retrieve them then get to San Francisco somehow. Darcy expected Carl to ask a million questions and to think her somewhat crazy. Instead, he just said he would help Kate anyway he could. He said he would get right to the airport and ready for the flight. He was so understanding and anxious to help his best friend's sister that Darcy had the last minute thought that, since she might be being followed, maybe Carl could stop at the library and get the book for Kate. "No problem," Carl had agreed, "I'll run and grab it now. I'll need some time to ready the plane and layout a flight plan. Go home, get Kate and her friend and meet me at the airport in three hours."

Darcy was relieved to see that no one seemed to be following her anymore, and that she had secured a flight to San Francisco. She was sure Clay and Kate would understand her delegating the book retrieval once she explained how close Carl and Thomas had been. She took a deep breath in the car and relaxed a bit for the drive home.

Carl headed straight to the library as he had promised. During the short drive over, he made one call on his cell phone, then checked out the book and headed to the airstrip. He jumped at every opportunity to go to San Francisco. 'Helping in the cause,' so to speak, was just a bonus.

***

Clay had been a bit uncomfortable with Darcy delegating the book retrieval, but he understood. In fact, he was sure Darcy was not being paranoid; she probably was being followed by one of Edward's men. There was nothing else to do but wait, so the three of them sat around the kitchen table while Clay and Kate tried to answer Darcy's questions as best they could, without sounding crazy.

Kate decided to oblige her questions with the whole story. She wanted to gauge her reaction to the incredible truth. Plus it freed Clay to think about how they were going to get past Edward and meet with Remington. The tough part was how to start. "Hundreds of thousands of years ago, all humans lived on Mars," Kate jumped into it, but knew right away it was going to sound unbelievable. It was also going to be difficult to convey such a long and complicated story in just the couple of hours they had.

She went on, nonetheless. "There was a huge cosmic event when a large planet named Ceres between Mars and Jupiter exploded and created the asteroid belt. Some pieces showered Earth, Mars and the moon. One fragment annihilated the dinosaurs on earth. That is how the moon became so pot-marked. The biggest piece hit Mars. It was so big that it changed Mars' orbit and made it uninhabitable. Humans on Mars at that point were as advanced as we are now. They fled like refugees but not as one group. Some fled to Earth; some prepared to live indefinitely in space; and some stayed on Mars and tried to create an artificial environment. It didn't work, and they came to Earth later."

Kate took a breath and tried to gauge

Darcy's reaction. So far, she was not laughing. "These humans on Mars," Kate continued, "had a slightly different physiology and psychology than what we know of as human. They had a life expectancy of roughly four hundred years; their women were only fertile about every forty years; and there were a few very subtle other biological differences. There were also some psychological and social differences that I don't really understand."

"So you're saying our ancestors are from Mars, and Earth has somehow changed our biology and psychology," Darcy guessed.

"Correct," Kate exclaimed. "But the people from the second group of refugees were not affected. They remained what is to them normal. They or their progeny have existed as something of a hidden sub-culture or pseudo-society all through history."

"If you two don't mind," Clay interrupted, "I'm going to step outside and do some thinking while Kate finishes."

"Sure," Kate sounded concerned and added, "are you all right?"

"Oh, absolutely," Clay assured her. "I just need to figure out how exactly we are going to get past Edward to talk to Remington once we get to San Francisco. It is not going to be that easy."

Kate was telling Darcy about Borden Island, about the controversy within Iatros society over giving the technology to Apoikians, and about the Movement as Clay headed out the back door. She went on to tell her about Thomas and Bethany getting involved, and she told them that they thought they knew who was behind the Movement and why they needed to get to San Francisco and report what they knew directly to Remington.

Clay paused to look across the lake, then began a stroll down toward the beach and gazed at the water. The lake, of course, was the same general area and had the same type of rocky shoreline as Bigstone Lake. It was surrounded by the same type of heavy woods and brush, but it was still overall very different. Bigstone Lake was secluded and undeveloped. Lynn Lake was surrounded by homes and a few occasional commercial establishments. The pandemic had quieted things down, but it normally buzzed with fly-in outfitters landing and taking off with their planeloads of tourists and sportsmen.

Still, it reminded Clay of the day he, Brooke, Bethany and Eric had boarded one of those planes to begin a relaxing week of fishing, swimming and hiking. The sadness, as it so often did, flooded back over him. Yet, the sadness was followed, as it was always followed by, a driving determination to understand. At first, it had been an angry determination, but it had slowly become more of a dutiful and urgent mission. Something he felt he owed to Bethany, Brooke and Eric, for sure. More and more it was something he felt he owed to something bigger. He couldn't quite put his finger on it. Perhaps he owed it to his own destiny, or perhaps to humanity.

A sharp gust of wind off the lake and the splashing of some wake waves just reaching the shore snapped Clay's thoughts back to Remington and how to reach him. He headed to the house, no closer to a plan than he had been.

Kate studied Clay as he entered the kitchen just ahead of the slamming screen door. She had finished, but Darcy was not showing much of a reaction. She sat silent staring into her coffee cup for nearly a minute then simply said with a determined voice that confirmed her understanding that it was time to get to the airport. As they headed out, Kate again asked Clay if he was all right.

"I'm fine," Clay assured her. "I'm just not sure how we are going to get to Remington once we get there."

"You'll come up with something," Kate said confidently as she held his arm.

***

There was no shortage of pilots in Lynn Lake, but nearly all the planes were equipped with pontoons instead of wheels and had limited range, and none of the pilots would have been as anxious to help Thomas. From what Darcy had told them, Kate was fairly confident that Carl Stanford was a good choice. She became certain of it when she first saw him standing by one of the few planes in town that could make the trip to San Francisco, an ancient DC-3 he had restored and sometimes used to haul freight into Lynn Lake. The classic tail dragger plane was actually show quality. Carl had taken it to a few air shows and had been to Oshkosh several times with the old bird.

Carl was a good-looking man, very woodsy and masculine. Trim, muscular, sharp features, and hair very much like Clay's; slightly graying at the temples and the day or two of growth on his face. He was tall, maybe a little too tall at almost seven feet, and he did not look like a pilot. He was wearing a well pressed black and grey striped dress shirt with black dress slacks. The only thing about him that struck Kate as pilot-like was the expensive looking and complicated watch slash chronograph slash compass slash tachygraph slash whatever else the thing could do, that he wore on his wrist. It amused Kate, as did his boyish and naïve almost goofy demeanor that seemed so incongruent with his appearance.

Clay and Kate followed Carl through the door near the tail. The interior of the DC-3 showed its age. Most of the passenger compartment had been gutted to accommodate freight. It had a bare floor close to the bottom of the fuselage with two parallel rails to support pallets. They all climbed a short ladder at the front to discover that the few feet closest to the cockpit had been left untouched. The floor was carpeted along the aisle with two rows of four gray seats, two on either side. There was no galley or lavatory, so the front row was placed fairly close behind the pilot and copilot seats. The plane's cockpit showed no signs of aesthetic consideration. The instrument panel was bare metal with thirty-five or forty gauges; more complex than the typical piper cub, but nothing like a modern jet either. The controls consisted of four oversized foot pedals, two for each seat; a center console that sprouted a bouquet of sticks and levers; and two steering wheels that looked like they came off a '55 Chevy except the arc at the top of the wheel was missing. The long flight would not be uncomfortable, but clearly, it would be a different experience than the private jet belonging to Remington that had taken them to San Francisco the last time. Instead of cocktails with steak or salmon dinners, Clay, Kate and Carl shared coffee from an old, green and silver, bullet-shaped thermos.

Carl waved Kate into the copilot's seat as he climbed into the pilot's position. Clay sat on the aisle immediately behind Carl. The arrangement should have made conversation easy, but the noise of the plane forced them to shout. Clay had tried to be polite asking questions about the plane as he feigned enthusiasm for the vintage aircraft. But he was anxious to dig into Thomas's notes that had been carefully placed, just as Kate knew they would be, in the worn copy of Taylor Caldwell's classic tale. Carl had even less interest in making polite conversation. He wanted to talk about Wilderness Fly-ins' and Thomas's other cabins. He had been trying to buy one for years, and once they were airborne he couldn't resist breaching the subject with Kate. He also, of course, wanted to talk about people dying en masse and what Clay and Kate knew about it.

"I have to tell you, Kate," Carl said as he determined to avoid a confrontation, "I was shocked when I heard that Thomas had sold Wilderness Fly-ins' two cabins on Bennett Lake. Thomas knew I had wanted to buy the A-frame out there for years. I was surprised that he didn't even give me a chance to bid on it."

Kate was caught more than a little off guard. "Thomas sold the properties on Bennett Lake," she said with shock. "I had no idea! When? To whom?"

"You didn't know?" Carl said in disbelief. "Thomas said it was an old family friend from New Haven. Some engineer he had known, so I assumed you knew him. Flarity or Flannery or something like that."

"Flaherty? Is that it?" Clay asked. His surprise was obvious when Carl confirmed the name.

"Are they on the way? Can we fly over and take a look?" Clay asked anxiously.

"Actually, they are about a hundred miles in the opposite direction," Carl discouraged the idea, and there is really nothing to see."

"I'm certain there will be plenty to see" Clay insisted.

Carl was not sure he should, but he complied with Clay's seemingly senseless wish and banked the plane into a full one hundred and eighty degree turn. "I don't see how those old cabins could have anything to do with all these people dying," Carl objected, even though he knew they just might.

Clay did not look up from Thomas's notes that he had been leafing through. Rather he turned the small journal and stretched out his arm so that Kate could read a particular page as he interjected. "I can answer that," he said somberly.

***

"Holy Mother of God!" Carl was genuinely shocked when the cabin on the north end of the lake first came into sight.

"It's a transmitter," Clay commented almost nonchalantly as if it was what he had been expecting. "It looks identical to the drawings in Thomas's notes. It is designed to transmit electricity, but there is a group of people that have been experimenting with the transmission of various isotopes." Clay recounted the little they had learned from Bethany's project management journal and added what they had just learned from Thomas's notes.

The transmitter was essentially a pyramid. It was metal of some sort as opposed to stone, but otherwise looked identical to the great pyramid at Giza. The only difference was a large pipe that rose out of the lake, straight up to a level slightly higher than the pyramid, then angled downward into the pyramid's side. A second pipe angled out of the pyramid's adjacent side and made a ninety-degree turn sloping back down to the lake. There were a half-dozen adjacent buildings, the largest about a third the size of the pyramid.

Carl banked to the right and turned toward the cabin on the south end of the lake, just four miles away.

This time, none of them were surprised to see an odd-looking obelisk nestled in the woods where the cabin once stood. It too matched Thomas's drawings, and reminded them of the demonstration they had seen at Borden Island. It was only about three stories high, topped with a small half sphere which made it look like a giant mushroom. A large round building formed its base. There was only one outbuilding, and it looked more like a shed than a building. As with the pyramid, there was no sign of activity. The installation appeared abandoned.

"It's the receiver. Actually, it works more like a cell tower. It receives the energy pulse then stores it and resends it out over a fairly short distance." Clay had barely spoken the words before two dark-blue jet skis came out of nowhere. They were a bit larger and seemed much bulkier than either of the jet skis Clay and Kate had used. They looked professional, and menacing. They took up positions just inches off the tip of each wing. Moments later, a third jet ski flew over them and took a position about twenty yards in front of them. They exerted no direct control, but Carl could not help but follow the lead of the jet ski in front of him. Their course was altered slightly so that they were heading west-northwest. They followed dutifully and expected to be forced to land near the installations below. They were surprised to find themselves following the jet ski's lead for nearly two and a half hours. Carl remained oddly calm and hailed the jet skis on the radio several times to exchange instructions. They spoke mostly in numbers and pilot jargon that Clay did not understand.

About halfway through the flight, after yet another calm radio exchange, it finally hit Clay. "Carl," Clay asked, "are you with the Royal Security Service?"

Carl gave a slight smirk, amused that it had taken Clay so long to figure it out, but there was no need for deception. "Yes, I'm almost finished with my mandatory service. When I was assigned to conservation duty in Lynn Lake twenty-two years ago, I expected it to be pretty boring and uneventful. Then your brother shows up," Carl glanced and Kate, "then your daughter, and the next thing I know I'm right at the epicenter of all the action. I've got to tell you, it has all been pretty exciting for me."

Clay thought for a second that Carl was going on like a fool until he finally got to his point. "Then I get a call, just three days ago, directly from the King. Imagine, I was speaking with the King! He says that if you two show up I am to call him immediately, and he gives me this special direct phone number. So I called him after I met

Darcy this morning, and he tells me to go ahead and get the book and give it to you and to take you to San Francisco. It sounded like he pretty much wanted me to do what you wanted. So, when you asked to fly over the cabins, I thought 'Ok, can't hurt.' Now I think that might have been a mistake 'cause, honest to God, I did not know anything about that installation. I was as surprised as you guys, and I think I might be getting into some trouble over it."

"You think that's what these jet skis are about?" Clay asked in disbelief.

"Oh no," Carl responded with a wave. "They said it is the standard procedure when flying into Kingsvalley."

"What is Kingsvalley?" Clay had to ask.

"You never heard of Kingsvalley?" Carl was dumbstruck. "It's the Royal Palace. I've been ordered to bring you there instead of San Francisco."

***

They finally began a descent toward a seemingly endless mountain range. Clay could not help but notice the large isolated lakes and asked Carl where they were.

"We're over the northwest corner of Tweedsmuir Provincial Park in British Columbia. That's the western end of Whitesail Lake to the north and Eutsuk Lake to the south," Carl sounded like a tour guide. "There are a couple of popular lodges in the area, and I have flown sportsman to the park before, but most of the attraction is to the north and east." The area they were over was a military reserve named Tweedsmuir Corridor Protected Area, not at all well known, but something like Area 51 in the United States. It was strictly off-limits to air or any other kind of traffic.

They turned south and flew what seemed like nearly a hundred miles before landing near Bella Coola. Clay could see a waiting fleet of the rickshaw-like vehicles they had toured around in on Borden Island. There was also a crowd of suited men awaiting their arrival. Clay assumed Edward would be among them, out front, ready to take Clay and Kate into custody once again. It was not Edward that greeted them at the bottom of the stairway, but Tom Benton. Kate actually felt glad to see him but Clay had moved him firmly back into the 'bad guy' column.

Clay only grunted when Benton held out his hand to greet him. Kate waited for the inevitable exchange of angry words. It never came. Instead, both Clay and Kate turned to look when they heard a familiar voice shout, "They'll ride with me." They were both frozen by astonishment to see Jason Randal calmly standing at the door of the lead rickshaw and waiving them inside.

◆CHAPTER 14◆

During the long ride, Jason explained his suicide attempt with little difficulty. "After Benton took you and Kate off the plane at Borden Island," he told Clay and Kate, "he left me alone with the two guards. They were planning to take me to San Francisco and put me on trial for treason. As with the Apoikian world, it is not always necessary to be guilty, it is often devastating enough just to be accused of something. The humiliation that my family would have suffered would have been too much to bear. It was a sloppy attempt, but I managed to get a gun from one of the guards. For a shot to be fatal to an Iatros, it must be precise to within a quarter of an inch in an exact spot on the side of the skull, otherwise revival is likely. I had to fire so quickly before being tackled by the guards, that my shot was just a hair off. They easily revived me, but as you might imagine, I was not the most compliant patient. After a day, I guess I made enough of a fuss that they flew me here, and the King exonerated me. He gave me significant insight into the Movement, and I have been working here ever since. The King arranged the whole San Francisco cell and suicide story as a cover up for his son's, excuse me, for Mr. Worthington's benefit."

"So it is *not* Edward leading the Movement," Kate said as she realized the implication.

"Yes and no," Jason's answer confounded them, "but that will be explained soon enough." He preempted any questions by pointing to the huge stone building they were now approaching. "For someone in the Royal Security Service, Jason boasted proudly, "duty at Kingsvalley is much like White House detail to someone in your Secret Service. You have no idea how fortunate you are to visit this place."

Clay had not noticed when it started, but they were now following a road paved in large gray smooth stones laid in a herringbone pattern. They had all fallen silent as they took in the scene. The road went perfectly straight and led to a huge stone archway about a mile ahead. As they came closer, Clay thought the gate reminded him of the Arc de Triomphe in Paris, but much larger. The images of soldiers that decorated the arch in Paris had been replaced by a collection of odd symbols and there was a single word, *Kingsvalley*, carved atop the arch. The road widened to the edge of the wide arch as they reached it then narrowed again as they passed through. The road inside the gate was tree-lined. Behind the trees for about fifty yards on either side were flowering gardens that gave way to wild sloping meadows, climbing to the mountains that formed the valley. A mile ahead, Clay could see a large round fountain, about a hundred feet in diameter. As they approached, Clay could tell that the outer wall of the fountain was made of granite, but his eyes were drawn to the much smaller inner circle capped with four statues, one of a woman, one of a man, and two of young boys, each looking to the sky. The statues were evenly spaced to form four arcs. One was formed from a large block of onyx. The second seemed to be made of ruby and the third of blue sapphire. The fourth was white. In the very center was a larger statue of a man pointing to the sky.

The paved road split and circled the fountain. Being the back seat driver that she was, Kate flinched when they circled to the left, going in a counter-intuitive, counter-clockwise direction. As they circled the fountain, they had an unobstructed view of the front of the palace. It was something of a cross between the Palace of Versailles and the Taj Mahal. There were turrets at either end and there was a dome. The front was ornate with what seemed to be hundreds of windows; each one framed in granite ornamentation. The entire building was built out of large brownish-orange stone blocks. Nearly halfway around the fountain they again veered left onto a side road that led them around the end of the building. They stopped in a small parking lot or courtyard, Kate could not tell which it was, in front of a side entrance that was grand enough to be the front of any other government building.

Jason led Clay and Kate through the large double doors followed closely by Tom Benton and the huge entourage that had met them at the airport. Inside there was a spacious reception area with a guard seated at a bank of electronics and monitors. The floor was marble, and the large group raised quite a racket as they filed in. Jason merely waived a badge at the guard and continued to a door on his right. Most of the group seemed to disburse except for Tom Benton and four other men who followed Clay and Kate through a passage and down the hallway. At the end of the hall, Jason entered a small office and took a seat behind the desk. There was little other decoration or furniture so Clay and Kate stood across the desk facing Jason.

After shuffling through some papers, Jason took one particular sheet in hand and read aloud. "Clayton Jeffries, Katherine Young, you are under arrest for the theft of a levcar and for disregarding a Royal 'stay-in-place' order. I have been ordered to hold you in custody until such time as an arraignment hearing is held. A hearing to that effect has been scheduled before His Majesty King

Francis Remington VIII exercising his preemptive powers. You have the right to an attorney either privately retained or selected from the State pool. Which do you choose?"

Clay and Kate both stared blankly at Jason, who waited a second before setting down the paper he had been reading from. "Look," he finally said, "these charges are just a legal formality and a political necessity. Nothing will come of them. Just pick a lawyer from the pool. The King can call for privacy during the hearing, and I suspect he will explain everything then. In the meantime, he does not want to treat you as prisoners, but neither can he treat you as guests; not politically anyway. I'm sorry we don't have more comfortable cells for you to wait in, but I assume you will only be here for a couple of days. Be patient and you will soon understand."

Tom Benton softly touched Kate's elbow and guided her to the door. He and the four other men led Clay and Kate down a hallway to a short flight of stairs where a guard sat at high tech desk/console. At the bottom of the stairs, he unlocked a door on each side of the hall then motioned Clay through one and Kate through the other. They could hear Tom lock the doors from the outside and climb back up the stairs.

***

The room was clearly a cell though not at all uncomfortable. The floor was painted concrete, light blue, and the walls were smooth stone also painted blue, just a little darker shade. There was a daybed doubling as a couch that Clay found uncomfortable. He sat instead, in the over-stuffed chair that faced, to his surprise, a television that had been set into a bookcase loaded with DVDs, magazines and a game console. The controls of the television included a small clock that showed the time and date in green LED numbers. There were no windows, and the door was solid.

As he sat, Clay sensed a subtle vibration in the room, like the air conditioner had just kicked on. Within minutes, the heel of his left hand began to tingle, though he barely noticed until his right hand and both feet began to feel the same pins and needles. He didn't think much of it until he tried to reach for the TV remote and found his arms paralyzed. He was asleep within seconds, drool running from the corner of his mouth and eyes wide open.

***

Consciousness returned quickly. Clay was suddenly awake and alert. He was no longer in the chair he had been sitting in. Instead, he was in a bed. It was the same dull cell, but equipment had been wheeled in and there was an IV line stuck in his arm. His focus went immediately to the clock on the television. If the date was correct, he had been sleeping for nine days.

The television was on, and it drew Clay's attention almost immediately. It was tuned to his favorite news channel. He remembered how he used to leave the TV in his office at the university turned on to this channel. It seemed like a lifetime ago. He was familiar enough with their format to know something was going on. It was not the typical talking head stuff with seemingly unrelated pictures occasionally inset on the screen with a stock ticker running across the bottom. Clay's focus was immediately drawn to the large red and yellow logo in the upper-right corner of the screen that simply read 'Pandemic'. He read the ticker at the bottom: '...pandemic currently striking South America...worldwide death toll now tops four billion...' Clay turned his attention to the host. It was that good looking guy from Louisiana. Clay couldn't remember his name, just that he shared Clay's passion for college football. The host was in mid-sentence, "...but what do we actually know? What are the facts, Doctor?"

Clay had missed the introduction, but clearly, the guest was a doctor involved in investigating the pandemic. "We know the disease is infecting a huge percentage of the population where it strikes: something between eighty-five and ninety percent get the disease. It is most often fatal, killing about eighty percent of its victims. We know it is moving in a pattern, spiraling across the globe from west to east and from north to south. It struck first in the Nordic states, then Russia, Canada, Europe, China, Japan, the United States, Northern Africa, the Middle East, Southern Asia, and is now in Central America and the northern portion of South America. It's like someone is peeling an apple." The guest went on with his litany of facts, "We know there is some kind of genetic factor. There has not been one single case reported of parents dying and their children surviving. There have been extremely few cases of children dying and a parent surviving."

The host interrupted as he often did. "There is also a lot of talk about there being some economic factor." The guest seemed to want to respond, but the host just charged forward. "Is there any basis to the claim we're hearing, that only wealthy people are surviving?"

"There does seem to be some basis for the claim," the guest conceded, "but we suspect it has more to do with lifestyle than with some secret immunization that is raising everyone's ire and causing the riots."

The host shifted the focus, clearly not wanting to talk about the violence. "What about the aftermath?" There was some drama in his voice. "How are survivors dealing with the mass of, and I hate to be crude, but with the mass of corpses this God-awful thing is leaving behind?"

"Well, as we all know now, this disease is not contagious so there has been little hesitation among survivors to pitch in and gather the deceased and bury them in mass graves."

"How can you say it is not contagious when it is killing so many?" the host sounded genuinely confused.

"The disease is being caused, we are certain, by some type of," the guest was grasping for the right word, "radiation or atmospheric disturbance."

"Is it coming from space? Many are claiming that we are under attack from some type of alien force. Could that be at all possible?" The host sounded doubtful.

"Actually, the way the disease is moving, spiraling across the globe, would suggest more of some type of airborne pathogen of some kind." The guest apologized but begged off saying that it was an area beyond his expertise. The host thanked him for being there and turned to the topic of an economic connection. He introduced a reporter who was in a small village in Northern Africa.

"Jessica, what's going on there seems typical of communities, large and small, all over the world." The host positioned his question. "It's a small village of about six hundred people; most of the men work in the diamond mines; they have one school and one doctor. So, give us a picture of what you are seeing there."

"That was a good description two days ago, Chip. However, today it is basically a cemetery." The reporter, who had been speaking to the host, now began speaking to the audience. "The pandemic hit during the night two days ago. The village was unusually quiet for seven o'clock in the morning." Several men began going house to house to investigate. They found what they had already feared: whole families that had died in their sleep; nearly half of the villages six hundred residents. By mid-afternoon that day all but seventeen residents had died. Households were undisturbed. Breakfast was still on the table in many homes. Candles in the local Catholic mission church still burned in preparation for morning Mass. The attached school still in perfect order with children's drawings pinned to the wall." The reporter's voice uncharacteristically broke for just a moment as the screen showed pictures of the school, the empty streets and finally what seemed to be a construction site. "Local leaders surviving the devastation, including the mayor, the Doctor and the missionary priest, have organized the remaining seventeen residents. They borrowed some equipment from the mine and dug a mass grave. There was what you might call some orderly looting as the remaining seventeen gathered valuables and keepsakes from the households of the dead. They are packing and plan to hold a small ceremony tonight as they have decided to burn the entire village and make their way to the nearest large city, Kananga.

**

Kate awoke to the same broadcast, and it brought her to tears. The horror of all those people dying, especially when they showed the young children in Africa, was almost too much. The only consolation for her was a small sense of relief that their short life of grinding poverty was over. She hoped and truly believed that they had passed on to a better existence. She was crying, but was too mesmerized by the scene even to wipe her eyes. The pictures on the television blurred as she fell back asleep.

It was only minutes before she startled at the sound of keys rattling in the door. She was still disoriented. She didn't know where she was, what time it was, or whether the horrible scenes on television had been a dream or real. She remembered the tingling. The memory of the dream about her father and Rupplemeyers still saddened her, though the depressed mood left her quickly when she saw Clay standing at the door with a group of four other men. Her head still took a few seconds to clear when one of the men told her it was time for their audience. They removed the IV stuck in her arm and told her to shower and dress quickly. When they returned fifteen minutes later, she stood and walked to Clay, took his hand and squeezed it tightly as she began to follow the men down the hall and back up the stairs.

At the top, one of the men leading was handed a note by the guard at the desk. He read it then half turned his head and spoke to Clay and Kate. "Mr. Remington has arrived for the weekend and has invited you to join him for dinner. I would guess that is a pretty good indication of how this hearing is going to go." His voice was full of contempt and sarcasm.

Clay took the opportunity to ask why they had been asleep for nine days. "When the pandemic swept across Canada nine days ago," the man explained, "your cure was apparently not complete enough to spare you. You gave everyone quite a scare, especially Dr. Rothlensberger. He had not anticipated the development and is still searching for an explanation." Clay's confidence in Dr. Rothlensberger was a bit shaken, but he apparently had more immediate problems to worry about.

***

Whitcolm Remington's father, His Highness Francis VIII, King of the Iatros people, Successor to the Leader of the Refugees, and Servant to All, was even a bit shorter than his son. He did have the same crazed-looking eyes, but his face was not as round, and it showed a few more years. He was not as trim as his son, though not out of shape by any means. He wore a deep-blue suit with a button down white shirt. His cufflinks were grossly oversized and matched the large medal hung on a ribbon where his tie should have been. There was also a narrow purple sash that went from shoulder to shoulder and hung just a quarter of the way down his back.

They had obviously been in a heated discussion when Clay and Kate entered the chamber with their escorts. "Father," Remington was almost whispering as he pleaded with the king, "have you ever wondered why I care so much for the mentally handicapped? It's because they keep me focused on what I think life is really about. Any Apoikian and any Iatros would agree that the mentally handicapped are ill. I work with them every day. I see some advantages to their illness. They are often carefree, unburdened by the demands of everyday life, and they are guileless. It is a trait that comforts nearly everyone they touch. Most importantly, they seem happy even if for what you and I consider a brief moment. They feel joy, and that is what it is all about. We can't reach into their minds and know what that is; what life means to them. And we can't reach into the Apoikian mind and know how they perceive life. Father, what you are doing is wrong. You must stop this!"

"It is too late for that. Besides, it is my burden to carry, and I will carry it as I am suited," the King barked back. "We shall talk of it again, but for now, that is the end of it." The King motioned with his head toward Clay and Kate's party and abruptly turned to climb the three steps onto what looked like a stage. The floor was marble and there were large banners hung on either side. The only other decoration was a single chair, ornate as it was, with small wings attached to either side that served as tables. It was obviously a throne. Remington bowed slightly as he turned and walked to a simple podium facing the platform on the left. Two of the men who had been accompanying Clay and Kate joined him. Two others followed Tom Benton to a matching podium on the right.

Kate looked around the room. It mirrored

the throne room they had seen in San Francisco, though on a much smaller scale. There was the same communion-type rail running across the front of the room, similar-looking pens on either side of the room with standing height tables, and the identical ribbon of carpet with its concentric circles. Kate was turning to look at the back of the room when she saw Jason Randal enter and march up the center aisle. He bowed deeply before the King.

"Your Highness," the man standing with Remington and who appeared to be the prosecutor began to speak in a very formal tone, "You are gracious to receive Mr. Clayton Jeffries and Miss Katherine Young. They have been convicted of vehicle theft and disobeying a Royal Mandate, and they now seek your grace and pardon."

Clay almost wanted to object since he knew nothing of having been convicted. He thought better of it since it was clear that Jason would be speaking on their behalf and because this whole foreign drama was hard for him to take seriously. He glanced at Kate instead, and could see she was finding it just as difficult. She seemed on the verge of a giggle.

Jason took over the podium. His voice was low, and he spoke in a less formal tone. "Your Highness, you know of Mr. Jeffries' and Miss Young's involvement with the Movement and that Chairman Remington had encouraged them to bring any information they obtained to his attention. While at Borden Island, Mr. Jeffries became aware of information that he presumed to be urgent, and that he believed could only be safely shared with Chairman Remington. Mr. Jeffries believed he had discovered information that incriminated Chairman Remington's temporary chargés d'affaires, Edward Boularde, as a key figure, if not the leader of the Movement. They further believed that the stay-in-place order was not issued by Your Majesty, but was fraudulently issued by Edward Boularde to prevent them from reaching Chairman Remington. Neither of them knew, nor could have known, that Edward Boularde was acting throughout this affair on your behalf and on your instructions." The lawyer's voice changed to a more pleading tone. "Your Highness, while Mr. Jeffries and Miss Young may have been mistaken and misguided, they were sincere and acted in good faith in what they believed were the best interests of the government and the Crown. It is on this basis that we beg your pardon."

The King turned and studied Clay and Kate. "Your Highness," Jason repeated, "It should be noted that no one, especially Mr. Jeffries, nor Miss Young, knew that Edward Boularde had been your own Chief of Staff and spoke on the authority of the Crown. Nor did they know that he served as Chairman Remington's chargés d'affaires *temporarily*, through your extraordinary kindness in lending his services while that vacancy was being filled. Had they known that he spoke on the authority of the Crown, they would have certainly obeyed the stay-in-place order."

"I am, indeed, familiar with the quandary Mr. Jeffries and Miss Young found themselves in, and the confusion that I may have created," the king spoke first sympathetically, then authoritatively. "Assuming the prosecutor has no objection, I am inclined to grant pardon, but wish first to invoke my Royal prerogative of privacy."

If the prosecutor did have an objection, it was clear he had better not raise it. Instead, the moment the king mentioned privacy, everyone simply began to file out of the chamber without a word. Clay and Kate started to follow Jason, but he motioned at them to stay.

***

Once the room was clear, the king stood and walked to a door on the side of the chamber. He opened and paused at the door, clearly suggesting that Clay and Kate should follow him. The room inside was not an office as Clay had assumed. It was a sitting room, beautifully decorated in Queen Anne style. There were two cherry cabinets, one on each side wall, with long curving legs and a glass center door with a brass wire woven into the glass. One was set with ornate crystal decanters containing liquor and matching crystal glassware. The other held several porcelain figurines set on a lace doily. There was artwork covering nearly every inch of the wall and an intricate burgundy, gold and blue woven rug that covered most of the cherry hardwood floor. The king sat regally in a classic Queen Anne chair with legs that matched the legs of the side tables and red leather upholstery tufted with brass buttons. He clenched the ends of the rounded armrests and told Clay and Kate to have a seat. They sat on a blue wool upholstered sofa that had an intricate pattern stitched into it with gold thread and a burgundy border. It too was of cherry wood on the legs and end of the armrests.

The king did not offer drinks or anything. He simply stared at Clay and Kate for several seconds, as if not knowing where to start. "Monarch is a lowly position in life," he finally began. "A king's decisions are dictated by the welfare, the preferences, even the whims of his subjects as they express them, or as he perceives them. Yet, even though he is not truly free to make decisions, to make choices as he would prefer, he alone is held responsible and accountable before God for those decisions."

Clay felt uneasy as if he were a small boy about to be lectured to by a disapproving father. He uncrossed his legs and placed a hand on the couch's cushion at his side, unconsciously assuming an attentive and compliant posture. He noticed that his palms were sweating, so he moved his hand onto his knee so as not to touch the expensive fabric of the couch. He was genuinely nervous and glanced at Kate. She looked terrified.

"There are, of course, those rare decisions that neither the people's voice, nor morality and ethics, nor a well-developed intellect, offer any guidance. They are those 'fight or flight' decisions that come only from the gut. Those types of decisions are almost always of monumental importance, and they are a heavy, heavy burden. It is bearing the burden of those decisions that is the essence of a monarch's place in society. It is when executing those decisions that the king best exercises his role as the leader. It is always preferable to rally the people behind such decisions, but it is not always possible." The lecture began to sound more like one delivered by a stuffy professor than one delivered by a castigating parent. Clay felt a little more at ease.

"The affairs with which you have recently become entangled are the result of just such a decision." The king finally paused. Clay and Kate both leaned forward the slightest bit. They sensed that the importance of what the king was about to tell them was immense. It was an unexpected admission that he *was* the Movement; that all along Edward had been acting at the King's direction. The pause became uncomfortably long, but no particular comment or question came to Clay's mind. He began to lift his hand from his knee, though not intending any kind gesture, when the king finally began to speak again.

"Mr. Jeffries, Miss Young," again the king paused and seemed unsure of what to say next. "For millennia the Iatros people have viewed

Apoikians as our brothers and have labored to understand and find a cure for the terrifying disease that affects you, so horribly, both physically and mentally."

"We do not feel afflicted," Clay interrupted defensively.

"No?" the king asked. "What of the millions in every corner of the globe that suffer from grinding poverty? You don't think they feel afflicted? There are children starving in your society Mr. Jeffries! What of the tens of millions caught in the ravages of childish and meaningless wars? You don't think they feel afflicted? What of the tens of millions whose bodies have failed them long before their time, who you call your elderly, who are abandoned and left lonely and in despair? You don't think they feel afflicted Mr. Jeffries? What of those who you would assume have every advantage but instead turn every meaningful relationship into a battle of animosity or get trapped by drugs or alcohol? You don't think they feel afflicted? And what of crime; one human being doing violence to another? You don't think the victims of those unimaginable acts feel afflicted? For that matter, what of the criminals locked in a small barren cell or even killed because society says they are not worthy to participate? Do you imagine they are living the life they would have chosen, Mr. Jeffries? What of the physical ravages: the Black Death, influenza, polio, cancer, Alzheimer's disease? Do you not realize that these are all merely symptoms of a far greater disease and do you not think that their hundreds of millions of victims feel afflicted?"

The king had built into nearly a rage and now sat silent for a moment as Clay and Kate absorbed the awful truth of what he had been saying. Clay weakly countered by reminding the king that there were also many joys in life. The king agreed but denied that there was any necessary connection between the joys Clay described and the afflictions he had described. "There are easily enough resources on this magnificent planet for everyone to possess every possible luxury they could desire, let alone meet their basic needs," the king argued passionately. "There is no need for financially motivated crime; envy and avarice should be obsolete. Imagine such a world!"

"I do not accept the notion that avarice could ever be obsolete," Kate interrupted. "Take, for instance, a piece of artwork? There can be only one original and men will always compete to possess it."

"That is a great example, Miss Young," the king became very animated. "The joy in art to the Iatros mind is experiencing it. One of the tremendous beauties of art is that it can be experienced by all. Anyone can view a great painting or sculpture. It is one of the distinguishing symptoms of the Apoikian disease that a man feels some irrational desire to possess, rather than experience with others, a piece of artwork."

"History is full of fools who thought just the way you do," Clay scoffed, "who promised to create the perfect world, and it always involved the mass murder of one group or another. You are no different," he added with disdain.

"Most of those men were indeed mad and bent, not on improving society, but dominating it. The other distinguishing characteristic of Apoikian disease," the king added, "is an equally irrational impulse to dominate others. No such impulse exists in Iatros psychology."

"Ah," Clay scoffed again, "this coming from a man who surrounds himself with people bowing and scraping to him every minute of the day! Come on…"

"They do not bow and scrape to me, Mr. Jeffries. Observe…" The king took off the medallion that hung around his neck and set it on a table next to the door. He then pushed a small button on the table. A moment later, a man entered that looked like a servant but didn't quite act like one. He simply asked in less than a formal tone if he could get anything for them. When the king asked for a pitcher of water, the man said 'sure', turned, bowed to the medallion sitting on the table, and left.

"We are people strongly affected by symbols, Mr. Jeffries. They bow to the office, not to me," the king concluded the demonstration.

"Then why not let nature take its course," Clay genuinely wanted an answer. He wanted to understand. "What is it in your psychology that makes you do this?"

"Despair, Mr. Jeffries." The king lowered his head, his words almost a sigh. "I have helplessly watched the suffering of your people for centuries and seen it, in this past century, reach an unimaginable level of horror. Twice the entire world at war; families, villages, whole cities gassed or bombed en masse"

"Consider this analogy, Mr. Jeffries," the king spoke confidently. "You are a doctor and you have a ward full of terminally ill children, say, for example, thirty children. They are in great pain, and their death is certain. You also have a drug that will completely cure one or two of them; which ones you do not know. However, you do know that if you administer the drug, it will instantly kill the many children who are not cured by it. Would you administer the drug Mr. Jeffries? Would you Miss Young?"

Kate answered without hesitation or equivocation, "No! Death is God's choice. Besides, how can you know that a cure is not just around the corner?"

Clay's answer was less certain. "It would depend on how long the children have to live. If we are talking about a few years or even a few months, then no, I would not administer the drug. If we are talking hours or even a day or two, then yes, I probably would."

The king sat pensively for a moment before commenting. "Your answer, Mr. Jeffries, is typical. What you are really saying is that your action would be determined by the measure of hope you could muster. You are equating the time and hope. You, Miss Young, are full of hope; it does not fail you until the very last. You could not imagine how much I admire and envy you for it."

"The analogy could not be more accurate," the king suddenly sounded like a professor finally getting to the point in a long and difficult lecture. "Unlike you, I am in a position like no one else. I know there is no hope. Beyond death, there will be no end to Apoikian suffering, and there will be no cure beyond what Dr. Rothlensberger has discovered. Many of your Apoikian theologies treat despair as a special kind of sin. I do not understand how one can call it a sin, but I do know firsthand that it is a special kind of affliction. I doubt if you could ever understand how difficult it has been to bear the burden of the decision fate forced on me without hope for a happy outcome."

The silence between the three of them was broken by the unexpected presence of a fourth. "I am probably the only person truly in a position to understand that," Whitcolm spoke up from the doorway he had been quietly standing in for nearly a minute. "I do not fully understand your despair Father, I guess I am a bit like Miss Young in that regard, but I do understand how difficult and heavy the burden of your decision must have been." Whitcolm Remington crossed the room and stood before his father like a small boy might. "I also understand that one of your motives was to spare me the burden of the decision when my time comes. You must know how deeply I appreciate that kindness."

The king did not respond. He simply reached out and held his hand for a moment before looking around Whitcolm at Clay and Kate. Whatever your thoughts or rage might be at the moment, they are moot. The process is complete. I have euthanized our Apoikian brothers and sisters." The king turned to Whitcolm and added as if he needed to know, "About six and half billion Apoikians have passed. Only three hundred million survive as recovered Iatros."

◆CHAPTER 15◆

The king excused himself rather abruptly. Whitcolm Remington apologized on his behalf and explained that the King would be addressing the Iatros people in just over an hour. He would talk about the deadly virus that had decimated the Apoikian population, and he would lay the moral groundwork for adjusting to a world without Apoikians. He would also discuss the very practical challenges that lie ahead, and begin to lay-out a plan for meeting them.

"It will by far be the most difficult speech of his reign. He will be addressing several of us here shortly afterwards," Remington informed them and added, "but I wanted a chance to talk to you two first."

"I have often felt bad about implying that

your brother, and your daughter, had been duped into cooperating with the Movement. You will see in a moment that they were not. As you now know, it was I that was beguiled." Remington appeared more than remorseful. Kate thought he seemed deeply saddened.

Remington massaged the back of his neck and sighed as he called and whispered to the servant. A large machine was wheeled into the room. It resembled the pedestals Clay and Kate had seen in San Francisco in the Hall of Iatros History. "You have seen our holographic projections," Remington said as the servant pushed the coffee table aside and parked the machine in front of Clay and Kate.

"There is a significant amount of footage that I am sure you will want to review at your leisure," Remington explained. "There are a couple of items that I suspect you two need to see now." He turned on the machine and selected 'Jeffries/Young – Lynn Lake – 9/3' from a long list of items. Both Clay and Kate were instantly mesmerized by the images of Bethany and Thomas as they came to life before them.

Remington fiddled with the machine while he spoke. "I placed security teams with Bethany and Thomas and ordered surveillance on both of them shortly after they had been cured. Unfortunately, the tapes were skillfully edited before reaching me. I have only just recently discovered the ruse and recovered the unedited versions. There are several scenes that I think you should see."

Clay recognized the location. Bethany and Thomas sat by a large rock on the beach just a hundred yards or so from where they had all stayed the night before Thomas flew them to Bigstone Lake. Clay remembered it from when he had taken a walk that evening with Brooke. The image reminded him of the night in Bar Harbor when they had worn those special night-vision glasses; the picture was bright and clear, yet you could somehow tell it was dark. The lake in the background was black, and you could hear the crickets chirping.

Bethany spoke first. "Staying behind is not going to be as easy as you think. I still think it would be a good idea for you guys to keep in touch with me by cell."

"It's too traceable," Thomas reminded her. "We need a backup left behind. If something goes wrong, you can still try to get to Remington and alert him to Edward's plan. Tucking you away at Bigstone Lake is going to be perfect. You'll be close in case we need you and no one is going to know to come looking for you there. Besides, I know that you are going to enjoy a week with your dad and sister."

"I already am," Clay thought Bethany looked genuinely happy as she spoke. "We all went to dinner tonight at that little diner in town and, really Thomas, I don't think my dad has been that relaxed for years. That's why I feel so guilty. I'm going to be having the time of my life while you guys are all going on what is practically a suicide mission."

Clay's throat began to tickle the way it always does when he fights back tears. Kate seemed in her own world, not even bothering to wipe the tears that were streaming down her cheeks. He took the tissue that Remington offered and passed it on to Kate.

"I would hardly call it a suicide mission," Thomas minimized the dangers. "The worst thing that could happen is that Edward gets on to us and locks us away somewhere so we can't get to Remington."

"And you're not suspicious of the delay?" Bethany asked Thomas to assure her once again as he had that afternoon when Allen, Steve, Jill and Karen had called about them being delayed in the office in San Francisco. "And you can adjust the plan?" she added.

"I'll fly you guys to Bigstone, then come back here and get them. I'll take Jill and Steve to the installation at Bennett Lake. They will need about six hours to get all the data and reports we need. It will give me just enough time to fly Karen and Allen to Borden Island. Karen will keep the plane ready while I go to our apartments and get our journals and laptops. The only one in any real danger will be Allen. He has to go the thirty miles to the plant, get the battery that contains the isotope, and get back to the airport. Then all I have to do is pick up Jill and Steve, and we're off to San Francisco." Thomas stood and brushed the sand from the seat of the loose-fitting khakis he was wearing. As he did, he took a light-hearted tone. "Relax Bethany. I'm more worried about how I am going to introduce Karen to my sister, than I am about this little adventure. It was probably pretty stupid of me to fall in love in the middle of all this, uh?"

"You never get to pick the time. Besides, are you calling me stupid for falling in love with Allen? I'm thinking there was more in that cure than what Dr. Rothlensberger told us about. Do you think the Iatros have come up with some kind of high-tech love potion or something?" Bethany was laughing, and it forced Clay and Kate to both laugh through their tears.

Remington paused the machine and returned to the index. "They were happy. I thought you should see that." Clay and Kate had warmed to Remington long ago, but only now did they realize how kind and sweet a man he was. They found it hard to believe that they first saw him as an enemy. They were comforted by the fact that Thomas and Bethany apparently had also come to see him as a trusted friend.

"I received word of a Borden Island breach the day after those surveillance tapes were made. Our security agents reported that a small battery had been taken and that Bethany's and Thomas's apartments had been broken into. Security had tracked the intruder's plane to Bennett Lake where it had landed for a few minutes and then taken off again. It was heading due west and was just south of Bigstone Lake when I ordered it shot down." Remington paused, waiting for some reaction from Clay and Kate, but they only sat silent. "You have to understand that I was fairly sure that the passengers on that plane were Iatros members of the Movement. What else could I have concluded? Shooting a plane down would not be fatal, the passengers, assuming they were Iatros, could be easily revived. I was horrified when security reported that the passengers were the members of your party, Mr. Jeffries. The rest you know."

Remington turned back to the machine and selected 'Young - Borden Island - 9/3' from the index. "Where the hell..." An image of a frantic Thomas appeared. He was throwing pillows and cushions from the couch in the very octagonal suite Clay and Kate had stayed in on Borden Island. He moved to the bedroom as the camera followed.

"How does it do that?" Clay asked Remington. "Move with the action, I mean."

"Our surveillance cameras are like... well, you've heard the old saying, 'a fly on the wall': well," Remington explained, "that is exactly what our cameras are. They are drone flies programmed to stay with an assigned subject. They're tiny little machines that do amazing things."

Thomas was rifling the bedding off when an alarm on his wrist sounded. He moved his hand to turn it off and glance at the watch. "Damn," he muttered and ran out the front door. The camera followed him along an uneventful journey back to the plane. A man in a grey Eisenhower jacket over a black shirt and dress slacks was waiting for him at the top of the stairs in the plane's doorway. "Allen," Thomas shouted, "I didn't get anything. Our papers and laptops were not in the apartments."

"Never mind now, we can transmit what data we have to Bethany," Allen shouted back. "We have to go. I set off an alarm!" Karen pushed forward on the throttle as Allen closed the hatch. They heard the clank of bullets hitting the fuselage as they taxied away. It all looked like a very predictable scene from some action-packed spy movie.

The scene did not seem to have much meaning for Clay nor Kate. The only reaction was Kate's comment that apparently Karen was a pilot too. "She and Thomas spent hours, even days after their cure in the air," Remington explained. "I assume he taught her, though I can't imagine what they did the rest of the time up there. I don't think the old de Havilland had an autopilot."

Kate held up a hand to Remington, "Too much information! I don't want to think about it." The tapes were somehow lifting their spirits. Nonetheless, Remington reminded them of their serious nature and returned to the index. This time he selected a heading that read 'Jeffries - recovery warehouse - 9/12' but paused before pushing the play button.

"I first learned of the existence of this tape just two days ago," Remington sounded apologetic. "I have not yet seen them, and I don't know if the implication will be immediately clear to you. I have labored over just how to break this news to you. One would think it would be easy, but it is proving very, very difficult. Watch the tape, then take a moment before you react."

Remington pushed the play button as Clay and Kate leaned in expectantly. It was another night scene. The camera was focused on the body bag laid before it, but at the top of the screen, the image clearly showed through an open tent flap, Edward climbing from a pontoon plane tied to a fallen tree. A man came into the picture, the man Clay had shot at this same place months ago.

The man read the papers and took a pen from Edward to sign them. "This is no problem, let's get to it." They both went on the plane and emerged a moment later carrying a body bag. They moved, walking sideways as each held an end of the bag, toward the camera. They set the bag down and immediately picked up the bag that Clay knew to hold Bethany's body. This time the camera followed the men as they made their way back to the plane where the two more body bags came into view. They set Bethany down and picked up another. The picture was still for some time until they reemerged carrying a body bag back onto the plane. They repeated the process one more time. The man finally waived at Edward and left the plane, closing the hatch after him. The camera showed Edward in the background climbing into the pilot's seat and manipulating controls.

Remington turned off the machine, and they all sat in silence for nearly a minute. "I don't understand," Clay finally muttered. "What were they...where...I don't understand." He paused again for just a moment, then spoke firmly. "Where is Bethany's body? Why did Edward take it?" He stood in front of Remington and demanded answers.

"Bethany, Brooke and Eric were brought here, to the infirmary at Kingsvalley," Remington spoke softly. "The bodies you saw in the recovery tent were clever fakes made of polyurethane, glass and plastic. They were made to fool me, not you."

Clay sat back down, looking even more confused. It was Kate that seemed to put it together. She stared at Remington and finally asked. "You said that reviving an Iatros from a plane crash would be easy. You said Thomas and Bethany had been cured. That means that they were Iatros." She stared at Remington even harder. "Were Thomas and Bethany revived? Are they alive?

Remington looked at the floor. "I understand that they have been a bit of a handful. They have not accepted my father's plan nor given him credit for anything other than madness. We were also able to revive Brooke and Eric. They, on the other hand, seem almost sympathetic to his little adventure."

Clay had jumped to his feet and ran to the door. "Where are they? For God's sake, take us to them now!"

***

Clay had been breathing hard. He realized how quickly it had dried his lips and throat to a cracking kind of pain. He soothed them by licking his lips and swallowing the saliva that had formed in his mouth. He had only taken a few steps into the hallway when he also realized that Kate was not following. He stopped and asked Remington why.

"As I just explained, Mr. Young will be brought here shortly. I thought these should be private moments for each of you. There will be time for introductions later." Remington seemed annoyed to have to repeat himself and even more annoyed when Clay started past him. "Mr. Jeffries, I'll need to show you the way."

Clay remembered Remington talking to them for a moment before they left the study, but he hadn't heard a word. Somehow he knew where they were going. They all walked at a fast pace down a long corridor then made a left into a hallway that Clay recognized. Remington had been talking all the way, but again, Clay had not heard a word. As they turned down that hallway that led to the stairs descending to the cells where he and Kate had been held, where he had watched the horrifying news reports, Remington took hold of his elbow.

"Mr. Jeffries," he shouted, "you need to listen to me."

Clay stopped; exasperated. He halted his march begrudgingly and gave Remington his tentative and temporary attention.

"They do not know you are here. They do not know you thought they had died. They think you were arrested shortly after they were taken into custody. They think you gained your freedom because you became sympathetic to my father's plans. Brooke and Eric will quickly forgive you, but Bethany, as I said before, and as I understand it, has been a handful."

"You son-of-a-bitch!" Clay pushed Remington hard in the chest with both hands. Remington fell backwards. "Screw the Iatros!" he added as he stepped over Remington, kicking his forearm half by accident and half on purpose.

The security aide at the desk atop the stairway started after Clay, stopping at the sight of Remington's outstretched hand. Remington simply nodded his head indicating it was OK. He morphed his hand from a palm-facing stop sign to an outstretched plea for help in getting up. The guard was bewildered, but obliged.

Clay saw the glass window halfway down the hall and headed straight for it as if he knew. He stopped at the window, obviously a one-way mirror because there was no reaction from Eric or Brooke standing on the other side, their backs to him. They were clearly speaking to someone on the far side of the room. Clay could not see who because Eric and Brooke were blocking his view, but he knew who. Then the tears began to well.

As Eric walked away, toward whoever they were talking to, Brooke turned to set a glass on a table just in front of what was, from her side of the window, a chrome framed mirror. The image of Brooke that Clay carried in his mind was, of course, idealized. In Brooke's case, Clay's mind-view and the very real view in front of him were like the two images of a stereoscope. They slowly came together and they matched almost perfectly. She was beautiful by anyone's standards. Full dark auburn hair that hung straight to her shoulders; a narrow face with sharp features in near perfect proportion; tall and thin, maybe a little thinner than Clay usually pictured her (she thought herself too skinny); and a confident, erect posture that could both inspire respect and intimidate at the same time.

Eric had taken a seat on the simple couch that hugged the far wall. He was talking fast, though Clay could not hear what he was saying. Clay sensed that he was trying to be persuasive. Once Brooke had turned and taken a seat in one of the two wing chairs facing the couch, Clay could see that Bethany was not being persuaded.

That stereoscope effect showed a bit more discrepancy between the real Bethany and the image of Bethany that Clay carried with him. It was the same cute round face with expressive round eyes and the same full eyebrows. But she had lost weight. She was now almost as skinny as Brooke. She seemed to have aged or, more accurately, matured. Her face and her posture suggested a very serious-minded person rather than the light-hearted person Clay so cherished.

He noticed how the shorts she was wearing still gapped at the small of her back. She had stood up just as Brooke had sat down, further evidence that they were not in agreement on some point or another. Remington shook Clay from his thoughts when he placed a hand on his shoulder and guided him to the door. Clay noticeably skipped a breath or two as Remington turned the handle and stepped through the door. Clay stood, arms to his side and head slightly bent, still on the hallway side of the door.

There was a moment of stunned silence before Brooke shouted 'Dad' and Eric shouted 'Clay' in chorus. Brooke ran and hugged him tightly; Eric followed with an outstretched hand but pulled him close when Clay reached for it, hugging him just as tightly. Once released from Eric's grasp, he turned back to Brooke, placed the palm of his hand on her cheek, then hugged her again. As if on cue, they all turned at once toward Bethany, once again sitting on the couch, her hands covering her mouth, tears forming.

She stood slowly at first, but rushed to meet her father halfway. Her arms circled him, pinning his own arms to his side, but he managed to free them enough to return the embrace. She laid the side of her head in his chest and cried.

***

Clay started to tell Bethany of the past months. She stopped him. "Mr. Remington has told us the entire story. I knew you could not be part of this! Dad," Bethany sounded apologetic, "I don't think we can stop them. They are going to kill billions of people, and I don't think we can stop them."

Clay reached down and took Bethany's hand as he glanced at Brooke and Eric. "No Bethany... Brooke... we cannot stop them. It is already done. Six billion people have died from what they are claiming was a worldwide pandemic." Clay glanced again at Brooke and Eric and could tell from their focus on Bethany that they already knew. Bethany let go her grasp on Clay's hand and pulled back a step, staring at Clay in disbelief. She stared at him for a good thirty seconds before Clay began to explain more.

She cut him off before he could get a word out. "I'm engaged. I met Allen during my orientation at Borden Island, and we are getting married."

Clay wanted to be happy for her, but he didn't know what to say about Allen or about the genocide that Bethany was clearly having trouble processing. Instead, he just reached for her. He held her just as her knees buckled, and she fell in his arms.

Clay guided her to a chair and started to kneel in front of her. She waived him off and seemed to recover. He retreated to the other chair while Brooke and Eric sat back down on the couch. They sat in silence that was finally broken when Bethany whispered "God grant me the serenity to accept the things I cannot change; courage to change the things I can; and wisdom to know the difference." They bowed their heads and silently repeated the eternal prayer.

It seemed the prayer was immediately answered when Clay asked Bethany to tell him about Allen. Her face instantly softened in a way that told Clay she really loved him. She told them of her last two years with Allen, mingling in stories of how she had been cured, how she had gotten involved with the Movement, and her months of being 'a guest' at Kingsvalley. She talked a lot about Thomas Young and asked about Kate. Clay talked about Kate endlessly and concurred with Bethany that the Iatros must have included some kind of love potion in the cure. They were all laughing when Remington entered.

They stood and walked to the door being held by Remington as he announced, "The King requests your presence."

***

They dutifully followed Remington back up the stairs where they were joined by Kate and Thomas. Clay and Kate hugged tightly before Kate introduced her brother to Clay and Clay introduced Brooke, Bethany and Eric to Kate. They all quietly resumed their nearly half-mile walk following Remington. The transition from an office setting to what was more clearly a palace had come suddenly when they passed through a set of large glass double doors and entered a wide, plush carpeted hallway lined with framed objects hung on the wall. The baseboard, chair rail and crown molding was a heavy and ornately carved dark wood. There was an occasional statue and several decorative chairs that drew their attention, but did not interrupt their march behind Remington.

"Mr. Remington," Clay asked as if it was an afterthought, "why us? Why did the cure work on all of us?"

"Dr. Rothlensberger is certain that it is a matter of genetics," Remington answered. "All of the survivors are at least one-quarter Iatros. Your father, Clay, is Iatros."

Clay tried to absorb that revelation as they finally passed through an open set of wooden double doors into a room similarly appointed but full of a dozen or so people. The gathering had the aura of a wake. Everyone was standing. Small groups were talking quietly. If it weren't for the absence of refreshments and music, one might think it was a party. Bethany immediately spotted and walked toward a man who looked every bit a marine: barrel chest, square jaw, close cut hair. He had been standing with a couple clinging to each other and a rather plain looking woman with remarkably bright eyes.

Clay and the others followed Bethany and

as the groups joined up she introduced the marine type. "Dad, this is Allen Kopeski, my fiancé."

"Sir, I'm sorry I did not get the opportunity to ask your permission."

Clay ignored the permission part. He would reserve judgment for now. "None of that 'sir' stuff, Allen. We're going to be family."

"Along those same lines...," Thomas interjected as he put his arm around the women with the bright eyes, "Kate, everyone, this is Karen Howell, my fiancée."

Kate hugged her and Thomas in turn.

"Oh, I'm sorry," Bethany told Clay and Kate. "This is Steve Heire and his sister Jill. We all got to know each other pretty well during our recovery at Borden Island."

Clay shook their hands and at the same time noticed that he had met almost everyone else in the room. Jason was there as was Tom Benton and the rest of Jason's security team. Dr. Rothlensberger was there with Brian Flaherty, who they had met at Borden Island. Remington came in just before Edward entered the room from a side door and spoke loudly as the rest of the room fell silent: "Ladies and Gentlemen, His Highness Francis VIII, King of the Iatros people."

The King entered the room as nearly everyone turned toward him and bowed slightly. He took only a few steps into the room before he began to deliver what sounded like prepared remarks:

My friends, today is a day of both

mourning and rejoicing; a day singular in importance and at the same time like any other day. For today, I have, as I strive to every day, fulfilled the most somber and sacred duty as your servant. Though I have met my duty through the grace of God and with clarity and confidence, my heart remains conflicted.

It is among my many fears that the same conflict might plague and injure our society through the very process of judging. It is for that reason that I beg your eternal silence on these matters. In this room is everyone who knows the full truth surrounding recent events. That knowing will surely require of you a judgment. I humbly submit to your verdict.

I offer in my own defense, and I beg you to remember in your private judgments, that my duty demanded the full measure of courage and wisdom with which God has gifted me. While you must know that measure to be sufficient for the challenges required of me, I can only offer my assurance that I have brought all of those talents, however humble, to bear on my decisions.

Along with my sacred oath, I give you that assurance, and several others:

First, no matter how great or small, I assure you that your participation in affecting my decisions was beyond your control. I beg that I alone face the judgments of God, of history, and of all men. You must know you are blameless, for guilt or innocence resides only in the heart of the accused.

Secondly, I assure you that those millions of souls who today have recovered from a long and frightful illness will be welcomed into our society and invited to participate fully as the brothers and sisters they are. The fullness of their worth was proven to us by their very creation.

I assure you and all of my subjects that life, in all of its goodness, goes on. The wonder and bounty of God's creation, and it seems our enjoyment of it, is endless.

Finally, I offer not an assurance, but a prayer. I pray that the billions of souls who have today passed from this life are finally free from the burdens that so afflicted them. I pray they are met with the fullness of God's goodness. And, should I have erred, I pray their forgiveness as I pray for God's mercy.

◆CHAPTER 16◆

Clay sat back and remembered the late King's words, what he thought of as 'the real speech'. The television was running file footage of what he thought of as the fake speech; King Francis VIII addressing the Iatros people that night ten years ago. The coverage on this tenth anniversary of what had simply come to be referred to as 'The Storm' was wall to wall.

The speech he was watching had a few moments of eloquence. The King began by likening The Storm to what Christians called the Rapture and ended with a moving prayer. Other than that, it was all business. He shared the gruesome statistics: world population reduced from seven billion to just under seven hundred million. Six and a half billion souls perished. The

Storm had some additional affects on the natural world, though none as dramatic. A half-dozen species of plant life became instantly extinct. The population among domesticated animals was barely affected. Species of wild animals felt the effects to wildly varying degrees. Reptiles took it the worst; sea life was virtually untouched.

The King talked about causes. There were no certain answers, but most scientists agreed that some type of inter-stellar storm had showered the earth with a deadly isotope. They were certain that it was the same type of rare phenomenon that had originally afflicted Apoikians thousands of years ago. It was then that the king delivered the real shocker. The phenomenon had cured those few Apoikians that had survived. 'How' would become the most prominent scientific question for centuries to come.

The bulk of the address called all Iatros to assist with the two monumental tasks that lay before them: orienting and assimilating the recovered Apoikians into Iatros society and the 'clean-up' that would involve no less than rebuilding the entire surface of the earth.

***

Clay thought back on that first seven years of cleanup and turned the channel to a show called "Transforming the Landscape." It was another tenth anniversary special that focused on the cleanup after The Storm. It brought back fond memories for Clay for several reasons. After 'the mass wedding' as the family liked to call it, Clay and Kate, Bethany and Allen, and Thomas and Karen had all gone on an Alaskan cruise for their honeymoons. Brooke and Eric tagged along just for fun. They were still celebrities, not because of their roles in flushing out the Movement, they never spoke of that, but because they were among the first recovered Apoikians. They enjoyed it while it lasted, but the celebrity status faded quickly and, to their thinking, just in time since Kate was by then pregnant with little Jason.

While they were on the cruise, the Iatros Congress had passed RAMSA (the Recovered Apoikian Mandatory Service Act). The law required all recovered Apoikians to attend intensive, nine-month orientation programs that were put on in each of the thousand or so communities that people had been drawn to. Then they had to enroll in LTO (long term orientation) for three years. The Iatros education programs felt very much like going back to high school. The real meat of RAMSA was that it drafted all recovered Apoikians into mandatory service. The House of Families had been contentiously divided over the length of service that the law would require and whether the law would mandate a set number of years or service up to a set age. In the end, they settled on service of thirty years or until age eighty-five, which meant Clay was almost half through his twenty-year tour. The rest of the family would be in for the full thirty years.

A lot of people saw mandatory service as something of a jail sentence, but not Clay. He liked it. Of course, being an officer didn't hurt and Colonel Jeffries had it even a little better than your average full bird since his celebrity had not completely dissipated. It was the duty he had drawn though, more than the rank, that endeared Clay to service. He had been assigned to urban recovery where he led a brigade of six hundred men and women. The process was incredible. Clay would assign an area, usually eight to fifteen square miles depending on whether it was residential or commercial. An artifacts team of six would enter a building or home and collect items they thought worth preserving: photos, artwork, and occasionally some personal papers. They would bag it, and it would be sent to an artifacts center for further judgment and cataloging. The team had only ten minutes to scour a typical four-bedroom house.

Once the artifacts team had finished they would move on to the next house. A demolition team of four would follow them. The demolition team operated a massive machine that was only ten feet wide but nearly three hundred feet long. At the front, it had a fifty-foot diameter disk on the end of an arm that could be rotated two hundred eighty degrees and lowered or raised by seventy feet. The driver would position the disk over the house or building. Once positioned, the disk would be activated, and the structure would fly apart and be sucked into the disk like a log going into a chipper. Computers would instantly analyze and sort materials from the structure, and they would either emerge at the other end bundled in a plastic-like material or be ground up and shot back into the hole where the building had stood. The bound material was stacked onto huge levitation barges that would eventually take the materials to a raw materials center for recycling. The entire operation would take ten minutes.

The demolition team was followed by a landscape team of five that drove machines similar to large commercial lawnmowers. One machine was specifically designed to remove fences, lamp posts, mail boxes and the like while another ground concrete and blacktop into a fine sand that added to the fill material. A third machine would mow down and mulch any large growth like bushes, hedgerows, and gardens, before a fourth machine tilled, raked and spread a seed mixture over the lot. The seed mixture was different every day depending on the geography and the planned use of the land. For the most part, trees were left untouched. When one or two did have to be removed from a lot, the team would have difficulty keeping up with the crews ahead of them.

Clay loved the feeling he got at the end of the day when he could look back at what was just eight hours earlier an abandoned sprawling suburban neighborhood, a rundown inner-city section or commercial park and see what looked like a forest. The trees might not be as dense and the ground would be covered in beige and brown and black seeds, but it was a satisfying sight. He especially liked to look back on areas that had been recovered four or six or eight weeks earlier and see an almost natural landscape where a city once stood.

***

Eric and Brooke arrived for the planned family barbecue just as the program ended. Clay was telling them about the program when Eric mentioned Bloomington and how he wished he could see it again. Early in Clay's mandatory service, Bloomington showed up as one of his assignments. It was to be completely eradicated and turned back to nature. He more than declined the leave he had been offered and actually accompanied the artifacts team that he had assigned to his former home and his university office.

Since people no longer needed to change their appearance every eighty or so years, photographs again took on their rightful meaning. Clay had grabbed everyone he could find. He loathed his own baby pictures, but took them as well since he thought his father might like to have them.

The Iatros emphasis on keepsakes also came naturally to Clay. He carefully folded the banana costume Brooke had worn in her kindergarten play and placed it in the box under his arm. On top of the costume, he laid out the furry blue Grover puppet with the big red nose that Bethany had called her best friend, and that Clay and Kara had feared she would never grow out of. He wished she hadn't. The jersey that Bobby Knight had given him signed by every member of the 1987 championship team softened his mood a little as he put it in the box. He slipped one item into his pocket instead of the box. It was the first gift he had ever given Kara, a cheap steel necklace shaped like a heart and engraved with 'Always and Forever.' His mood shifted back to a haunting peacefulness as he renewed the pledge.

Strangely, he found it even more difficult going through his office. Clay loved his work. He loved the writing. He loved the research. And he especially loved the teaching. As he packed away the framed copies of The Declaration of Independence, The Gettysburg Address, Roosevelt's 'day of infamy' speech, and JFK's inaugural address, he wondered how the social sciences might see this new world.

Economics certainly changed. There was still the rich and the not so rich, you really couldn't call them poor anymore, but the spread was really pretty narrow. The rich could afford season tickets to pro-football games; the not so rich might be able to afford two or three games each year. The rich would likely take a luxurious vacation a couple of times a year; the not so rich would take one, at best, every two years.

Social status was still important, but was

defined very differently. In the old world, status was given by how well an individual performed the task at hand. A great teacher would be given higher status than a mediocre principal. However, in the new world, status was conferred by progression through a profession. Some teachers were still better than others and given greater status, but the worst principal was given greater status than the best teacher. The progression through one's chosen career was, of course, inalienably tied to age. You couldn't be a principal unless you had been a teacher. Whether this was good or bad, Clay thought, would make for a good research project and book someday.

The nature of social relationships in this new world was much the same as it had been in the old world. People no longer identified themselves by nationality because there were no nations. Things like patriotism, nationalism, and international politics were a thing of the past. Good riddance, Clay thought. Instead, social relationships were defined by family. There were still only about two thousand families, but each extended family now averaged about four hundred thousand members. Even more than belonging to a particular family, people identified with the city that they lived near. There were about a thousand cities around the world, all with a population less than one million. Government was centralized, but culture and social norms varied widely from city to city.

One of the keepsakes Clay carefully packed

in his box to save was a copy of a book one of his grad students had published. The student had written an inscription to Clay noting how the book was directly inspired by one of his classes. The book was about crime in America, and the class had been *Bloodletters and Badmen* based on an earlier book by Jay Nash. Clay was struck by how irrelevant the book had become since The Storm. There was still plenty of crime, but only crimes of passion. Financially motivated crimes simply did not occur anymore. Clay chuckled to himself as he thought how it made for honest-to-gosh sincere politicians. That fact alone put a real dent in his social sciences field. How much of history would be erased if there had been sincere politicians around? None of the wars Clay could think of.

***

Clay was so lost in his thoughts of that last day that he had spent in the former Bloomington that he didn't even hear Eric ask if he should change the channel to the game.

"Clay," Eric asked again, "is it OK?"

"I suppose," Clay had finally snapped his mind back. "Even though you know we are in for a real spanking."

It's a long shot, I know," Eric just couldn't bring himself to give up that last shred of hope.

"It's not a long shot," Clay had retorted. "It's an absolute no shot. Our boys are just hoping they get through this alive."

Rugby was still pretty new to North

America, and the Chicago Ramblers were only in the playoffs because of the geographic format. They were given no chance against the well-seasoned Brisbane Broncos. It turned out to be one of the league's most historic games. People would still be talking about that upset in a thousand years. Eric had yelled and cheered so hard that he had literally lost his voice.

Thomas was as delighted with Eric's silence as he was with the Chicago win. He had arrived with Bethany and Peter, Clay's five-year-old grandson, just as the game had started. Brooke and Kate had nearly ignored the game, choosing instead to keep Peter and little Jason occupied. Clay never stopped being amused at the sight of his seven-year-old son playing with his five-year-old grandson. They all headed out to the patio after the game, and Clay went straight to his hammock, not because he was tired, but because Jason and Peter liked to make a game of jumping on him and swinging wildly.

**

It had all made for a nice holiday weekend. Eric and Thomas did the grilling while Kate, Brooke and Bethany seemed to find an infinite number of subjects to chat about. They talked, as people often did these days, about how much the world had changed. It was only natural. Even after ten years everyone seemed to confront, almost every day, new things, new ways of doing things, or new situations.

It started with Brooke. The ladies had all gone shopping earlier in the week and Brooke again shared how amazed she was by the experience. No lines, no parking problems, and especially no crowds. There were still enough people at the mall to keep it from being creepy, but there were no salespeople. Actually, there were still a few that sold higher ticket items like levcars or appliances. In most stores though, there was just a manager. Scanning was on a whole new level. If you decided to make a purchase, you simply scanned the item with your personal device, which would process the transaction and put the store's delivery system into action. The item, unless you overrode with special instructions, would be waiting for you, nicely packaged, at a kiosk by the mall's door where you had come in.

"And still you can never find your size," Bethany chided her.

"No kidding! I swear, there is someone at the door that yells when they see me coming: 'Quick, hide all the petite talls. Brooke Louth is coming'." Brooke just shook her head.

"I sure don't miss the traffic," Bethany added. "I can remember times when I would spend half my day parked on the New Jersey Turnpike. Now it's just hop in the levcar and go. I love it"

Outside of the cities, there were no longer any roads or highways. Levcars flew above the trees with little if any input from the driver. Since the country is where most people lived and homes were so spread out, you would be lucky to see even a few dozen other levcars on a trip from Chicago to New York. In the cities, streets were replaced by decoratively paved walkways and greenways. Levcars followed those paths, but in the air, which meant no traffic lights. Traffic was still sparse anyway.

"But there are still billboards," Eric interjected. There were still billboards. And there were still directional signs and even some graffiti. Not physical signs, of course, but signs that were broadcast by small chips embedded in the walkway and displayed on the levcar's navigation screen.

Since Eric had joined the undeclared game of sharing favorite changes to the world, Thomas also chimed in. "That stuff is all piddly," he scolded. The big change has been the environment. No air pollution, no water pollution, no shrinking ozone, no global warming. Though you know what really excites me?" Thomas was launching into one of his famous lectures. "No outdoor lights. I never thought much about light pollution, but the sky is amazing now that everyone just wears night glasses. For thirty-five years of my old life, I had never seen a natural night sky. Now I can't go to bed at night without first going outside without my night glasses and gazing up for a minute at the sky blanketed in stars. It's incredible!"

Clay was reminded of that night in Bar

Harbor when he had first worn night glasses. Now everyone wore them whenever they went out at night.

"Actually," Kate added her view of the most notable change, "I think it is the people. Do you notice how everyone is like a neighbor in a small town? There's no crowding and rudeness. Of course, not everyone is your best friend, and some people are nicer than others. Everyone is civil though; outright polite. People aren't always trying to get the better of each other. I think that's been the biggest change."

Everyone agreed then laughed when Clay added, "Unless it's a rugby match."

***

Clay started for his hammock just as the sun was setting after the long summer day. This time it was to relax, not to bounce the boys around. He was content. It had been a nice day, until...

After the boys were asleep; after all the idle chatter had died down. In a moment of peaceful silence, Kate told everyone she had some news.

"I spoke with Dr. Rothlensberger last night," she had said somberly then took a long pause. She again thought she probably should have told Clay first, but the news was going to impact Thomas and Bethany perhaps more than anyone since they were among the first recovered Apoikians. She decided to tell everyone at once.

"I'm pregnant," she finally said.

There was stunned silence. The enormity of the news was just too large for any of them to get their arms around. Clay finally spoke: "Has the King been told?"

◆EPILOGUE◆

Takis Remington maneuvered the cigar-shaped capsule with tiny bursts until it aligned perfectly with the entrance to the wormhole known as UAS4. The journey from New Mars to the entrance, a distance of about thirty-eight astronomical units or six billion kilometers, took nearly a year. Just to accelerate to full speed had taken over a month. Once aligned, Takis retracted the cone-like sail that extended beyond the capsule. His crew of two men and two women braced in their seats as Takis began a countdown: "Insertion in five...four...three...two...one... He slammed the fore-thruster forward as the capsule began a high-pitched vibration. He and the crew blacked out almost instantly.

They traveled across the nearly seven

thousand astronomical unit length of the wormhole in about fourteen seconds. When Takis awoke he immediately deployed the sail. It was a cone-shaped piece of plastic pushed along by the billions of particles of cosmic dust entering the cone. While most of the energy held by the dust was used to propel the capsule forward, a small amount was converted to electricity to power the capsule's life-sustaining systems. He again used tiny bursts to aim the capsule directly toward the sun of the solar system that the worm hole emptied them into. He reached for the telescopic viewer as his crew awakened and focused it on the fourth planet from the sun; the dead-looking red planet just thirty astronomical units away; the planet his ancestors had fled thousands of years ago; the planet he presented to his crew simply but dramatically as 'home'.

The crew stared in reverent silence as they thought of the history coming to life before their very eyes. Their ancestors bravely traveled this same path on a journey to find New Mars. The journey had been difficult as they drifted among the outer reaches of this solar system. They fearfully navigated through those same thousands of pieces of the exploded planet Ceres. They had faced a near revolt as many of them entertained second thoughts about fleeing to the blue planet that Takis now beheld. The water they carried unexpectedly decayed with each recycling. Without it, they would not have been able to sustain the artificial environment they had so carefully planned, and that had otherwise operated perfectly. They had thought themselves doomed until their crude ship happened upon the wormhole purely by chance.

***

Real time, two-way communication with New Mars was not possible once they had passed through the wormhole. As an alternative, they would launch a communication drone back through the wormhole each month. When through, the drone would transmit its recorded data to New Mars. The system kept mission control appraised of their progress, but didn't allow mission control to respond until the capsule became stationary. Even then, responses would take fourteen months to reach Takis.

Twelve years earlier, mission control had launched a similar drone that had remained stationary at the exit from the wormhole. This drone collected data from the solar system with an emphasis on Mars and Earth. It measured the atmospheric and geological conditions of each planet, surveyed life forms, and recorded seismic and meteorological events. Takis ordered the download of the data. Once complete, Takis would add his first Captain's log entry, then launch the drone back through the wormhole to transmit to New Mars. His entry was simple: "Disporia I arrived destination solar system; proceeding to Mars."

Their mission was twofold. They were first

to land on Mars where their species had originated so many thousands of years ago. They were to determine if any humans, descendants of those that had chosen to stay, survived. If so, they were to establish contact and initiate relations with them. The mission to Earth was the same. Some of their ancestors had fled to Earth after the atmosphere on Mars had been destroyed, and they were to confirm or refute the theory that their descendants had survived. If they had, Takis was also charged with establishing contact and initiating relations.

With the momentum they had gained from the wormhole, the trip to Mars would take only three months. It would be barely enough time to analyze the data collected by the drone. Up to now Takis had been more a passenger than a captain. Now, with daily reports on the ongoing data analysis, navigating through the asteroid belt, landing on Mars, launching from Mars, landing on Earth, launching from Earth, navigating back through the asteroid belt, and returning to the wormhole, his life was about to become hectic. Just this first day of real captaining had been eighteen straight hours. He debriefed the crew to ensure everyone had fared well through the wormhole transition then ordered lights out. It was important that he maintain a daily structure and routine.

***

Lights out on the small capsule was the

highlight of the day. It was not that any of them was lazy or thought their daily duties unpleasant. It wasn't even thought of as rest for bodies that were actually more active than they would be on New Mars. It was not at all seen as a moment of escape. It was the highlight of the day because it was a moment of serenity unlike anything any of them had ever experienced.

The capsule's bunks were lined up against its inner hull, each with a full-length portal that could be opened or closed, made transparent or opaque, at the touch of a button. Except for Takis, the crew all liked to close their portals and sleep in absolute darkness. Takis could appreciate the mind-liberating experience, but he preferred to keep his portal open. It wasn't just the incredible dome of stars that so irresistibly drew his gaze and inspired grand thoughts. It wasn't even the imagined slight sensation of motion, like gentle swinging, that tricked his muscles into relaxing. What Takis really liked about gazing into space during that moment before sleep was the contrast between the cold, dark deadliness of infinite space and the warm, cozy comfort of his tiny bunk. It was the same feeling he had gotten once when he was a young boy, and his father would take him on fly-in fishing trips. He vividly remembered one stormy night on one of those trips. The storm was ferocious and they were in the middle of a great and foreboding wilderness, huddled in a flimsy tent, and still he felt profoundly safe and comfortable and content.

The feeling was always followed within what seemed an instant by revelry blaring from the speaker at his head. At once, artificial gravity would be briefly suspended and lights that simulated daylight would turn on. Takis would pull off his sleeping gown and reach for the odd-looking funnel at the end of a hose. He would relieve himself before pushing the switch that activated the bunk's vacuum system. Within a nano-second his body would be vacuumed clean of dead skin cells, dried salts and any dust he had picked up. He would then hurry to pull on his jumpsuit and comb back his hair before artificial gravity was restored. He would pop the fizz pill with its fluoride, cleaning bubbles, whitening agent and breath freshener as he climbed from his bunk. The entire routine was so quick and rehearsed that all the crew members would emerge together.

After a Waltons-like exchange of 'good mornings,' Takis would lead a formal briefing on the day's plans over tea and breakfast. The first part of the briefing rarely changed. As First Mate, Beton would update the crew on current velocity, distance from Mars orbit, and the status of ship systems. He barely fell under the astronaut program's height maximum. Any taller and life on the capsule with him would have been impossible. Even now as he stood to deliver his brief, he had to hunch forward a bit to keep from bumping his head.

Navigator Laria would report on any solar

flares, asteroid activity, and, since there was no communications officer, she would include progress of the communications capsules being sent back to New Mars. She actually entertained the thought, albeit for only a brief second, of passing on the mission rather than cutting her once thick long black hair. She was still beautiful, Takis thought, but he could understand how difficult it must have been for her to sacrifice those gorgeous locks.

The more interesting parts of the daily briefings came from the science officers, Alida and Galen. The talkative and perky Alida would report on the historical data that had been captured on the atmospheres and geology of both Mars and Earth. She would also include any environmental information that might be of interest. The crew was at first alarmed by a warming of Earth that seemed to be occurring. Alida explained that it was probably the normal warming after a glacial period and was no cause for concern. Earth, it seemed, was just exiting an ice age.

Galen would report what little data was coming in on each planet's life forms. He was a biologist who fit all the stereotypes. He delighted in discussing things that the crew, or any normal person, for that matter, found disgusting. Their reactions amused him to the point of laughter. He was both intelligent and geeky beyond reason, would occasionally neglect his appearance and would more than occasionally so immerse himself in his data that he seemed absent-minded. Yet,

Alida found him cute; she had developed a bit of a crush on him that had made the sometimes monotonous work fly by.

It was barely a week after they had exited the wormhole and begun their flight toward Mars that Galen had reported the devastating news that there was no life on Mars. The crew was stunned into silence. Takis could sense the determination that grabbed hold of each of them. They would find out what had happened to their ancestors. Their first clue, Galen had told them, was the other startling data he had been analyzing.

***

The early data was confounding enough. They knew how many were in the original refugee expedition and had calculated what the maximum population should be if all had gone well. They reasoned that if the population was lower, there had been a problem. How much lower, they reckoned, would possibly give them at least some insight into what the problem had been. They were mentally prepared for anything, they thought. They had even entertained the possibility that the population would be zero, indicating the refugees had encountered some type of disaster sometime in the thousands of years that had passed.

They were not prepared for this. No one had even considered the possibility that the population would be higher than the biologically based calculations indicated as a maximum. It still struck Takis and Galen as impossible. The population was not just larger; it was more than ten times what they had expected!

They checked and rechecked and rechecked the data. They had poured over the software and hardware that had gathered the data looking for what must be a flaw, but they could find none. Takis sent special communications capsules back through the wormhole, hoping that the scientists on New Mars might have an answer, even if that answer would not catch up to them for months.

Indeed, the early data was confounding enough. Then, just weeks away from Mars orbit, Galen broke the news. The entire crew had startled when he drove his fist into his data console that afternoon and shouted "Shit!" The weekly data packet he had been analyzing could not be right. First, the data packets showed a ridiculously high human population count. Now they were beginning to show a sharp decline. The population was falling by the millions on a daily basis.

They double checked, and triple checked the data. They went over every line of the software and every nut and bolt of the hardware. Again, they could find no flaw.

***

They had proceeded to Mars orbit and had landed on a desolate and dead planet. They gathered data somberly; looking over a dry and dusty landscape that they knew once looked very different; that long ago was filled with skyscrapers, roads, gardens, stores, offices and the homes of their ancestors. They had planted the plaque they carried from New Mars and left even more determined to find some answers to the confounding data they were getting from their next stop.

By the time they established Earth orbit, onboard supplies had become an issue. The mission plan was to wait in orbit until communications capsules from New Mars caught up to them, then land on Earth where they could replenish. There was a year's worth of contingency supplies that Takis knew he would have to stretch over nearly two years if he proceeded with the plan he had been considering since they had left Mars. Before finally making the decision, he reminded himself of the factors he must consider: the data was still just as confounding. They invented a dozen scenarios that might explain the population data; there might be some kind of war going on; there might be a native species so genetically close to humans that the sensors were not distinguishing it; there might be some type of planetary upheaval in progress.

Whatever the explanation, Takis saw it as a significant threat. He briefed the crew and recorded an entry in his log. As he was finishing the entry, he reached for the small red button below the mission clock. The crew watched as he pushed the button at the same time as he recorded the last words of the entry before launching the log back to New Mars. "Data remains ambiguous and suggests perilous landing," he had reported. "Disporia I mission clock holding at EL minus fifty-two hours, thirty-six minutes, twenty-one seconds. Crew is awaiting further instructions."

Takis and the crew would stare at that frozen clock for nearly two years while they orbited Earth. Watching and wondering.